D1140710

The
KINDNESS

POLLY SAMSON

The KINDNESS

BLOOMSBURY
LONDON · NEW DELHI · NEW YORK · SYDNEY

First published in Great Britain 2015

Bloomsbury Publishing Plc
50 Bedford Square
London
WC1B 3DP

www.bloomsbury.com

Bloomsbury is a trademark of Bloomsbury Publishing Plc

Bloomsbury Publishing, London, New Delhi, New York and Sydney

A CIP catalogue record for this book is available from the British Library

Hardback ISBN 978 1 4088 6187 5
Trade paperback ISBN 978 1 4088 6188 2

10 9 8 7 6 5 4 3 2 1

Typeset by Hewer Text UK Ltd, Edinburgh
Printed and bound in Great Britain by CPI Group (UK) Ltd, Croydon CR0 4YY

In memory of my father, Lance Samson
(1928–2013)

WYCHWOOD

August 1989

Lucifer flew well for her in the fading light, falling through the sky when she summoned him and away again towards a great bruising sunset. She was alone on the ridge at first: just her, the bird and the wide-open view. It was one of those nervy summer days of sudden strong winds that fretted the hawk's feathers as he stared at her from his perch on her gauntlet.

She was wearing a long red shirt over jeans and sandals, her hair was breaking free of its band. A leather pouch hung from her belt and a whistle from a cord around her neck. The hawk braced his feet on her wrist, making a leather tassel swing from the gauntlet. She felt the breath of his feathers on her face as he departed and she watched him go with the wind right under his wings, scattering crows like drops shaken from an umbrella.

Julia was trying her best to get it right for the bird, the morsels were small to keep him active. A shaming twenty-six ounces he'd weighed on the scales that morning. She called him with the whistle, two sharp bursts and there he was: a dark Cupid's bow firing straight at her from the heavens.

She continued along the ridge, Lucifer steady on her arm, his manic eyes never leaving her face until she gave the signal. She sent him reeling to and fro and neither of them knew that this was to be their last dance.

The evening started to chill. She'd almost forgotten that Julian was supposed to be meeting her there or perhaps she'd just given up hope. He was panting when he arrived, still red in the face from the run up the hill, his bike and its useless tyre abandoned. He had the air of a boy who'd crossed three continents to see her, his sweatshirt knotted round his waist. Impossibly young, with hair falling over his eyes, and an uncertain lope, one leg of his jeans still tucked into a sock. He didn't dare kiss her, he said, with the hawk glaring at him like that from the end of her wrist.

The hawk shrugged his shoulders and she sent him flying. They kissed and when Julian stopped to glance nervously at the sky she took off her gauntlet and pushed his hand inside. She urged the hawk with her whistle, moving Julian's arm up and down, the gauntlet's tassel dancing, but Lucifer only soared higher, the wind whispering murder into his ear and deafening him to her call. Julia ran cursing, Julian lolloping beside her. She grabbed back the gauntlet as the hawk fell to his kill. Julian's hands were warm on her waist and it seemed to them both that the scream of the rabbit went on for ever.

It was almost midnight when she got back to Wychwood. She'd have stayed at Julian's digs until morning if it hadn't been for Lucifer, bloody bird.

She parked the car in the lane, coaxed him from his crate and clipped him on. Lucifer shook out his feathers, a little irked that *somebody* had carelessly creased his cape.

Fallen twigs cracked underfoot as she cut through the copse, the bird a resentful weight on her arm, the accusatory glitter of his eyes the only brightness beneath the trees. The darkness dropped, the branches stilled: Wychwood stood alone in the clearing, as unexpected as a Grimm Brothers' cottage with its wonky black boards and crooked windows. At once she could see a light was on, though was certain she'd switched everything off.

Her face owlish white, Julia slipped through the back gate, whispering to Lucifer as she transferred him to his post in the shed, and on alone up the path. Heart beating, a skittering loose stone at the steps, she pushed the door open with her foot and straight into the kitchen. A gasp, mostly relief: Chris, her husband, streaky hair flat to his head, his giant grey trainers kicked halfway across the floor, chinkering his spoon in a cup.

She took half a pace back. 'Why the look of surprise?' he said. 'I live here too, you know.' Maggie, his lurcher, quivered in disgust beside him, her nose pressed to his knee.

'So here I am. Ho-ome.' He made a mockery of the word, bristling with it, pointing his spoon at her.

'I wasn't expecting you.' She hung the leather gauntlet on its hook, brain racing for an alibi and stalling. 'You gave me a fright. You could've been anybody.'

He cursed her for the welcome, baring teeth older than his mouth: Nescafé and tobacco.

'What did you do, did you leave Lucifer in the boot while you . . .?'

'I couldn't get the car to start.'

He snatched the leather pouch from her and threw the leftover bits of meat to his dog, then pulled it inside out. 'If you don't clean it out there'll be maggots again.'

He had eighteen floors in Dagenham to paint, that's what he'd told her. One hundred and eighty offices, little hutches, all rollered the same drab grey that was spattered over the overalls from which his torso was hatching. He was supposed to be away until Christmas, by which time Julia had promised herself to be gone. His overalls fell open to a Ramones T-shirt so faded you'd have to already know the name of the band and down to a belt with a large metal buckle. He unloaded his pockets over the

5

kitchen counter: tobacco, Murray Mints, rolling papers, dope tin, change clattering. His hair was dotted with the same grey paint, like flies had been laying eggs in it.

'It's great you're so pleased to see me,' he said. 'A real treat.'

'Likewise,' she said but as he turned she caught a glimpse of an earlier version of Chris, a sudden trick like a hologram strung between them, something about the crease of his forehead and his overhung brows, a glint in amber eyes. His overalls had been unbuttoned just this way the first time she set eyes on him, in the playground as it happened – where he was part of a team painting the Nissen huts that would become the new classrooms. His hair was streaked in spikes of peroxide and ash. They all called him Sting. The girls of the fifth form took to gathering around the huts at break when he slunk over to talk to them, his chest golden brown.

She'd lain in bed after the first night with him, her hairbrush pushed under the door so the sound of it opening would wake her should her father come stumbling in. Through the floor the noise of the bar had been an unwelcome soundtrack as she thought of Chris's tiger's eyes, of how he could skin up a joint with one hand, leaving the other free to stoke her into a stoned frenzy.

Now he was wiping her kiss from his cheek as if she'd stung him, coffee sloshed all over the counter.

'Lucifer killed a rabbit tonight.' She was trying to act normal, unzipping his holdall and subjecting the contents to strict apartheid before the washing machine: a pile each of whites (so-called) and coloureds (balled-up pants, sweatshirts and socks stiff with rigor mortis).

'I don't suppose you brought it home,' he said. 'The rabbit?' His lip curled. 'No, of course you wouldn't, would you.'

'It was bad enough fighting Lucifer off it.' She shuddered at both the memory and the smell of him. 'Your clothes are rank.'

'Some of us have to work for a living.' He glared at her and checked the freezer, pulling out a metal tray of frozen little pink corpses, banging it on to the counter so they bounced free of the frost. Had she filled in the chart? What had Lucifer weighed in at that day? The day after that? How many hours had she flown him? How many kills?

'He's your bird,' she said eventually, wishing the sick feeling in her stomach away. 'You're lucky I make time to fly him at all.'

From the corner of her eye she saw him select a couple of stiff baby mice and place them on a dish. When thawed their defeated heads would hang as he took them from puddles of spreading pink to pull them apart with his fingers. His jaw was tight. 'At least one of us earns proper money.'

He was wiping his hands on the seat of his overalls: 'So, when were you planning to tell me about wonder boy?' He crashed the metal tray back into the freezer and came towards her rising out of his overalls. His arms were muscular for someone so skinny, something she'd once found attractive.

Her hands flew to protect herself. 'Stop it, Chris.' But she stood her ground, rocking back on her heels in front of the washing machine and holding her breath as he kicked himself free and roared into her face: 'I suppose you've been flying my bird with him, haven't you?'

She turned her head, afraid that she might laugh. He cared more about the hawk's fidelity than her own.

'Did you?' He grabbed her shoulders. 'You've been gone this long. Did you let him fly my bird?' His face was a roaring hole, his breath rotten.

She shook her head and he flung her from his grip.

His jaw was so tight the skin was stretched white on the bone. A sudden realisation followed by a jolt of terror sent her shooting to the bathroom where she slammed and locked the door.

Had he already checked and found her Dutch cap missing from its plastic clam in the cabinet? She pulled down her jeans and squatted over the pan. He was yelling from the kitchen about how she'd been seen with the 'little college boy', ranting on about money and MOTs and all the things that couldn't possibly be wrong with her car. Her body was flooding with shame at the names he was calling her. She hooked out the Dutch cap and ran it under the tap.

The instant she emerged he sprang at her, yelling, 'Liar!' Grabbing her by the hair, he wrenched back her head. 'You let lover boy fly my bird.' He continued yanking, making her eyes smart. 'Don't believe you haven't been seen. And you're a fucking cradle snatcher, a fucking joke.' He twisted his handful of her hair until her face was pressed hard against his chest. She could smell his sweat and the turps he used for washing his brushes. She could hear his heart pounding.

'Let me go.' She managed to knee him, though she missed his balls. She heard more than felt the searing at the back of her scalp as she broke free, leaving him with a fistful of her hair.

He stared at it in surprise for a moment, then sprang at her as she tried to drag the door open, pulling her away and wrestling her to the floor.

He had her pinned face down in the scattered clothes. 'Don't leave me.' His anger turned to raw pleading. 'Don't go,' he said.

'Let me go.' She tried to stop her voice shaking. 'Please let me go. Let me go, let me go.'

'Promise not to leave me and I will,' he said, as though this was just play-fighting and it was simply a matter of getting her to say 'Submit'.

'Let me go!'

He was attempting to kiss her.

'Leave me alone.'

She was exhausted and lay impassive, though her heart was still knocking. She could feel his slobber and tears on the back of her neck.

'Take down your jeans.' Her favourite red shirt was now ripped in several places.

'Don't be stupid, Chris.'

'For old times' sake before you go.'

Julia knew she'd wear the shame for ever, but she was suddenly just tired.

He pulled her jeans to her knees as soon as she stopped resisting and spat into his hand.

The loose frame of the back door rattled; the wind was building up again outside. Her stomach churned as she thought of another night, windy like this one, the same part of the Downs where she'd flown Lucifer earlier.

They'd been 'lamping' with a powerful light fixed to a truck and a helpless rabbit in the beam. Chris's hawk swooping low into the ring of light, like a skater in an elaborate cape and hooking its talons into the rabbit's spine, shielding it with its mantle as it screamed. Chris on his haunches stretching the rabbit's neck: 'It's kinder this way.' She didn't hear a crack and it continued jerking its hindlegs, running nowhere. 'Just nerves,' he said, presenting it like a sacrifice, and the bird ripped strings of meat from its throat while its legs kept pumping.

He took his time. She begged him not to come inside her. But he did.

At last he relinquished his grip and rolled away into his sea of dirty laundry. She stood shaking and pulling up her jeans, and flew at the door and over the steps with no one to run to but Julian.

FIRDAWS

August 1997

One

There are no photographs of Mira now. A drugged sleep, a ringing phone, a room full of daylight that has been cleansed of her existence. Julian surfaces, arms flailing, and wakes to a morning with no reason for waking. There is no sticky bottle of Calpol by Julia's side of the bed, no chewed copy of *Goodnight Moon* by his. The doll baby has disappeared along with her cardboard-box cot from the corner where Mira played. Even the extra little pillow they had kept between their own in tacit approval of the nights she crawled in between them has been tactfully removed. Julian ignores the phone and buries himself deep beneath the sheets, sinking back into a fug that smells only of himself so that he has to curl into a ball to bear it.

Another August day dawns blasphemously close to midday with his arms and hands so groggy it is an effort to silence the phone when it starts up again. It's stuffy. He has to keep the windows shut against the creeping night-scented jasmine because it's been giving him a headache of late. Birds squabble among its vines, something scritches at the glass, a distant cow bellows. A flare of light cuts through a gap in the curtains, dust motes swirl and though the picture is missing from his bedside table, Mira's face is the first thing that swims into focus: Mira, with a crown of daisies and sunshine in her hair.

He's clumsy on the stairs, grabs the handrail to stop himself falling. He's an old man of twenty-nine before the double hit of nicotine and coffee. Crocked up and scratching beneath yesterday's T-shirt and boxers, automatically stooping his head beneath the beam at the turn and again at the door to the kitchen. The dog dances around him, out of kilter with his mood, tail whacking the back of his legs, oblivious to anything but the emergency of its bladder. It bursts like a cork through the door when Julian opens it and runs sniffing among the fruit trees. Before setting the kettle to boil, he scrapes meat into the dog bowl and lands the fork with a clatter into the sink.

Outside there's the slam of a car door, the indignant cough of an ignition. He heaps coffee into a pot. The drawn curtains at the front (which, of course, Julia had wanted to change) are gauzy with sunlight. He keeps them closed so the people who come knocking might believe him not in. At last the car drives away.

There remain Sellotape traces on the fridge door. They show up more on bright days like this, tiny ziggurats at the corners of spaces where once had been a cut-out zebra daubed black and white; a face painted on a paper plate; an abstract in pasta shapes; a nursery timetable; a strip of photos from a booth, Mira's eyes surprised by the flash and big as flying saucers; a red and yellow painted butterfly; the merry wave of her handprint.

Inside the fridge there's nothing much to want apart from the milk for his coffee. Half-wrapped butter sits stippled with crumbs. There are meals that his mother has prepared, not knowing what else to do, their contents marked on cardboard lids. Lemon chicken, lasagne – things he especially liked as a boy – banoffee pie and Persian stews with nuts and oranges, barberry, almond and lamb. She's added extra labels: *You must eat* and *Made with love*. It's a wonder there isn't one declaring: *You will get over this*. There is a tray of eggs that Katie Webster's mother left at the front door, speckled browns from her Marans. He thinks briefly of boiling a couple but his stomach tightens, leaving little space for anything other than salty grief.

He wanders, slurping coffee, to his study. The dog trots in from the garden, finds him sitting there with his chin in his hands and slumps at his feet with a deflated sigh. Julian's desk is about as welcoming as a pool of stagnant water, its surface littered with Post-its. His computer is poised for action; a bunch of pens offer their services from a green glazed jar. Again there's a space to which his eye always wanders, where once had been a photograph in an ebony frame. The picture has been taken away along with everything else. There will be no asking for it back.

The jar for his pens was made by his mother, the glaze partially oxidised in sawdust so it is almost metallic where darker rivers run through it. He has everything he needs: Pentel V5s in black, blue and red, new foolscap, ink and toner for the printer, packets of gum, tobacco, Rizlas and all the time in the world.

He reaches a hand to the bottom drawer of his desk. Resists. Daily he must stem the urge to check it's still there. One scuffed shoe: the left. Soft leather. Mira's with a T-bar and a silver buckle that she'd almost learned to do by herself.

The dog stretches, shoulders twitching, throwing his master baleful looks. Julian's mother will ring, she won't mention Julia, she won't talk about Mira: everyone agrees it's for the best. She'll ask if he's eaten, if he's managed to take Zephon for a walk. 'It would do you good, walking always does,' she'll say and the forced brightness of her tone will bring an extra bleakness to his day.

He slides open the drawer. *You will get over this*. The shoe is the only thing there. Cut-out diamonds in the leather and a whitish crêpe sole. Her heel has left a grubby print where it says *Start-rite* inside. She was a good little walker right from the start:

he remembers the tug of her hand, the determined hoppity-skip of her steps. Her shoe is a little rough across the toes, worn down on the outer edge of the heel. She'd walked too soon – at eleven months and thirteen days. He remembers the feeling of slight loss that quite shamed him as she made it triumphantly across the room. Mira, the jutting of that determined chin announcing that she wouldn't stay a baby for long. Always keen to be somewhere else. Her ever-pointing finger: 'There, over there ...'

He closes the drawer, tries to make himself focus on work.

Above his desk is a window, jasmine wreathes across leaded glass, vines reaching and twisting in double helixes. The sun throws patterns across the flotsam of yellow Post-its. Their corners curl, his scribbled words have faded and some are circled by coffee from his mugs. Sometimes he reads what's written – a short description of something, a phrase, the odd metaphor – and tries to make sense of it.

'And so it came, this dark messenger, flapping towards him like an omen,' says one in ancient biro. What omen? But it is his writing.

'Gather a cloud around us to secretly make love (Homer?),' scrawled across another like ancient code. Time passes.

In the kitchen he shovels down something slippery from a tub. As for walking, the poor dog lives in a state of dashed optimism, darting to the door each time Julian stands from his chair to ease his back or pace, scooting back and forth like a cheerleader, prodding him with his nose.

'OK, OK, let's go out,' he says, opening the door. They get as far as the outbuildings, the dog twirling around his legs, before Julian is defeated by voices along the lane.

He returns to his desk, wakes his computer, makes himself check his inbox but fails to answer a single email. It doesn't help that the pills are making him muzzy. The dog stays outside, barking at swallows to annoy him. He stares at his mystifying notes, though they might as well be written on papyrus: 'They disappeared into the mist, arm in arm, like lovers walking into the pages of a book.'

He wonders what it all means but for now can do nothing much but rest his head in his arms and think about Mira.

Missing pictures haunt the spaces they once inhabited. Indelible, though gone from her ebony frame, Mira is a sunny baby in Julia's arms. The front door to their flat in Cromwell Gardens is ajar, a mild April morning with the dust just starting from the plane trees and Julia concerned that the baby's eyes might get irritated. Mira has the gummy smile of a pixie, on her head a flecked red wool hat with a green stem at its centre, like a strawberry. She's in a white billowy dress for her party, across which Julia has managed to get her name appliquéd in red felt.

Mira Eliana. Mira for the miracle and wonder of her birth (from the Latin *mirus* 'surprise'). The second name sprung on him by Julia on the day they registered her at Hornsey Town Hall. Eliana. According to the book of names it had Hebrew roots meaning God-given, or Greek ones relating to the sun.

It had a good ring. Mira Eliana. And it made sense, for he had been present for the miracle: the midnight sunshine of her birth.

Julia had made him promise to stay away from what the midwife called 'the business end'. But the South African doctor was calling: 'She's crowning!' And Julia's face was turned away. 'Quick!'

A membranous dark dome was forcing its way through the lividly splayed folds of Julia. Her thighs were bloody and the head was emerging, pushing and stretching her into a purple scream. She was propped on her elbows panting, hair clinging to her forehead (tentacles it was his job to hold back), as the crown pressed towards him like a giant eye from its socket and was born in a splatter of blood.

'Oh God, Julia,' he cried three times, overcome by a sudden flood of remorse.

'My baby, is my baby all right?' her only concern.

Julian can see it all: the birth room that had seemed so without charm when they arrived, the stern bed and banks of monitors, the optimistic primrose-yellow walls, squishy bean bags piled in a corner. As she's placed in his arms, Mira's quavery wails shoot to his heart and a golden light – impossible because it is the middle of the night – starts spreading throughout the room.

He sits beside the bed and someone tucks a white waffle blanket around the baby and slips a tiny cotton cap over her head. He cradles her in the trembling hollow between the crook of his elbow and his chest and she stops wailing with a quiver of her lower lip. A look of deep concentration takes over, her fingers play an invisible harp. They are opening and closing around the astonishing lightness of air and her forehead furrows into a deep V beneath her new cap while she considers this strange phenomenon. He lifts her closer to his face to reassure her, pressing his lips to the softness of her skin, breathing her new smell of warm bread and hot blood.

The South African doctor, who seemed a little grizzled only hours before, takes on the sun-kissed sheen of a movie star, his coat and teeth pearlescent. 'She's a beauty,' he says. Mira is moving her mouth, trying out shapes and pursing her lips, her cheeks surprisingly rounded and as soft as new mushrooms. Julia wears the pale face and pellucid eyes of a saint, turning her head on her pillows, cooing to the baby girl in his arms while the doctor finishes stitching. The anaesthetist, who Julian had only partially registered previously (when the gauge of the needle she'd pushed into Julia's spine had made him go genuinely weak at the knees), has a pretty Irish voice and a halo of red curls. She clucks over the baby. Mira yawns and locks on to his gaze, her eyes so steady he feels she is reading his mind.

'There, you can give the baby to Mum now.' The doctor snapped off his gloves. 'You've done very well,' he said, patting Julia's thigh as though she was a favourite filly. Even that failed to rile him as Mira continued staring into his eyes.

Almost reluctantly he broke the contact to place her into Julia's waiting arms and sat beside the bed quietly in awe of the pair of them. Watching them falling in love. Murmuring. Crying. Julia unbuttoning her nightdress.

A tractor has started up nearby, its droning amplified and falling as it drags the baler back and forth along Horseman's Field. A distant shout brings him back to his desk. His emails remain stubbornly unanswered. Michael is cautiously broaching one or two outstanding questions: the design for a slipcase of his entire *Historical Dogs* series awaits his approval; his film agent wants him to sign up to write *Fletch le Bone III*.

He ought, at least, to deal with Michael. Michael has every right to think of himself as his stepson's saviour as well as his agent, but the last thing Julian wants right now is anyone turning up to save him.

Not so when he was twenty-one. Then Michael's offer of a job had come as a blessing. Julia was pregnant and they were about to be thrown out of his student room when Michael flew in. Julian was working every shift he could at the Crown and Julia was in the sort of debt that made her scribble hasty sums on bits of paper. She was constantly tearful and Chris, her fuck-up of a husband, kept turning up at his lodgings (where Julian wasn't supposed to have overnight guests), dumping bin bags of her clothing in the hall and pushing wads of bills that he'd maliciously decided were hers to pay through the letterbox.

London was as good a place as any to start their life together. They found a cheap room with its own bathroom at the end of the Northern Line. Julia, washed out with the morning, noon and night sickness of that short-lived first pregnancy, was hired by a horticultural centre a short bus ride from their street. Julian was glad that she at least could be in the fresh air. Unlike him. First the tube, then on to the subterranean world of the children's books slush pile in the basement at Abraham and Leitch. The Abraham being Michael, his mother's husband, the man he was supposed to think of as a father.

His employer then, his agent now and bursting with questions that need answers. Julian scrolls on past Michael's emails. There's something from the new girl in publicity, a school has requested he open their library: couldn't someone there ensure he wasn't bothered by this sort of thing? From the shelves beside him garish copies of his own books leer down at him in their cartoon covers.

This career of his, built on a knack for reducing history to the level of pets, started to pall even before Mira was born. When Julia needed to go back to work, he was more than happy to take a break from the hairy rogues' endless gossip, the goings-on in the kennel at Hampton Court, the New Model Army of bull terriers, the sycophantic little dogs in the laps of their Queens. Yap, yap, yap.

Oh, but he should be grateful. Without them he could never have raised the cash and loans to reclaim Firdaws. But even Firdaws, which he used to think he loved as much as any person, had not been enough to override the flare of humiliation when a writer he admired congratulated him on the success of his most recent, *Ponsonby*. This last, a Restoration comedy told through the eyes of Charles the Second's spaniel, was finished without enthusiasm shortly before Mira's birth.

He attempts a couple of emails, but still has difficulty settling. There are several from his old mate William. They are cautious in tone: 'I am sorry to disturb . . . I'm sure it may not be the right moment for you to think about this . . . Please do not hesitate to call if it would help to talk, any time, day or night . . .' Julian rocks back in his chair and closes his eyes.

'Mira', a miracle. They started trying for a baby soon after Julia lost the first one, but it took Mira five years to arrive. They were in the bathroom of their flat in Cromwell Gardens, trying not to care, when she first made herself known. He was in the shower when Julia peed on the stick (as she did most months because her periods liked to taunt her by being late). She called to him over the beat of the water, pointing to the white stick on the cistern and a blue line that was deepening from a hint of pale forget-me-not to a navy certainty. They both stared at it, hardly daring to speak, and Julia had to sit back down on the loo. He quickly did the maths on his fingers. 'Paris!' he said, and biting her lip she looked up at him and nodded.

She broke away, urging caution when he knelt to hug her. She asked him to get a second test 'just to be sure' and when he ran back with it, out of breath, with the bag from the chemist in one hand and a bottle of champagne in the other, she was in the kitchen and, still wrapped in her towel, was sitting on the little stool beside the telephone, crying.

The day disappears much like the ones that went before it. Firdaws sinks into the dusk until eventually he switches on the lamps. He manages crisps, heats up some sort of stew and finds the scent of the jasmine has grown stronger when he returns to his desk with a sturdy Duralex glass and the remains of a bottle of red wine.

In their bedroom above, Julia would throw open the window to let in the scent. He imagines she's up there now, her lustrous hair kinking and purling, Mira framed beside her in the golden square of light, holding out her arms, calling down to him: 'Dadoo . . .' to make sure he can see her there in her favourite pyjamas. He pours the wine.

Soon he'll go out for some air, find the dog and together they'll cross the garden by moonlight. He takes a gulp from his glass, the smell of the jasmine giving him a headache already. He can summon the taste of the sleeping pill he plans to take. Upstairs the empty bed waits.

He has nightmares about Mira falling. He'll wake in a sweat, his arms grabbing at the air like a newborn. Then emptiness. No Julia, no Mira.

He rolls a last cigarette, calls to the dog. Mira skips back into his mind, avenues of trees unfurling leaves and promises, the afternoon sunny enough that he can't resist her pleas for the playground when he picks her up from nursery. Pigeons hanging around like boys at the bus shelter hoping for a few extra crumbs from her lunchbox, and Mira hurtling down the bigger children's slide, her face screwed shut until he catches her. Blinking with shock, her eyes meet his and instantly she's confident as she gauges that he is smiling. All will be well: 'Brave girl,' he says as she slips from his grasp. 'Again, again.' Running back along the concrete to the steps, a loose strap of her dungarees flying, grabbing her to secure it; she watches his fingers intently, always learning. Her funny skippy steps and his mix of pride and terror whenever she tries anything new. Swinging her straight up to the top just so she doesn't have to work so hard climbing the metal steps, swooping her skywards and blowing a raspberry on her neck to make her laugh.

All of this over and over until he glanced at his watch and realised that it was Friday and Julia would be back at Firdaws already.

Mira looking down at him from the brink to where he's ready to catch her: 'OK Dadoo?' – that's what she called him and neither he nor Julia could bear to correct her. 'Ready?' Quite solemn. Seeing her from a new angle, from the crepe soles of her shoes up, no longer a baby. And then down she comes, a starfish hurtling towards him, and he braces himself ready to catch her.

He set Mira on the foot of the slide to help her get a stone from her shoe, her sock a little sweaty as he straightened it. He slipped the shoe back on to her foot, bowing nobly, 'Is your name Cinderella?' And she giggled, told him: 'Don't be a silly.' He showed her again how to thread the strap through the buckle. Her breathing grew heavy as she concentrated on the task and he held her foot steady.

He reaches to the drawer, opens it a touch just to be sure it's still there. It's impossible to resist. He takes it out and holds it as he does every day. The creases across the toes have shaped it; the soft leather sole has yielded, the heel bulges, so it is almost as though he has her little foot in his hand and not just her shoe.

Around him familiar shadows watch, the friendly ghosts of four generations of Vales. It's snug in here, with beams so low they just clear his head, a couple of ancient armchairs, Turkish rugs on the floor that have had their corners chewed by a succession of his mother's dogs. 'Hey, how about this as a playroom for Mira?' Julia tried suggesting the first time he showed her the estate agent's pictures of Firdaws.

'Oh, but that was always my den.' He couldn't help but be crestfallen. 'It's probably the best place for me to write.'

It's cosy, this room of his: the familiar west-facing window partially covered by the vines, lending a suggestion of a cave or an arbour.

He replaces Mira's shoe and closes the drawer. This desk was once his father's. On the day he and Julia moved in, his mother had all the old furniture taken from storage and sent around in a van. Julia was uncharacteristically grumpy as it all came through the door: the big kitchen table, the Welsh dresser and its brightly painted pottery animals, chests of drawers, armchairs, rugs, this desk. Sitting here now, he's struck by the thought that perhaps nothing had happened to him. For a moment he is a boy again, looking up at the same patch of sky through the same leaded glass, waiting for his mother to call him to the kitchen for soup. He drains the last of the wine, closes his document, puts his computer to sleep. He won't be far behind.

Two

Firdaws is the last cottage along the lane that winds from the village to the river and since the schools have broken up it seems there is never a day someone isn't around, whistling to a dog or shrieking on the way down through the water meadows. Most of the other houses have front paths and gardens, but Firdaws is reached across a small meadow of scrubby grass filled at this time of year with yellow wildflowers, cornflowers and dog daisies. Its chimney rises tall and crooked and in the evenings soft mist rolls in from the river to surround it, giving it the appearance of a house in a dream. Of a gentle weathered brick and hanging tile, it was built into a natural nook, so if you lie on the riverbank looking up towards the village it's the first house you see, tucked close into the bosom of the landscape with nothing but dark-green conifer woods at its shoulders and the spire of St Gabriel's pointing to the sky.

Beyond the meadow the lane from the village comes to a meandering halt at Jerry Horseman's fields, whose rusting gates with their elaborate bracelets of baler twine are of no consequence to locals long decided this access to the river is common land. Occasionally Jerry Horseman livens things up by grazing a bull in one of his fields but on the whole he is amicable and leaves this part of his empire to a rough hay which is always too full of buttercups.

At the back of the house a small wooden porch faces the downward slope of the garden across the fields with their waving fronds of yellow and rusty dock and on to the river that glints through the trees. When it rains it's good to sit in the porch, to smell the wet earth and smoke and listen to the water dripping off the roof and leaves. On a really still night you can hear the owls at the river, and around the house the squeaking of pipistrelles that flit among its creepers.

There's a small terrace for herbs and beds for clambering roses, a few fragrant shrubs. The rest is down to fruit trees and seedy grasses; that is, if you can manage to ignore the three formal flower beds the Nicholsons left behind, where massed bushes of candy-pink roses have flowered all summer long, the air made heavy by their scent.

Strung between the furthest pair of apple trees the hammock mocks him with a low-slung smile for the hours he spent feeling safe, Mira cradled beside him begging for stories. There's a worn patch of grass beneath it, down to the earth in the middle, scuffed by his foot pushing them to and fro beneath their canopy of blossom and leaves.

The garden was wet with rain after they had been and gone, as though it too had been rinsed of her presence. Their efficiency was astounding. He became increasingly agitated as he tore through the rooms, opening drawers and searching behind cupboards. That night, unable to sleep, he wandered barefoot across the wet grass. The sky, cleared by the rainstorm, was ablaze with stars. The granary windows glinted silver at him and he shivered as something rustled in the apple tree. His bare arms looked freakishly white as he reached inside the hammock. Mira's shoe was caught in its folds, the strap still buckled, so it must have slipped from her foot, a damp wad of blossom stuck across the toe.

The blossom is gone from the trees now, replaced by hard little fruits, the hammock is streaked with mould and should probably go too.

In the orchard the air will be sweet with ripe plums, but he doesn't go there to pick them. Beyond the plum trees and the damsons there's a tree that Julia planted. He tells himself not to be ridiculous – of course it's still there – but can't bring himself to check in case it isn't. It's a pear tree, carefully transplanted from Cromwell Gardens, special because it was given to Mira at her Naming Day.

Julia had written their daughter's name in silver italics on the invitations: *Mira Eliana*, and they waited until April to throw the party so that people could spill out on to the patch of lawn. They had stumbled over what to call this event since *Christening* would have opened the door to frenzied entreaties from Gwen, Julia's Catholic mother. They settled on Naming Day and Mira's snowy dress was lovely as any christening gown.

Mira was carried round the sitting room like a doll by older children, Julia more relaxed about this sort of handling than him. She was a robust baby, already able to support her own head, but still . . . The bluish pulse, beating like a guppy beneath the tender skin of her fontanelle, had caused him deep pains only a few weeks before when invited to hand her to anyone other than Julia. When Julia's father Geoffrey waddled in to the hospital to incant her with his brandied breath, he wanted to find a way to say: 'No, she's too new.'

Lucky for them Geoffrey rarely left the shambolic caravan behind the recreation centre in Vernow where he sometimes got work on the grass but more often didn't. At Mira's naming party he wasn't to be parted from the table where the champagne was poured for the toast. Julia's mother Gwen fixed her gaze pointedly at her daughter's chest: 'Are you sure you're producing enough milk for the baby?'

Mira barely cried all day. You'd have to be a fool, or just plain spiteful, to suggest she was hungry. Julia was so strung out by her parents' presence that a twitch started at the outer corner of her eye.

Everyone wanted their photograph with the baby, he had to leap in to shield her eyes from their flashes. Turn them off, he said. His own mother in a black dress and glittery tights arrived bearing armfuls of bright tulips and Michael, his hand proprietorially resting on the small of her back, was beautifully courteous in his weekend tweed with leather patches on his elbows.

Un-Godmother Freda brought her guitar as well as the pear tree and in her thin breathy voice sang a song she'd written for Mira. It was from the point of view of the tree and made Julian want to laugh and Julia cry. 'Mira, my dear, a golden pear just for you ...'

From a poster on the wall beside his desk a cartoon Skye terrier with heartbroken, improbably fringed eyes looks out from beneath the scarlet petticoat of his Queen. *Geddon, Her Majesty's Best Friend*. Julian shakes his head at him. His knack of giving family pets daft accents and acerbic opinions was never supposed to have become this: *Geddon* and a whole pack of historically well-placed pooches all at your service, book after barking book. *Hello, how lovely to meet you* – and screenplays, many more than ever got made, *Fletch le Bone, Laika's Moon*, a remake of *Greyfriars Bobby – yes, I'm the one who writes in dog voices.*

Children cried when they read Geddon's story and for this Julian was applauded.

He had read Antonia Fraser on Queen Mary Stuart and wrote in the evenings after work: laughing at his own jokes and typing in fingerless gloves. They were still in Burnt Oak then, and despite all four rings of the gas cooker sputtering away there was frost on the inside of the glass. Julia reading her plant manuals at her end of the table, rocked back in her chair with a blanket hanging from her shoulders and her hair tied back with one of her raggedy scarves, him typing away.

To be honest, at that point, *Geddon* had been little more than an enjoyable retort to the slush he waded through day after day at Abraham and Leitch. He never would have dreamt that *Geddon*, along with the swiftly imagined *Mrs Pericos* in his wake (written in the treacherous vernacular of Elizabeth the First's lapdog), would so heroically light their way out of Burnt Oak.

And open the door to Cromwell Gardens, a short, leafy walk from Waterlow Park. Julia loved that flat. Who wouldn't? At Cromwell Gardens there was an original fireplace in the sitting room, picture rails that had survived the conversion, plaster fruits along the cornicing which she painted in luscious colours. They woke each morning in a room she had stained deep raspberry with dark velvet curtains shining like cordial in the morning sun. He loved it too.

At Mira's Naming Day when Gwen sidled up to him – 'I hope my daughter's garish taste doesn't give you a headache' – he had to step away from her rather than reply. Freda's singing pear tree was being politely applauded and next up was William.

It should have been Karl doing the godfatherly honours that day, not William, but Julia had vetoed him: 'Absolutely not!' her vehemence stopping him in his tracks. Mira had been suckling and let out a cry. 'I mean, why him? Oh look, now you're interrupting the flow,' she said, stroking Mira's head.

So William, who he'd never especially thought of as his best mate, was there instead, going on about Larkin's poem for Sally Amis, 'Born Yesterday'. Bloody cheek! Julian wouldn't wish for his daughter to be anything other than extraordinary: for her, kingdoms would be renounced, incurable diseases cured, world records broken. Mira whimpered and Julian shushed her with her head snug as a nut between his shoulder and cheek, whispering: 'Oh, darling, don't listen.' People recharged their glasses and drank to Mira's health, all except Julia, who remained perched on the arm of a chair, looking out at the street, stray strands of hair catching the light from the window.

He remembers it all: Julia's breasts leaking milk through her thin silk dress; a big fruitcake; his mother's eyes rarely leaving his face – trying to read him – as he hands plates to and fro; people spilling things and dropping crumbs; Julia's dad stumbling into a lamp, breaking it; Julia's nieces lolling on the floor; Mira at the breast and him longing for everyone to leave so that it would be just the three of them again in the milky fug of their bedroom.

Three

Cromwell Gardens seems as unreal as a dream to him now and it's an effort to snap himself out of it. He wills himself to stay at his desk while a wasp frays his nerves, traversing the inside of the window, smacking against the glass, zigzagging itself into a tizz and drunkenly falling, resuming angrier than before.

As a boy Julian would have knocked that noisy hooligan into a cup, imprisoned it with clingfilm in the soporific cool of the fridge with a few of its friends. Before the chilled wasps regained consciousness, and though it was fiddly, he tied threads around their prone bodies and waited until they warmed up and took flight so he could soar behind them, momentarily shrunken and almost drunk with happiness, making them dance to his tune, a devil-winged coachman tugging at the end of their silken reins. Their harnesses were the gossamer threads of Queen Mab's coach. Or was it Thumbelina's?

Wasps were readily available for cryogenics that summer; people talked of them as a plague. Sometimes they seemed to be stinging children just for the fun of it. Nobody went near the fig trees that grew alongside one of Jerry Horseman's hay barns and sometimes the wasps' meat-lust became so severe that people gave up flapping and shrieking and telling each other to ignore them and took their Sunday roasts back indoors.

At the height of their frenzy his mother was stung on the foot while doing nothing more aggressive than working on some pots in the granary. She took a pause from the slip she was mixing, came crashing into the house to change into something less spattered and drove to the farm shop where she bought the last three wasp traps they had in stock. Others she made from jam jars. Together she and Julian filled the traps with a mixture of golden syrup and water and lined them along the sills, where soon they sweetened the deaths of multiple invaders. At the kitchen window he spent many a pleasant evening watching as they fought the inevitable, the sinking sun turning their fool's paradise to living amber.

But still more came. They nested in the shrubbery behind the granary. His mother was in there dreamily emptying her kiln of a week's work when he came to alert her. 'Hmmmm,' she said. 'OK, will you do something about it?'

So he did. He didn't 'ask someone' as she suggested with her gaze already on a new pot. There wasn't a 'someone' to ask.

'So is it OK,' he said, 'if I siphon the petrol out of the lawnmower?'

'Ummmm-hmmm.' Jenna wasn't listening, as he knew she wouldn't be. So, what did she expect?

He was stunned and elated by the magnificence of his Molotov cocktail, almost starstruck by the great orange *woomph* that bloomed from the shrubbery, sending a swirling mass of smoke and wasps and bits of rosebush into orbit.

To escape Jenna's wrath, he tucked his air pistol into his shorts and cycled three miles to his friend Danny's house. A couple of other similarly armed boys were already there and as usual they all ended up in the woods out back taking pot shots at each other – and woe betide any bird – dodging in and out of the trees, lucky, really, that nobody lost an eye.

When it came, the attack was as sudden as someone tipping

a carton of wasps straight over his head. They arrived in one vicious stinging cloud, savaging him as he hid in a dip. He ran in his shorts through the trees, batting them off, arriving breathless back at Danny's with wasps fizzing at his legs and clinging to his hair. Systematically he began killing the ones on his shins, waiting until he could feel their stings going in so he'd be sure of getting them, which only made their compatriots nastier. His skin was blazing as he careered into Danny's bathroom. There was a strange itching at his throat and in the mirror he could see red lumps across his neck and wondered stupidly if it was heat rash. Within minutes the redness spread. He stared in wonder at this map unfurling across his arms and chest and, pulling down his shorts to check, yes, down there too. Short of breath and with a whistling in his throat, he insisted that he was fine when Danny's doctor father ran out of his study and told him to lie down.

Dr Andrews saved his life that day with a shot of adrenaline before Jenna arrived, breaking every speed limit taking him the eight miles to Casualty. He remembers the blaring of horns at roundabouts. He was unable to reassure her. His throat contained a balloon that was being slowly but surely inflated, his swollen skin was the colour of ripe plums, but he felt so light-headed he found the whole thing only novel. At the hospital he was fitted with a mask and nebulised, then kept in overnight in case his breathing took a turn for the worse. He was told that he must never ever be without an EpiPen.

Naturally Julian never carried an EpiPen.

It was on a languid day post-exams that he was stung again. His assailant got him, with Exocet precision, right on his Adam's apple. He'd done nothing to provoke it. Sunshine and cheap plonk, the pages of his book fanning gently over his face as he breathed in the smell of the mown grass and the girls' Ambre Solaire. William was there too that day, helplessly in love with

33

Cara, a girl from their course with a sexy gap between her front teeth. There was a radio nearby and a noisy game of rounders. Cara was being mildly irritating: 'Here's a bunch of flowers,' pulling grass through her fingers and casting the seeds into the air. 'Now here's the April showers.'

The entire college seemed to have chosen this spot to celebrate the end of exams. This time last year he'd gone straight back to Firdaws – his mother's cooking and the warm folds of his girl-friend Katie were hard to resist – but this year he decided to stay on in the town, which pleased neither Katie nor his mother.

He had only recently given up being faithful to Katie. The summer stretched before him. A couple of the girls he'd not been faithful to Katie with had just wandered over holding hands and plonked themselves in front of him not wearing much in the way of clothing and he felt the warmth of the sun concentrate pleas-antly at his groin.

And then it got him. 'Shit.' He leapt to his feet, trying not to panic, rubbing at his burning neck. The pain subsided quickly and he told himself that everything would be fine.

'Bastard wasp!'

'I got stung on my bum at a very embarrassing moment,' said one of the girls.

'Haha, pain in the arse,' said someone else. Julian hoped he was imagining the tingling itch already creeping from his neck.

'Shit, I need an EpiPen, I think,' he said, attempting to stay calm.

'An epi-what?' Cara looked up from picking grass seeds out of her bra. Everybody else propped themselves on elbows and stared at him.

He spelt it out. 'I may go into anaphylactic shock. I need to get to a hospital.'

He could feel the warm rash spreading, a new tingling sensa-tion across his stomach.

'A and E is at the back of the cathedral, isn't it?' William said, slowly.

'Actually, this may be urgent.' Julian began walking away from them, the act of putting one foot in front of the other already making him woozy. It wasn't the wine, sadly not that. Something about his mother's constant entreaty had made him stubbornly irresponsible on the subject of the EpiPen. *I am immortal*, he teased when she nagged.

His breathing was growing shallow by the time William sprinted ahead to the road trying to spot a taxi, the others scooting round the park calling frantically for a doctor, an EpiPen, a lift to the hospital.

His throat was tightening, every breath shallower and more whistly than the last, his tongue swelling. The road beyond the park was becoming a blur. As he reached the gates he heard a shout and stopped.

A shortish man in a flurry of rumpled clothing flew into view, panting and waving a syringe.

'You'd better let me get to your thigh,' Karl said and as Julian fumbled with his belt he felt himself fall.

'Never mind.' Karl was kneeling over him and stabbed him straight through his jeans with the needle.

'Now we have to get you to a nebuliser.' Karl had already alerted a friend with a hospital pager. 'I'm not sure I can quite manage a tracheotomy today,' he said, propping him up, a grin twitching at his lips.

The others caught up as Julian staggered to his feet, Karl lending him an arm, saying: 'Take it easy. There's an ambulance on its way, they'll be here any minute.'

Julian was still finding it hard to breathe. He stared at Karl, trying to remember if he'd ever met this calm, mild-voiced man with John Lennon specs and tufty hair before. Karl's face seemed to go in and out of focus: beneath thick quizzical brows his brown eyes were humorous, which made Julian feel less panicked.

The sound of the siren was deafening as blue lights flashed across his saviour's face.

'Here we go,' Karl hefted him upright, while William and the others milled uselessly. 'I'll come with you, if you like,' Karl said, taking his weight. 'Don't worry. You'll be OK now.'

Julian abandons the modest anaesthesia that sorting through the mysteries at his desk might offer and calls to the dog, whose joy is out of proportion to his planned breath of air in the garden. The noonday sun is obscured by clouds. Outside is muggier than in. The dog spins in ecstasy as he heads for the far corner and the rougher grass. The granary stands squat on its staddle stones, still home to his mother's old stone kiln, though there's no sign the Nicholsons ever fired it up. They've added various shelves and flat-pack cupboards where Jenna's work benches used to be and he misses the way it was when he was a boy, with its wheel in the centre and all the industrial bins of minerals, the smell of burning sawdust mingling with the dankness of fresh clay, her work drying on shelves. The pots and figurines are all gone now, as are the old-fashioned spike on which she impaled her orders and her tins of glazes each with its own coloured tile hanging on a nail, sorted so they ran along the wall in a rainbow.

Julian turns his face as he passes. He's yet to set foot inside, still can't help regarding any proof of the Nicholsons' occupancy as vandalism.

He visited them here once, by mistake, the day he travelled from college, bringing his rotten two-timing heart for one final kicking by the girl he'd forsaken. Katie Webster was taking the news of Julia's pregnancy so badly she'd come home from Manchester so that her mother could at least try to get some good food into her. Her voice was shaky when she called him at his digs and he'd agreed almost at once to come.

He arrived in the village the following day and cycled straight from the train to Katie's house. He was shaken by the brute physiological effects of his betrayal on her: she looked so diminished in her raggy leggings and T-shirt, all angles where once had been curves. She remained curled miserably on the sofa the entire time, balled-up tissues to her eyes.

He stood awkwardly across the room, hopelessly making excuses. 'We've been together since we were fifteen. You didn't seriously think . . .'

He didn't rise to anything she said, put his head in his hands to hear her call Julia 'some old slag who gets pregnant.' He let her rant on, shrugging and wincing, until she ran out of words. What else could he do? Katie's parting shot was vicious: 'I'm glad Firdaws has been sold,' she said.

He found himself there on automatic pilot. Mrs Nicholson was looking out of the window and must have guessed the identity of the doleful young man with the bicycle leaning against Jerry Horseman's rusting gates.

Walking into Firdaws that day was a waking version of the old childhood nightmare of getting home to find there are only strangers who don't know who you are: it didn't smell right, the pictures were all wrong on the walls, no dogs, everything so sharp and clean and lemony. Mrs Nicholson led him through to the kitchen. The Rayburn was gone, the wonky apple-green cupboards too. The Nicholson twins sat with their straw-coloured plaits and colouring books at a round table at the wrong end of a shiny new space laboratory of white and steely appliance.

He turned his attention from Mrs Nicholson's hideous children – what was their problem, why were they staring at him like that? – to the steaming rose-patterned mug placed before him on the table. Noticing the gleam of his knuckles beneath the stretched skin, he made himself unclench his fists. He drank the tea scalding and pedalled to the station with it burning inside him and the wind stinging his eyes.

Four

Firdaws swelters, no air escapes from the valley. Every day bluebottles battle the glass, things scrabble and buzz, the butter he left out has gone rancid so he has to throw his toast to the dog. Someone is tapping on the kitchen window when he comes down, forcing him to skulk at the foot of the stairs where the postman has left yet another slip for a parcel, which he tosses to the top of an untidy heap of packets and letters. From beside the front door his father is unconcerned, blue eyes twinkling for ever in Jenna's smudgy oils.

Maxwell is paler than Julian, who has Jenna's Persian skin that tans with one lick of the sun. He looks confident, amused; large hands resting on a green-topped card table; a good-looking man with a delicate colour, sandy lashes and shaggy hair. He's wearing a blue shirt with an open Nehru collar and, most noticeably, the sort of almost-smile that makes you believe he's about to tell you a secret. Maxwell Julian Vale is so bursting with vitality it seems impossible he will be dead within three years of this being painted.

There are hooks for coats and wellies, several pairs, still caked with dry mud from the winter. Mira's red ones are, of course, missing. Her fleecy duffel, striped hat and nursery rucksack no longer hang from the brass peg that he'd screwed into the wall especially low so that she could reach her things herself.

The knocking seems to have stopped and Julian darts into the kitchen, willing his visitor far away so that he can retrieve the milk from the step and get on without being spotted. Already he's shaky, in need of a smoke. He's down to the last of the bread now and, more importantly, tobacco but can't face the clucking he'll be subjected to by either or both of the Miss Hamlyns at the village shop. His headache reminds him that he's out of wine too, out of booze generally: last night ended in the custardy embrace of a bottle of Advocaat.

Inside his car is Stygian, but the dog insists on accompanying him into town and sticks his head out of the window with the wind whooshing past so his ears look like the flaps of Amelia Earhart's flying cap. Insects splat themselves against the windscreen and the wipers process them into a pus-coloured cream to smear in arcs across the glass. His screen wash manages only a tiny spurt of foam.

Some men are repairing the humpback bridge leading out of the village and Julian has to stop at a barrier to let a white Volvo pass. It pulls up beside him with a menacing crank of handbrake and he has to suppress the urge to reverse when Penny Webster's pink and white head pops out from the window. With one fat hand she fans herself. 'Phew, so warm. Oh, Julian. We thought maybe you'd gone away, but here you are.'

There are children in the back of her car. Penny Webster reaches through the window to give his shoulder a squeeze, her bare arm mottled mortadella by the sun.

'Are you OK, pet?'

Katie's boys regard him from the rear seat with blank blue eyes. He tries not to look. 'Katie's left the little devils with Grandma,' Penny Webster says unnecessarily, gesturing so he has to.

Billy is sucking his thumb with a blankie to his mouth while Arthur kicks his legs to and fro against his car seat. Julian manages to nod and they carry on staring at him. They don't ask where Mira is, so they must have been told something.

Billy's blankie stays hanging from his mouth even when he removes his thumb. What have they been told? They couldn't have forgotten her so soon. Billy, Arthur, Mira, squealing and splashing each other with hosepipes, running around in their pants, bouncing on the trampoline, yelling newly acquired rude words. The three of them calling from the hammock: 'Come and swing us, come.'

In the back of the Volvo Arthur leans across to whisper into Billy's ear.

Why don't they ask for Mira? Katie brought them to the hospital that Saturday in April: it's only been a matter of weeks. They brought her some new comics and balloons . . .

Penny Webster is talking. He mumbles something about a meeting, fixes his eyes on the road ahead.

'Did you get the eggs? I left them on the step . . .'

The truck behind Penny's car flashes for her to move on.

'Come for a meal, pet. Katie's worrying about you. We all are,' she says and he has to look away from her now that her eyes are welling up.

These Webster women cried easily. Katie failed to hold back her tears when she came to the hospital, arriving on the ward with Billy and Arthur trying not to stare as they drew closer, tucking themselves behind their mother like goslings sensing danger. He wondered what it was they were seeing. Mira was pale, surely that was all, and free on that occasion of anything too alarming in the way of canulas or drips or feeding tubes.

The balloons they brought were helium, a monkey and a Winnie-the-Pooh, and Mira sat grinning, propped against her Disney pillows, set alight at the sight of them bobbing. Katie leant over and kissed her gently on the forehead then embraced Julia, who looked brittle clasped to her bosom.

'Here, you have the chair,' Julia said, standing and hitching up her clownishly large trousers, 'but we mustn't let Mira get exhausted.' She started pulling her hair back, severely winding the band round and round, making Julian think of snagged knitting. Katie frowned and took her place beside Mira's bed. Julian was stiff still from his night on the hospital camp bed and needed more caffeine. He pushed his hands into the small of his back, wondering if he could escape for long enough to grab a coffee from the cafeteria downstairs. The boys edged along the bed and Julia busied herself tying the balloons to its frame. The nurses thoughtfully brought pink milkshakes with straws when it was time for Mira's protein drink. Julian made up voices and a silly conversation between her stuffed toys and Mira's laugh came easily. He stopped the bear mid-speech and stared at her. Her eyes shone huge, enough to break any heart. Enough that Katie cried.

'This must be so hard for her,' she whispered, turning her head, and at first he thought she meant Julia. 'Have you any idea when they'll let her come home?'

'If they can keep her blood pressure down and the tests continue to go the right way it could be soon,' he said. Please God.

Katie grabbed Billy to stop him bouncing on the bed. Julia perched, fiddling with her necklace.

'Poor love.' Katie allowed a slippery curtain of hair to fall across her eyes.

'But Mira's doing fine,' Julia pulled a face to make Katie shut up. 'She's watching everything that goes on and she's never alone because me or Julian sleep beside her every night.' She reached for Julian's hand and he pulled her close.

Mira led the way to the playroom. Her enthusiasm was painful to witness. He and Katie followed the others, Julian working hard to swallow.

'Julia's staying tonight and I'll be off to my mum's,' he was saying. 'Did you ever come to Michael's house? In Barnes? No?'

Katie shook her head. At the sanitiser they stopped to squirt their hands.

The playroom was bright enough, light streaming through the windows along with the din of the streets. Low tables, baby-bear-sized chairs, felt tips in Tupperware boxes. Mira led the boys to the boxes with their primary-coloured lids. The wipe-clean toys were lined up on the shelves.

'Michael and Mum talk all the time, and argue, like they always did.' His hands mimed a pair of yabbering heads. 'And her dogs are constantly doing terrible things to his lovely furniture. It's a bit of a strain,' he said, pulling out a miniature chair for Katie as Julia took to her knees, sorting through a crate of train set.

'They never seem to grasp that I could use time alone.' Catching himself whining to Katie like this made Julian realise how grumpy he'd become, how worn down.

'I'm much better the nights I stay here,' he said, plonking himself in his own tiny chair.

'It must be awful for Jenna too,' Katie said.

'It's tough for us all.' He stooped to rescue a runaway train. He passed it to Julia, gave her shoulder a squeeze and for a moment she put her cheek to the back of his hand. 'We haven't had a night together since this started,' he said. 'And I'm stuck with my mother who jumps every time the phone rings. She's right at my side: *Is it the consultant? What does he say?* Drives me nuts.'

'Oh, poor Jenna,' Katie said and Julia rocked back on her heels and snorted.

'Mum is also very pissed off that Julia doesn't stay in Barnes with her on the nights I'm here,' he said.

'Yeah, it's intolerably selfish of me to want to be as close to my daughter as possible,' Julia said, unsnapping some pieces of track. The children had grown tired of the trains and were climbing in and out of the Wendy house windows.

'Oh, dear,' Katie frowned. Julia started chucking carriages and bits of track into a box as Julian explained.

'Julia's got her room in Lamb's Conduit Street, it's just five minutes' walk away.'

'Oh, right, that's where you've been staying in London ...' Katie said, turning to Julia, and Julian interrupted her: 'Yeah, with my friend Karl's dad, same as before. Three nights a week before any of this ...' and he waved his hands to include Mira, the whole hospital.

'It's a nuisance Firdaws being so far,' Katie was rummaging for something to wipe Arthur's nose.

'It's worked out well for Julia, and Karl's dad is a lovely old fellow. I'd much rather camp there myself, but you can just imagine how much Mum would go for that.' Julian sighed and tried to slump in his Lilliputian chair.

'Actually, talking of Firdaws,' Katie waved a triumphant tissue at Arthur, 'my mum thought I should offer you some help in that department. What's happening with the builders? I imagine there's quite a bit to be done since they ripped out that awful kitchen.'

Julian ran his hands through his hair, making it stick up at the front. 'I've not been able to get there ...' he said, and Julia stopped what she was doing and stiffened. 'I, I need to at some point soon.'

Mira, he could see, was starting to tire. She was sitting in the doorway of the plastic house dreamily fiddling with a piece of ribbon. Shadows clung to the hollows of her face. Above her, dangling their rounded legs from the roof, Katie's boys looked ruddy, indecently healthy.

Katie turned to him. 'I'm in the village most of the time now,' she said. 'Can't I help? You know, chivvy the builders, or something?'

Julia's response was huffy, he thought, and almost certainly

44

audible. Arthur jumped from the playhouse roof and Katie dived to deal with his nose. The boy squirmed in her grasp.

'Billy, you come back down too,' she said.

Mira wrapped the ribbon around a dinosaur's tail like a bandage. She yawned and Julia went to her, scooping her up like a baby.

A nurse rattled by with a trolley. Julian turned to Katie and nodded. 'Thanks,' he mouthed.

Later, in the hospital cafeteria, Julia worked herself into a rage. 'How could she look at Mira like that?'

He was tired, the fluorescent lights sucking the life out of him. Everything tasted faintly of hand sanitiser.

'Does she not think it might be just a bit distressing for Mira when people walk in and start blubbing like that?'

Julian held up a hand to her. 'Stop that, Julia, please,' he said. 'I think she was trying very hard to be breezy. It was a shock. I should've prepared her better.'

'And did she ask a single thing about how Mira's treatment is going?' Fresh tears were pooling in Julia's eyes and he leant across to blot them with a paper napkin, but she pulled away. She was so thin that the necklace she had taken to wearing, a tiny gold sun, swung from her clavicles. He couldn't remember where it was from, this necklace. She touched it often, running the gold sun back and forth along its fine chain during their meetings with the consultant.

'Don't forget, it's difficult for other people too,' he said while she drained her tea in one angry gulp. 'It was good of her to bring the boys. Look how happy Mira was to see them.'

Julia stood up, brushing imaginary crumbs from her lap.

'All she asked about was Firdaws,' she said, gathering her purse from the table and marching out of the cafeteria and along the corridor to the lifts. He caught up, but she'd already pressed the button and the doors were sealing her off. He stood watching the arrow rise to Mira's ward on the ninth floor. There Julia would settle herself on the camp bed in his sheets from the night before with her hand reaching up to hold Mira's. He in turn would go to Barnes where he would have to deal with Jenna's juddering nerves and talk business with Michael, because Michael always had so much to tell him. He would be back for breakfast, but still he felt abandoned when Julia huffed off, and shaken, as he stood there staring at the lift, that she hadn't kissed him.

She kissed him with tears the next morning. But then: 'Hey, I can't even begin to think about this,' batted him away as soon as he brought up the subject of Firdaws. It had been a bad night on the ward, he didn't need her to tell him: it showed in the reds of her eyes. Mira had woken several times complaining of pains and refused breakfast. A child, Oscar, had fitted in the night and was in PICU. Oscar was on his third bout of chemo and, despite being nearly six and interested only in the train set, often played with Mira.

'He's still down there in Intensive Care.' Julia wouldn't stop spinning that sun on its chain, her eyes had run dry and the tip of her nose looked raw in a face that was mainly sallow. They left Mira sleeping and went down in the lift.

They silently sipped their coffee while people came and went, trays crashing, cutlery clattering. Someone walked in whistling. After a while Julia sighed, rubbed her forehead, then mashed her eye sockets with the heels of her hands.

'Look, I don't care, OK? If Katie's so keen to help, why don't the two of you just get on and get it done.'

'Right. I get the message. I won't bother you with it.' He ripped the corner from his croissant and stuffed it into his mouth to staunch his words. Their eyes met until he made her look away. He was thinking only of Mira leaving the hospital and getting her home to the fresh air of Firdaws, her familiar things, her books by her bedside and her dinosaur lamp . . . He couldn't stop himself smiling as he chewed.

He met Katie two nights later. The hotel was in Marylebone: red pelargoniums along every window ledge, a carpet of mustard- and ketchup-coloured swirls. He waited for her at the bar and felt a stab of dislike that took him by surprise when she entered in a shiny blue dress, so tight that it creased along her thighs as she walked. He felt it again when she kissed him and he inhaled the forced nostalgia of the hyacinth scent she had worn as a teenager.

She was wearing pink lipstick and he reached instinctively to wipe where her mouth had touched his cheek. The sight of her made him ache for Julia. He thought of Julia beside Mira's bed, the straggly rook's nest that her beautiful hair had become scrunched in that band at the back of her head, the long tail of her leather belt without which her trousers would fall down.

Katie led Julian from the bar to a corner table. The bar waiter knew her name and Julian cocked an eyebrow. 'I've had to stay here a few times when Adrian's had the boys,' she said. 'It's not worth going all the way back to Horton, not with all the delays on the line at this time of year.' Then, flushing slightly: 'Besides, I intend to empty our joint account before he gets any funny ideas about spending it all on holidays with *her*.'

Julian gulped and asked for a whisky, a drink he didn't espe- cially like. Katie ran a finger along the condensation on her wine glass. Now they were alone, she questioned him closely about Mira's treatment and listened intently. Now they were alone she called him Jude, as she had in the old days, and he was glad Julia was not there to hear it.

'It must be awful to watch them doing all this stuff to her,' she said, reaching for the back of his hand.

'Mira's so brave, honestly it's endless. Some days are better than others. Poor little thing has hardly stopped sleeping today. And every time she wakes up there are pains in her tummy and legs.'

Katie's hand came to rest on the back of his wrist. 'It was good the boys got to see her. They miss her,' she said.

'She's supposed to be able to go home, but every time it looks as if things are going well, something else goes wrong,' he said, pulling his arm away and in one movement swallowing the burning whisky and signalling to the barman for another.

'There's still weeks more treatment and the operation to come and, whatever's been happening, that tiny girl hasn't complained, not once.' He felt his eyes sting at the thought of Mira's courage and stood up to bolt for the Gents. Katie got to her feet too, reaching up and bringing him close enough to comfort.

'She's a real fighter,' she said, her head only reaching his chest despite her heels.

He could feel the press of her breasts, her warm breath through his shirt and tears sprang from his eyes.

She pressed him closer still, her hyacinth scent cloying. He took a step back and pushed her away.

At the basin he splashed his face with water. 'Right,' he told his reflection. 'This was probably a mistake.'

And yet . . . Firdaws did need to be put right by the time Mira got home, and that could be soon. Now the Nicholsons' kitchen had been demolished, someone had to be on site sorting it out. He turned off the tap and, looking in the mirror, told himself he saw an honourable man. Patting his face dry with a paper towel he offered himself a parting shot: 'She said it would make her *happy* to help,' and pushed through the swing doors and back into the bar feeling much better.

It appeared that a slim man in a leather jacket had already noticed Katie all alone at their corner table, probably took her for a hooker (Julian immediately regretted the unkindness of the thought). The man was handing Katie a business card; she was tucking her hair behind her ear, briefly studying the card, eyes reaching up to return the man's smile. Julian stalled at the bar, reading a joke from a mat. The man was pointing to Katie's glass and in a moment that lasted no longer than the flare of a match Julian was back in Paris with Julia: a darker, moodier bar than this, with red-leather banquettes and dimly lit chandeliers, trance music, spice-scented candles and Julia shamefully seducing a stranger in a brown corduroy suit for his enjoyment. He shook his head to clear it of the memory as Katie waved at him and the man moved smoothly away to the lifts.

'I see you've pulled already,' Julian said.

How would he have managed without her? Between them Katie and Penny Webster knew all the right locals. While he and Julia struggled on at the hospital, dust was cleared at Firdaws, cupboards painted the correct shade of apple green, the glazed tiles above the worktop were the exact smooth buttermilk. The kitchen was put back together with historical accuracy because in almost ten years Katie hadn't forgotten a thing, sending him photographs of their progress (which Julia refused to look at, infuriating him until he snapped: 'Must you keep sulking? Someone's got to do it'). Katie found a cream enamel Rayburn at the architectural-salvage place, the same model as the one the Nicholsons had junked; perhaps even the very one, it had been there a while. The pottery animals were ready and waiting with their twins on the shelves of the Welsh dresser, the saucepans on their nails above the cooker, the wasp traps ready for invasion along the sills. Everything put right and not a sign that the Nicholsons had ever been at liberty to wreak their ideal-home fantasies upon the place.

The drive to Woodford is gory. A pheasant flies out of the hedge intent on suicide. Julian has counted six pheasants, eight rabbits and two squashed foxes since he left Firdaws and now ahead here's a badger on the verge. He can't help but slow down to study it. Flies frenzy at a patch of congealed blood beneath its ear and in the grimy runnels of its cheeks, the stains like dried tears.

One of Julian's least favourite childhood memories is of a dead badger in the lane almost directly in front of the Firdaws. The evening they found it, his mother went to Horseman's Field with the dogs and heard the crying of its babies deep inside the sett and could do nothing to help. The next morning their crying was very faint and by the following lunchtime they were silent. That night she cooked Julian the same supper twice.

Then, one full moon, when they were just sixteen, he and Katie watched some young badgers playing in Horseman's Field. They'd scattered Maltesers around the mouth of the sett because his friend Peace Convoy Raph told them that's what badgers liked best. Maltesers and a full harvest moon. As dusk fell they sat together, Katie and him, listening to the various hootings and screechings. They were wrapped in a blanket because the evening had grown chilly. Mist slid from the river as the darkness settled around then. They remained motionless beneath the dampening blanket, her head on his shoulder until finally they were rewarded by a pair of badgers who came sniffing the air, picking through the grass and roots, snouting out the Maltesers, scampering and somersaulting.

He and Katie walked up from the field still huddled together beneath their blanket cloak, their breath a single cloud. The mist had seeped right into their bones and it seemed the most natural thing in the world for them to warm up together in his narrow bed. The tip of her nose was as cold as a frosted button. He stifled a scream when she rested her icy feet between his warm thighs and again when she leant across and her slippery hair tickled his face. She had never stayed overnight at Firdaws before. In their haste they hadn't drawn the curtains and from his bed they could watch the night uncurl and trace the silvered outlines of the trees. She slept with her head on his chest while he grinned to himself in the afterglow, the moon at the window like a peeping Tom.

The Nicholsons converted that bedroom into a bathroom, complete with an egg-shaped stone bath. He refused to go in there, though Julia claimed to like it and took long soaks with the door locked.

Once the builders finished ripping it out, Katie rang him at his mother's to let him know that his old room was ready for painting. Julia was at the hospital and didn't have to witness his delight that she remembered. 'Robin's-egg blue?' The room would be just as it was, even the original midnight-blue muslin curtains embroidered with silver stars that – joy – she'd found in a box in the attic. She'd easily get them repaired and rehung. Katie had thought of everything. Every picture was restored to its rightful hook. Mira's new room was all ready for her return to Firdaws post-treatment: her things, her books, her teddies, her dinosaur lamp. He had written to Katie to thank her. That would have to do.

Driving on through Woodford, the people on the pavement appear slow and drunk as if the sunshine is something that must be waded through. Trailing children whine for ice-cream, men with proud bellies emerge from the Six Bells car park with their shirts off; one of them stumbles into the road, his friend waves at the dog. Julian can't face the choice of the big supermarket's shelves, so heads out of town for Lipton's corner shop, scooping up biscuits, butter, bread, chewing gum, tomato soup and cans of disgusting dog food. At the off-licence he decides to buy some big bottles of R White's as well as more wine and beer: he's been quenching his thirst too often with bottles of beer throughout the heat of the last days and nights. He almost forgets tobacco.

Fresh road kill lines the route home. He drives with all the windows open because the heat has defeated his cooling system. The dog pants on the seat beside him, tongue lolling. Sweat pricks the nape of his neck; the back of his T-shirt is pasted to the seat. He lifts his arm, sniffs his own stench and curses. Now that Penny Webster has spotted him, what's the likelihood he'll find Katie waiting when he gets home?

A blackbird flutters up before him and he swerves to avoid its mate on the road; in his mirror he sees the little blackbird darting at the spatchcock of gore and feathers.

There is not a breath of wind. The tarmac shimmers as he comes over the brow of the hill to the village.

At Firdaws he struggles inside with his shopping, leans against the door to close it and stays there a moment, catching his breath.

He chucks a couple of his beers into the freezer, takes a long tepid gulp from the neck of another. In the sitting room he throws open the door to the garden before slumping in the window seat. As far as he can tell no one has been near apart from another delivery man who has left a large crate in the back porch, which he already knows he won't find the energy to open.

His head is thumping. The dog cowers, quivering and miserable, in the corner behind a chair; the birds grow silent. He smells the storm before he hears the first timpani echoing around the valley, nothing more than a rumour playing through the leaves of the trees before a blast from the east inks the sky and lacerates it with a crack of lightning. The rain comes beating and sizzling.

Drops the size of marbles bounce from the grass as the storm rips through the valley. Trees lose control of their limbs, every leaf an electric green so against the black sky they appear luminous as stars. He is unconcerned by the din of the thunder, the whining dog, the ringing phone. Vines batter the window and rain slashes to the glass. He watches drops break and scatter, their trails mesmerising, his fingers pressed to his cheeks, almost peaceful. The air is fresh with earth and electricity and he's transfixed by the liquid motion. The drops collect and burst and skedaddle, tadpoles of rainwater flickering before his eyes, transporting him to another night. Karl's student room. The night before he first laid eyes on Julia.

Five

Karl clicked the Anglepoise off and beckoned to Julian. On his desk the microscope glinted in the high-tech promise of its own light. Julian handed the joint to one of the girls lolling among the cushions and Indian bedspreads on Karl's bed, felt himself sway as he rose to his feet.

'Here, be my guest,' Karl said with open palm, prompting him to step up to the microscope. Julian found himself more self-conscious than he could remember and stupidly nervous, not helped by the CD, which took a momentous turn with massed strings and oboes exalting him onwards. He felt ridiculous, stalled in the spot between the girls on the bed and Karl's desk, struck by something like guilt or stagefright. And also quite stoned. The music crashed and crescendoed, propelling him forward like a wedding march in hell, and vampiric bridesmaids – the girls – clambered up and hovered behind him, so close he could feel their breath at his neck.

Karl checked his viewer once more, minutely twisting a dial back and forth, humming tunelessly under his breath. 'There, that should be focused for you now.' He glanced over his shoulder and something about Julian made him reach out and hold him, to take his weight, as he had that day in the park. 'It'll be OK,' he said, his shoulder steady. 'I've set it at 400 times magnification on a dark field. It's like an aquarium in there.'

'Hurry up,' Verity was poking him in the shoulder. 'I'm dying to look.'

They were a strange gang that summer, united only by their parts in Julian's earlier little anaphylaxis drama in the park.

Almost everyone else had scarpered when term ended, but Julian was staying on until at least the middle of August to clear his debts working shifts at the Crown. Cara too.

'Save a life and it's yours for ever, something like that.' Cara tried to remember a Chinese proverb for Karl, and looking side-long at Julian, deliberately provocative: 'And by the way he's been carrying on, you're welcome to him, I say.'

Karl had his research project and Verity was too hooked on Medicine to leave the faculty after her first year. She turned up wherever Karl went, nodding at every word that fell from his lips, positioning herself by his side whenever possible, picking his considerable brain. Verity had what Karl called a 'laboratory tan' and a bubbling complexion that betrayed a diet of wine and crisps. Most of her clothing in some way of cut or colour resembled hospital scrubs or doctor's coats. Cara, by contrast, was slinky. That night at Karl's she wore a black satin blouse with buttonholes crucially just a little too generous for its pearl buttons and a stolen black bowler hat that gave her the look of Sally Bowles.

'I was the one who found the lady with the EpiPen,' she was reminding them for the hundredth time, cocking an eyebrow with mocked indignation. 'I keep telling you it's me you need to thank.' She twirled the ill-begotten hat on the end of her index finger. 'Not Karl.'

Karl was grinning at her, intoxicated. Steady on, Julian wanted to tell him, you'll frighten her off. He had yet to discover that women rarely resisted Karl. It was not the way he looked – girls didn't, on the whole, favour short untidy men with comedy eyebrows. It was something else.

They'd finished the bottle of brandy one of Karl's housemates had swiped from a party. Cara prowled the borders of Karl's room, pulled books from shelves, studied the random objects ranged around. Picked up some old vertebrae and put them down fast, blew dust from flowers desiccated in wine bottles, her hat fixed at a jaunty angle. She came to a standstill at Karl's microscope: that's what started it. Tracing her finger along a box of slides and looking back at them over her shoulder but addressing only Karl: 'Someone I know had a boyfriend who liked to study his own sperm under the microscope.' Outrageously flirtatious: 'Do you ever do that, Karl?'

'I do it every day,' he replied, suppressing a smile. He'd unhooked his glasses and was polishing them on the hem of his shirt. He looked up, stopping to meet her gaze, blinking in that way he did without his specs. 'Mine and other people's.' His face was bare without them, vulnerable like a boy who has lost his mother.

Verity stopped leafing through piles of CDs and rocked back on to her heels, alert as a terrier at the rattle of the biscuit tin. 'Really?'

'Yeah, that's what I'm researching. We're testing sperm and its reaction to various chemicals and drugs.' He grinned at Cara again. His chevroning eyebrows were the most attractive thing about him. 'Motility, it's called. Or not. It's complicated.'

'You've kept that quiet,' Verity said. 'Is it a contraception research project?'

'Yeah, that's why I'm still here.' Karl gestured at the room and shrugged. 'It's got a small grant, so I get paid.'

'And you collect your own samples?' Cara looked sideways at him from beneath the brim of the bowler.

'We work from frozen mainly,' Karl shot a quick glance at Julian and grinned. 'Though we're always looking for donors.' Julian snorted, felt himself grow hot. Verity plonked herself close beside him among the cushions, rubbing her hand back and forth along the inside seam of his jeans. A sample was needed.

Another bottle of brandy was discovered, followed by chasers of ouzo from Karl's housemate's holiday. On repeat was that tape of Karl's favourite soundtrack, *The Mission*. Julian could hear it through the wall as he sat on the edge of the lavatory, his jeans round his ankles, Verity on her knees keen to assist, tugging at him with all the delicacy of a milkmaid. He looked at the glass jar in his left hand and thought of Cara in the other room with Karl. Somehow that helped. Cara had a gap between her front teeth and swingy hair that smelled of apricots, and that shirt on the verge of unbuttoning all evening. Karl had been leaning over her, finally removing the hat as Verity led him from the room with the jar. There was one last look as Cara edged herself up Karl's desk, her skirt sliding to the top of her thighs, Karl's hands already in her hair and Cara leaning back so Karl had to stoop over her to kiss her and at last her shirt fell open and yes, no bra . . . and with that Verity got her sample.

The extractor fan whirred and clanked as Verity inspected his cloudy offering, holding the jar to the light, tipping it this way and that until he begged her to stop, felled by pudeur and suddenly sober.

Karl prepared the slide and set up the microscope. He slooshed the sample with saline, telling Cara: 'It has to be around the same salinity as sea-water because the sea has the same mineral balance as our bodies. If I mixed it with plain water they would die.' On hand beside him, Cara was like a dental nurse in disarray, her shirt buttoned up wrong.

Verity hovered, refusing eye contact with Julian, while Karl continued making tiny adjustments to the microscope, peering through the eyepiece, raising and lowering the platform. Julian was almost tapping his foot with impatience when Karl started jigging, doing a 'pee-pee dance'. 'Sorry, I'll be quick,' he said, dashing from the room. 'Don't touch anything.'

While he was gone Cara rolled a spliff, Verity slumped beside her. Julian fiddled with a deck of cards, trying to remember a trick that his old friend Peace Convoy Raph had shown him the summer he first came in his brightly coloured wreck of a van to his verge on the road out of Horton.

Raph's was a good trick because not many people knew it. If he could remember how, he'd make all four aces rise from the pack. Cara and Verity kept spluttering with laughter. Cara put her hat on to Karl's skeleton. The joint was finally passed back to him and tasted hot.

They heard the chugging of the flush and Karl sidled back looking flustered: 'Why don't the three of you finish smoking that thing while I sort this out.' He resumed his work with the microscope. 'I might need to change a bulb. Never had one go before,' he said, mumbling, shaking his head over the thing.

Julian really was very stoned by the time Karl called him over. Karl gripped him by the shoulder. 'Take a look,' he said. 'All swimming around with no particular place to go.' And he shushed Verity, telling her to wait her turn.

Julian bent to the eyepiece. He was oddly moved by what he saw. This constellation – no, more than that, so many of them, each with its own halo as though lit from within – sparkling, darting, flickering. His very own universe composed entirely of comets. They seemed so purposeful, so bright and full of promise, that for a moment he felt sad for each and every one of them, for their urgency, for the messages they would never get to deliver.

Six

Julia arrived in his life the very next day. It was as if she had sprung fully formed from his forehead. Julia, like a prize for the climb he'd taken to get there, standing on the crest of the Downs with three counties falling away behind her and her long hair flying. Just moments before he had been dreaming her up, this very woman, as he clambered up the chalk path, his shame receding as he climbed higher but still a little breathless from Karl's brandy and ouzo of the night before. He'd summoned her from the depths of his hangover. Wished her into being. Ta-dah! She was everything he desired: right down to the muscular brown calves that emerged from her cut-off blue jeans.

The wind blew in chaotic gusts, bowling him along the grassy ridge towards her. She was walking with her back to the wind, chin tipped to the sky, and didn't notice him until he was close enough to make her jump.

'Hi,' he called out and as she turned with startled brows he saw that her face was just as he'd dreamt it, neatly featured with a tan skin and, out of dark lashes, her eyes as unexpectedly blue as a Siamese cat.

'Whoa, it's blowy,' he said, amazed to find he could speak. She nodded and gestured to the sky: 'Hey, look out.' And only as she raised her left arm did he notice the leather gauntlet. He followed her eyes skyward to a bird that was falling, turning and turning, like a heart that had leapt free. It fell, and as it did it became a falcon. He was transfixed. His was the raptor's gaze. He was hurling himself straight at her from the heavens. The beat of its wings was the beat of his heart. It landed on her outstretched arm, claiming her, snatching her wrist with its yellow and black feet, jealously shielding the meat she gave it beneath a mantle of wing and tail feathers.

'Wow, a falcon, I've never seen one up close.'

She laughed at his astonishment. 'Manners, Lucifer,' she said as it tore the meat from her. 'Actually, he's a Harris hawk.' The bird looked at her with psychopathic eyes.

'Don't be so greedy,' she scolded, and Julian noticed her shirt billowing, the sheen of her skin. She held a second morsel of pink stringy meat in the gauntlet. A leather tassel dangled from her wrist, jerking as the hawk stripped the meat.

'What's that you're feeding him?'

'Don't ask,' she wrinkled her nose in a way that made his heart tender. It was delicately freckled just across the bridge. Another mischievous gust revealed a leather belt and above it the momentary distraction of a long narrow stomach, smooth as new brown paper. Perhaps he was dreaming?

'All the way up here to fly him, and it's perfect, this wind, but he hasn't caught a thing this morning.'

He listened for clues to her exotic looks in her accent but found none. She pulled a face at the hawk and it took the cue to fly from her, imperious feathers ruffled, reeling away to the trees. 'Off he goes again,' she said and Julian watched the swing of her walk as she headed for the copse, the loose folds of white shirt gathering at her waist. The pouch from which she'd taken the bits of meat bounced against her hip. The gauntlet was comically large at the end of her slender brown arm.

The hawk landed in a tree and Julian found he was holding

his breath, his own arms outstretched, cruciform, willing it to fly to her, his every muscle tensed. It veered off and Julia started to lollop, then to jog, following the flight of the bird.

She was almost out of sight. He panicked, unable to think of a thing to shout. He patted his pockets impotently. All he had on him was the key to his bike lock and a wrap of tobacco. There was nothing he could pretend she'd lost. He watched her vanish round the edge of the trees, hands helplessly hanging at his sides as she disappeared. He ran to the copse, stumbling across mounds of grass, but there was no sign of her. Brambles snatched. Out of breath, he leant against a tree trunk. Through the leaves he could see only crows circling, their callous cries echoing.

Several times in the days that followed he went back to the Downs, but there was never any sign of her. He attempted to read the necessary books at his digs and at night he worked his shifts at the Crown among the insolent drunks, pulling pints and mopping slops. As he closed up the following Friday, Karl asked him what was wrong.

'I have fallen in love,' Julian said. 'It's giving me pains here,' and he pointed to his heart.

'Don't talk to me of your heart,' Karl said. 'It's your pituitary gland you've got to thank for this madness. Dopamine, oxytocin, adrenaline, norepinephrine, vasopressin . . .'

'Oh stop it!'

'. . . and serotonin,' Karl said. 'People who say they're in love have serotonin levels the same as OCD patients, that's the reason you can't stop thinking about her. Same as people who have to keep washing their hands, long after they've grown sore.'

Julian snorted.

'You may laugh, but consider for one moment the prairie voles.' Karl was warming to his theme, his hands miming two little rodents. 'Constant hots for each other. Ooh, so in love. At it far more than is strictly necessary for reproduction, little love nests in the long grass, seeking out special tidbits . . . however, give this lovesick male a drug that suppresses vasopressin, and he's off, Mrs Prairie Vole the last thing on his mind.'

'It happened the moment I saw her,' Julian said, ignoring his friend.

'Yes, your pituitary gland threw a little cocktail party for you.'

He couldn't stop thinking about her. He remembered the leap of his heart the moment he saw her, all sorts of less poetic places leapt too. Kidneys, stomach, gall bladder, bowel. The shape of his love was littered with organs.

His mother called to remind him about coming home for her birthday and his mind drifted constantly to the girl with the hawk. How would he ever find her again?

'Seeing you will be better than any fancy present,' Jenna was saying. 'I miss you . . . And swimming. You're the only other person brave enough. We'll cook fish in the tin bucket, chill the wine in the river.' She promised all the usual Firdaws things and he tried not to hear relief as well as delight in her voice when he told her that he wouldn't dream of missing it.

'I'll be there.' He sounded terse to his own ears. Sometimes he felt he was offering his mother scraps from his table.

There would be plump artichokes ready for him in the garden, trees heavy with plums, soft roses, the river flowing, and between the crab-apple trees the hammock hanging like a smile in a landscape as familiar to him as the face of his mother.

Every birthday Jenna swam a mile or so down the river. She dived from the high bank where they picnicked on a mid-August day on which the sun never dared not to shine. The river was wide there, a pool of glassy black water with purple loosestrife fringing its banks, a few swan feathers scattered around. She never once shrieked from the cold but surfaced shouting incitements to those brave, amorous or drunk enough to follow her in. It looked inviting, always, with lily pads and flowers blooming among the reflections of the trees, but it was cold enough to ache your bones and further along it became sinister and weedy as the blackthorns closed in.

Nettled banks rose vertically and the density and barbed branches of the thorn bushes made it impossible to clamber up until almost a mile or so downriver. From there, she strode bare-foot through the golden stubble fields, shaking water from her hair, exultant in her black swimsuit. Her annual triumph. There was always an obliging sunset and usually dear old Michael would play his harmonica. As his mother talked, Julian could almost summon the taste of the fish that they ate with soft brown bread and watercress, the smoky smell as Jenna lifted the tea towel from its tin bucket of hickory embers.

'I've found an incredible present for you,' he lied. 'I can't wait for you to see it . . .'

The quest for Jenna's 'incredible' present shook him from his mope. In Swallow Street he chained his bike to a lamp-post by the head shop, waved to Pete the hippie, and headed for the antiques and bric-à-brac arcade. The first thing to catch his eye was a collection of brass padlocks at Geldings Antiques – some Victorian, some earlier – and all polished to such a shine he felt like a magpie, he liked them so much, one in particular shaped like a heart. The price tag hung from a thin strip of red ribbon. He winced at what was written there. These shops were not priced for students.

He wandered from the padlocks to check that his favourite fantasy buy was still on display. And there it was, flamboyant on its stage: a wind-up mahogany gramophone with gleaming trumpet like a strumpet kicking her skirts.

He stood for a while, just staring at the gramophone and musing, rolling his cigarette. He'd been bad-tempered all week because of that girl with the hawk, was beginning to wish she'd stayed in his dreams. He'd been ungracious with his mother, even though she had offered to fund his train fare to Firdaws. He imagined the gramophone on the grass beside the river: Billie Holiday or Patti Page. How astonished Jenna would be.

Crosby, Stills and Nash floated from a radio, their celestial harmonies soothing him. He felt almost peaceful for the first time in days as he perfected his cigarette. He tilted his head to lick the paper and glanced at a large oil painting hanging on the back wall of the shop in which a cormorant dried its wings against a background of emerald green. His eye was instantly diverted to an ornate gilt mirror standing beside it. His girl was reflected there: Julia. Rusty-brown sundress, hair tumbling and bare shouldered, she was watching him silently, biting the corner of her lip.

He was standing right beside her, close enough to touch. 'It's exactly right,' he said as she described the mirror's fine provenance and he tried not to gulp as she told him the price. He studied her eyes in its reflection. Her pale irises had liminal rings of darkest blue, like ink that had seeped to the edges.

'What I like best is that the angel's face shows such tender concern,' she spoke in a near whisper. Her hair looked so soft he wanted to touch it.

'The frame,' she reminded him. The carved angel whose folded wings enclosed one edge of the mirror could've been a crow or a crone for all he cared.

'He looks a bit like Marlon Brando,' she said.

'Huh?'

'The angel. Don't you think?' She kept her gaze steady and they continued staring straight at one another in the mirror.

Seven

He missed Jenna's birthday by a week. He travelled with the mirror and the drunks on the last train out of town. The train of shame.

The moon kept pace as the train hurtled west and the air was heavy with the perfumed-garden-of-hell of the toilet. He took Yeats from his pocket and put him on the table and, twirling a matchstick between his teeth, rested his head to the window and stared at the moon, but saw only Julia, thought only of her.

He shook himself from a dream of falling and woke with a start just one stop before his station, Julia's steady gaze still floating before him. He shuffled sideways with the mirror in his arms to the front four carriages, cursing himself aloud. Horton's platform is shorter than the train: of course it is, *stupid*. The mirror was an awkward travelling companion and a tear had started in a corner of its wrapping. Together they tumbled on to an empty midnight platform. Oh for fuck's sake, why wasn't his mother there to meet him? Did she really think he meant it when he said he'd be happy to walk?

He briefly considered kicking the package but settled instead for speaking sternly to it as he trudged from the station. Would his mother even like it? It was a bit fancy: 'Rococo', according to Julia. Mist rose through the village and the sweet smell of silage and manure reminded him he was home. A dog howled across the valley and was answered with a chorus of barks. The wrapping tore a little more: at one corner the wing of an angel was trying to escape. He marched on, clutching it like an unwilling dance partner, trying not to bump it with his knees, avoiding the ruts in the road that suggested he trip and earn himself seven years' bad luck into the bargain.

His conscience loomed out of the mist, keeping pace beside him, sneering at the gift whose very expensiveness now seemed tawdry. *Think that'll absolve you for ruining the whole day? Fancy not making it home for her birthday. You promised. She even sent you the fare . . .*

He adjusted his grip on the mirror. In the darkness there was a sudden screech and his scalp tightened. The bobbing lights and the distinctive rattle of his mother's ancient Land Rover had never been more welcome.

'Hang on, Mum, I need to stash this in the back,' he said as she cranked open the door. She hopped out into the road, exclaiming about his lateness, the length of his hair. He batted her off, scooting round for the dog blankets to wrap around the mirror.

'Go away, nosey, it's your present.' He blocked her with his shoulder as she reached up and tried to part the hair that had taken to falling across his eyes.

She ground through the gears as they headed for home and he sensed her stifling a sob. 'What is it, Mum?'

'Something. Later . . .' Again the choked sound.

'I'm sorry I didn't make it for your birthday.' The road was bumpy, the smell of the dogs all-pervading as always.

She shushed him. 'Oh, that. You're not to worry about it, not at all.' But he couldn't make out her face in the dark.

He began telling her about Julia – the hawk, her startling beauty, the luck of finding her again – but it was all sounding too fanciful and all she said was: 'Uh-huh. Uh-huh.'

Arriving at Firdaws the smell of home turned him tender: wet earth and roses, honeysuckle, farmyards, cows as before, newly cut hay and fruit on the trees burnished by the summer he'd all but missed. He took several deep breaths, each as satisfying as the air gulped down after crying.

He gave in then to Jenna's hugs, a long sigh: 'It's so lovely to be here.' Some geese started up on the banks of the river. The earth and stones crunched beneath his feet and skittering terriers leapt at him, nipping at his pockets.

Inside Firdaws, woodsmoke and chintz, the familiar welcome. Bowls of roses dropping petals to the floor. He propped the mirror carefully against the wall in the kitchen and thought: I'll tell her everything.

'. . . So, there she was, this beautiful woman I'd only just met, waiting for me to finish my shift, sitting on the bonnet of her little Fiat reading her book by streetlamp. And that' – he nodded to the package – 'all wrapped up and waiting for me on the back seat.' Julia had promised to deliver from the shop, and she was true to her word. It was ready for him in layers of shiny red paper, even a bow.

'All part of the service,' she said, and when she jumped down from the car he found himself lifting the fingers of her left hand to his lips and kissing them. She made a joke of his courtly behaviour and smiled and curtsied but didn't pull her hand away. On her fingers he could smell the leather of the gauntlet she wore to fly the hawk.

'Oh, shush.' Why wouldn't his mother listen properly? She was all but drowning him out clattering about: filling the kettle, water from the tap thumping, interrupting him to offer stew, a sandwich.

'Or would you prefer a gin?' She gestured to the green bottle wrapped in white paper on the sideboard.

He nodded, and when she'd poured the gin and cracked the

ice they clinked glasses. 'Ah, I'm sorry, I should've got an earlier train.' Jenna looked well past her bedtime. As she lifted her glass he noticed grey pouches at the corners of her mouth. The cat yawned rudely on the table between them, confident that neither of them would dream of shooing it off. He wasn't sure what, if anything, she'd heard. He changed the subject.

'So, who did you persuade to swim with you down the river?'

'Oh, Michael, of course,' she said, sloshing another couple of fingers of gin into their glasses.

Julian snorted. 'You're lucky it didn't kill him.'

'I am,' she said.

The cat's purr was almost deafening as he nubbled it under the chin. For a moment he found it hard to keep looking at her. She appeared so strained: thinner than at Christmas, a little deflated in her dress of worn-out-looking daisies. He used to see it when people said that he was her spitting image but not so much since her bones had started showing through.

He stalled for a moment, unable to decide what to tell her of that glorious first night with Julia. In his haste it all came tumbling out. Leaping up the stairs to his digs, Julia behind him, scooping papers, books, socks from the chairs to make a space, wishing he had fresh milk in the fridge.

All night with nothing to judge them but the slimmest rib of a moon. In the morning waking to Julia tiptoeing for the door. He sprang from the sheets to wrestle her back, pulling down her sundress, but she fended him off: 'No! I can't be late. I've got the hawk to see to before work. I must defrost some chicks and mice. Ugh.' Wrinkling her adorable nose: 'To be honest I'd rather not deal with Lucifer and his disgusting diet at all, but when my husband's away there isn't much choice but do it.' Husband. It was the first time she said the word that made his spirits plummet. Husband. When he kissed her goodbye he thought that no smell would ever be more erotic than the smell of leather on her fingers, an indication that Chris, this husband of hers, was away and Lucifer in her care.

'Married. Julian, what the . . .?'

His mother's disapproval was etched on her face and he had the sudden urge to giggle inanely. 'She was leaving him, he was leaving her, it'd been going on for ever.' He held out the innocent palms of his hands, but she tutted at him and looked away to the kitchen clock. 'Anyway, it's done now,' he said. 'After twelve miserable years, she's left him.'

She turned to him sharply then. 'How old did you say she was?'

'I didn't.'

She waited, her eyes still upon him.

'She got married at eighteen. Yes, she's older than me, a few years. Does it matter?' he said as she openly did the calculation on her fingers.

'So, that makes her what? Thirty?' she said and a silence fell between them.

'It's getting awfully late,' Jenna broke it, extending her arms, fingers linked, above her head. 'And there's something I really do have to tell you.' She stretched her neck until it clicked.

'But first,' he was straining for gaiety, 'you *must* open your present.'

They both turned to the parcel leaning drunkenly against the wall beneath a hectically Blu-tacked retrospective of Julian's artistic endeavours. On the shelves of the dresser clay animals roamed two by two in various states of expertise. He and Jenna made them every year, though he always felt discouraged when he saw his lined up beside hers. His earliest effort, age four or five, was barely more than a blob of clay with a trunk and a tail, but last year's leopard was almost lovely. A pair of new creatures brought into being every Christmas, he and Jenna sitting together with the put-put of the portable gas heaters in the granary and frost patterning the windows, the excitement and chemical stink when she uncovered the kiln, telling him to keep his fingers crossed . . .

There was a lump in his throat as he slid the present towards her. 'Come on, Mum, open it.'

A terrier whined, stretched, and jumped into one of the stuffed chairs beside the Rayburn. He imagined Julia sitting there, her legs dangling over its arm.

'I'll open it in a minute, but first you must finish what you're saying and then I do need to tell you something before I go to bed,' Jenna said. He replaced the package and started to pace. It was hard to find the words for what had happened: Julia coming to him in the early hours, her shirt hanging from her in ribbons, that bastard's finger marks on her neck.

'He had her by the hair and there's a bald patch where he ripped it out. I couldn't leave her and come here.' He looked imploringly into his mother's face. 'You do understand, don't you?'

'Julian, stop pacing!' She ordered him into his chair, grabbed his hand and squeezed it hard across the table. Even simple eye contact was now a self-conscious act.

'We hardly slept that night and I was supposed to get the train . . .' he was starting to falter. 'I'm so sorry I wasn't here.'

'Julian! Will you stop apologising! I had a lovely day,' but still she looked downcast. He noticed the tendons of her long skinny neck, was surprised by tears which she wiped impatiently with her wrist as she blurted: 'On my birthday Michael asked me to marry him and I said that if he swam the river with me I would.'

He felt something twist. 'Michael?' Fat little Michael with his corduroy jeans and hairy hands? 'Did he? Did you?'

She nodded and smiled. 'Yes, and after the wedding I'll be living with him in Barnes, where you'll always have a room.'

Julian was almost winded at the thought of Michael's house

with its polished staircase and fussy, valuable furniture – of his mother waking each morning to embarrassing oriental erotic art and Michael's extensive collection of netsuke that were not to be touched (but towards which, as a boy, Julian had been irresistibly drawn, resulting in the shameful theft of an ivory monkey).

'You're moving there?' Julian sloshed more gin into his own glass.

'Darling, Michael wouldn't be able to commute to his office from here.'

'Why now?' He took a swallow of gin. 'What about all this . . .' He gestured around the kitchen with his glass, a sliver of ice sliding down his throat. He was choking and she leant across to bash him on the back.

'It's been a worry.' She kept getting to her feet and sitting down again, doing that straining thing with her neck. He was frightened by her tears now and concentrated instead on the sleeping dogs curled Yin and Yang into the cushions of the chair.

'What will happen to Firdaws if you're not here?'

She struck the table with her palms, making him jump. 'The Vales have made me give up the lease.' It came out as a wail. She hit the table again and the cat leapt to the floor. 'I never thought the greedy buggers would go through with it but . . .' Julian was suddenly faint. 'If your uncle was still alive they wouldn't dare,' she said. 'But it was only ever in trust to me until you *came of age* and now you have. You're twenty-one years old. A man.'

Firdaws was lost.

Eight

Julian stays drinking beer in the window seat long after the clouds and rain have rolled away. Swallows and house martins tick across the sky, the grass steams after so sudden a soaking, leaves drip. He opens the door to the porch to let the refreshed air in, gets himself another bottle, a packet of crisps and a lump of Cheddar. He eats the cheese, biting chunks straight from the packet, gulping them down with beer, and watches a blackbird tug a stretchy pink worm from the grass.

The dog crawls out from its hiding place, foolishly shellshocked. It is panting and trembling, slightly tragic in its cowardice but not averse to cheese. Patting the cushion, he invites it – him – to sit. Here was always his favourite place to read as a boy, dogs curled around. The window-seat cushions now are much larger and more splendid than the bobbly ones that went before. Papal velvet: Julia's choice.

The small carved-ivory monkey calls to him from its place on the bookcase. Julian picks it up. Quite a thing, this netsuke creature, with its polished jet eyes and lewdly curling tail.

Michael never once remarked upon its theft, did not even acknowledge the letter of apology that Jenna had made Julian write as soon as she discovered it hidden beneath his pillow. Over the years, Michael's silence had only enhanced Julian's shame and he made excuses to stay behind at Firdaws whenever his mother went to Barnes.

The netsuke monkey's eyes sparkle with malice. Your poor mother, it says. It's no wonder they waited until you were gone to get married. 'Fat hairy Michael'. That wasn't very nice, was it? Look at everything he's done for you. Picked you up from places, dropped you off. Crammed you for your exams. And all those tricks, poor man. What sort of person squashes real flies into someone's Garibaldi biscuit? All those phone messages you never passed on, the time you wiped your arse with his . . .' Julian closes his fist around the netsuke. 'He's been better than a father to you,' says the voice within. 'Where do you think you'd be without him?'

Michael's good deeds run unbidden: arriving at Mrs Briggs's in a Rentavan with the promise of a job for him at Abraham and Leitch, stopping at Geldings Antiques for Julia to drop off her keys and buying the wind-up gramophone for Jenna because she needed something to cheer her up. Without Michael there would be no books and no film deals, no lucrative screenplays to write. No Firdaws regained.

Julian drifts back to the first time he swam the river – he'd have been twelve or thirteen – and a salty feeling rises from his throat. Something his mother told him that day had made him want to cry. He sees her kneeling on the plaid blanket among the rubble of their picnic, her arms outstretched. And him: 'Stop it,' shunning her attempt to console him. Over what? He can't remember. Standing up, quite suddenly, and without another word, she took two scissoring paces and dived in.

Pinkish clouds lent the surface a pearly sheen and in she went, a long, perfect arc in her black swimsuit straight to the heart of the river, the deepest part, with no thought for those she left behind. Vernon, their Battersea Dogs Home Alsatian, yelped and leapt down the bank to save her.

'Oh my God! He's like a big bear.' Jenna swam in a circle laughing at the dog gulping his way through the lily pads. 'Call him back!' she shouted. 'He can't make it all the way down to where he can get out.' Michael slipped but, disappointingly, did not fall as he hauled Vernon up the bank by his neck, water-logged and snapping, his need to rescue his damsel entirely undiminished.

While Michael wrestled with the dog, Julian stood at the edge of the riverbank, its fringing of purple flowers at his feet. Way down, in the darkest water, his mother held her arms out to him and this time, without really thinking, he jumped and half fell towards her.

'Are you sure you'll make it all the way?' she asked as he gasped at the cold. 'There's no way out and nowhere to put your feet down until Swan Bank.'

He was treading water, unsure, but she had already set off, carving long strokes through the water. Michael was shouting to him from the bank: 'Here, let me pull you out. You'll freeze your bollocks off!'

She was a powerful swimmer, parting the river before him. He was spooked when it became so narrow and eerily silent. They swam through a tunnel of choking blackthorns and weeds with long tendrils and he started to panic, coughing and swallowing water. She told him to imagine the fingers winding around his scrawny arms and legs as 'a lovely massage', reassuring him that soon they would be clear of their slippery caresses and in another wide pool where he would be able to float on his back and rest.

It grew deeper as they set off again and he asked her to slow down so they could swim side by side as the weeds slithered beneath them.

'We're clear of them now,' she said, urging him on. 'You know, the weeds are nothing to get in such a flap about. It's the snake that worries me more.'

'Didn't I tell you?' she continued, glancing back at him over the wing of her shoulder, timing her words to the rhythm of her stroke. 'A couple of weeks ago I took Vernon for a walk to Swan Bank. I sat with him there for a while to watch the damselflies dance. Oh look, darling – like those two over there,' she gestured across the reeds but Julian was blind to their disco dazzle, could look nowhere but at the water, only darkness visible.

'Vernon was drinking at the edge when this enormous snake swam by. It was as thick as my arm and so long it made three loops.' She demonstrated by undulating her arm, fingers pressed together giving shape to its head through the water. Julian cried out and was rewarded with another mouthful of river. 'It gets worse,' she said as he kicked his legs, splashing too much to get anywhere fast. 'I was still staring at it when it doubled back and as it reached Vernon it rose from the water and hissed straight in his face.' She said something about fangs. 'Must've had young nearby, I suppose,' she added as she swept on ahead.

He was panting when they reached the bank, couldn't haul himself up its muddy sides quick enough. They lay on the grass catching their breath. He'd scraped himself getting out and there was a little pink blood puddled along his shin.

'Why did you tell me that about the snake?' he asked her. She sat up and touched his forehead with her palm, looking concerned, as though he might have a temperature. 'I don't know, I suppose I was frightened,' she said, and she pulled him to his feet so they could walk back to the fire she felt certain Michael would've lit on the riverbank to keep them warm.

It was Michael who first mooted that the Vales might not have been entirely within their rights to retain all the money when they sold Firdaws out from under them. He took Jenna's documents to his brother, a QC who liked nothing better than a wrangle over an inheritance.

It was Christmas Day, in Barnes, three years after Firdaws was lost that Jenna handed him the cheque: 'We won.'

Michael was looking on, with a smile that tried not to take too much credit. 'It's your share of Firdaws.' Both he and Julia stared in disbelief at the sum that was written there.

It was enough for a hefty deposit on Cromwell Gardens. White walls, fancy cornicing, glorious windows, a garden at the back. When Mr Pym, the flat's owner, showed them through the kitchen: 'I'm a conservatory designer by trade, hence . . .' and threw open the kitchen door, instead of the garden they were expecting they were greeted by a greenhouse so large and ornate it would not have looked out of place at Kew. There had been no reference to a greenhouse in the estate agent's particulars. 'My orangery' was what the sleekly satisfied Mr Pym called it while they haggled and Julian wished that Julia's desire for it was not so plain. She was rooted to the spot, practically suffering an attack of Stendhal syndrome. Double doors folded back the entire width at the front of the green-house and the white-painted ironwork was scrolled and crested at the apex with unfurling ferns. Pym showed them the clever steam watering system and the opening windows that were controlled by a thermostat. Inside he had a bamboo cocktail cabinet, suites of wicker furniture and several formal rows of lemon trees in green ceramic planters lined up like bearskin guards.

'Almost time for my gin and tonic,' he said, touching a finger to his gold watch. 'I've got the perfect space for it where I'm going. It's not included.'

Julia's eyes were bright with unshed tears and she was mouthing at him: 'This was meant to be.'

'Anyway, the agent thought most people would prefer to use the space to have a proper-sized garden, flower beds and a swing for the kiddy if you have one.' Mr Pym glanced nervously from

Julia to Julian. He had no way of guessing the true reason for her ardour.

Once it was hers, at a price that meant Julian would have to find another script to write quick, Mr Pym's greenhouse became the hub of Arbour, the specialist indoor horticultural business Julia was starting with her friend Freda. Freda paid for the van on which Julia painted the company name within garlands of fruiting vine, and they got their business cards printed.

Poor plants! He didn't know how Julia and Freda could stand it. From where he wrote in his alcove he could see them through the window as they loaded their van one way with pots of glossy clipped box and lollipop trees, open-throated clumps of lilies and branches of orchids swarming with blooms. The return barrows were filled only with sadness, as broken-limbed specimens made it back home from the City, some scattering leaves dry as raffia.

And the flat! By the time Julia had finished with it, entering any room of Cromwell Gardens was to be dazzled by sorbet: every wall was rag-rolled and glazed intense squashed-fruit colours. She made friends with a local upholsterer, rescuing unlikely furniture from dusty shops in Archway. In the sitting room cup-shaped chairs of pale-green velvet and a long table with carved and gilded edges, lamps with shades of painted silk, a plum-coloured sofa on brass lion's feet. Opium den or strip club, he thought. But in a good way. The central light hung from a moulding the shape and colour of a pomegranate and the plane trees along the street threw their patterns across the walls during the bright summers.

There's something contradictory, he thinks now, about Julia's desire for sumptuous opulence in the home. She clothed herself as though to disappear in a crowd. She covered herself up in mannish shirts, stone-coloured trousers rolled up at the ankle, crewneck jumpers in muted shades. Her shoes were either brown loafers or plimsolls. Lipstick was worn only as some sort of special favour to him and somewhere on the journey between Burnt Oak and Cromwell Gardens Julia's flimsy dresses had simply floated away.

She had wasted no time in getting to the paint shop. He enjoyed how animated she became, flying through the aisles with colour charts, plonking the tins on the counter, him just nodding away, lost in rapture. Sparks flew about her. It was all written in the stars, he was sure. The night before they'd wrestled each other within the flat's white expanse, rolling on the polished boards like excited children. Their first night there, a few boxes of belongings scattered about. Michael had sent a case of champagne so they sat in their bath towels on acres of floorboards, Julia's hair damp from the joyously deep claw-footed roll-top. The flames of their first fire made shadows dance around the walls. Clinking the tumblers they'd hastily unpacked, they toasted everything they could think of. They had the central heating pumping; the shivering cold of Burnt Oak would be forgotten in one night. No more typing in fingerless gloves, the sputtering of the cooker's gas rings inadequate against the December frosts. At Cromwell Gardens he still wrote in the kitchen, but at a desk in an alcove, his viewing screen set up on a stand beside him.

He had a book and a script on the go; Julia was happy to do most of the painting. They toasted their canine benefactors Geddon and Mrs Pericles and the soon-to-be box-office smash that was *Fletch le Bone*. She lay with her head in his lap while he worked his fingers through her drying hair and asked her to marry him, as he so often did. She shook her head, and laughed, confounding and contrary, sitting up and saying what she always said: 'But don't ever stop asking me . . .' kneeling to kiss the end of his nose. 'I love it so much when you do, and if I marry you you'll stop asking . . .' nuzzling him so he had to kiss her back.

'To not being married,' she said, clinking her glass to his.

'To Michael, for all his good advice,' he said and as Julia raised her tumbler, her towel started to slip and he reached out and tugged it away.

'To us,' he said, touching the rim of his glass to her nipple.

Later, with the fire dying and their mattress unrolled in the centre of the room, they whispered to each other about the son or daughter whose little room waited across the hall. Streetlamps projected falling snow on to the white sheets they'd tied at the window, shadow flakes swarming, her lips to his ear.

He was doubtful the next morning as he eased off the first lid with a screwdriver, staring at the bright-pink paint and glancing up to see if she was still certain. Julia nodded, a blue scarf knotted around her head to cover her hair, exposing the precise planes of her face, light catching the bud of her chewed bottom lip, very Vermeer, he thought.

She spent weeks on the ornate cornices, her crazy whim, paints spread on to the board that she used as a palette and artist's brushes stuck through her hair. She coloured and glazed, purple grapes, sunkissed peaches, every leaf and curl of vine, standing perilously on a plank suspended between two stepladders. She found it meditative, she said, and he massaged her neck when it grew sore. She played her old Bowie CDs – to which she knew all the words – and after supper, while she was singing away with her paintbrushes and *Hunky Dory*, he settled at the kitchen table and into the vernacular of his latest canine alter ego, a glass of wine by his side and from the greenhouse the scent of flowering citrus.

There were velvet curtains at Cromwell Gardens, hung from high and pooling at the floor. In their bedroom a dark mulberry, almost black at night, but richly red with the sun shining through.

Every morning a rubied awakening: Julia naked beside him, shaking the night from her hair, the pink light catching her shoulders as the sheets fell away . . .

They played rounds of Perudo, which Julia won more often than him, though, unlike him, she did not apply mathematical principles to the fall of the dice. Their life settled into a pattern of tea breaks where he read bits of his scripts to her, Julia and Freda in and out in the van, potted trees and plants filling the greenhouse, takeaways and fry-ups, shared baths when they scrubbed the day away from each other with flannels, Julia's soaped body slippery as a mermaid.

Such happy sheets at Cromwell Gardens! Going at it like, what was it Karl had said? Oh yes . . . prairie voles. Julia with her thermometer and ovulation charts, their bedroom the colour of a womb. Stockings, lace, the kitchen table, the garden fence. Elegant proportions, tall windows, Julia leaning out across the sill wearing nothing but that jumper of hers, his eyes drawn to the rosy moon beneath the lavender wool ribbing, candles making a monster of his shadow, a noisy brass bed.

Not long after they moved in, Karl came from Rotterdam to see them, his jacket creased from the flight, comedy eyebrows chevroning high.

Julian plays it back through his mind. Julia perched on her plank across the room and Karl shielding his eyes with his hands, pretending he had to put on his sunglasses to save him from the brightness of the paint. He brought with him from Holland a pair of identical twins in matching tight T-shirts who spoke in stereo. All of it making Julia scowl.

'Anki and Hendrika.' They were tiny as dolls and Julian had to stoop to shake their hands. How would he be able to tell them apart?

Karl calling to Julia, gesturing: 'It's a palace,' attempting to win back her favour, walking to the ladder to grab her hands,

'Jump?' And Julia pausing to lay down her palette, cleaning the brush with a cloth before poking it through her hair. 'Come on then, one two three . . .' Karl said and she grasped his hands so he could swing her to the ground.

The twins perched like bookends beside Karl on the plum sofa. He had put on weight, in fact, Julian noticed the middle button of his shirt had come undone or, knowing his friend's high-minded disregard for his appearance, was probably missing. He went to the kitchen to open wine. Julia came to fetch glasses and to hiss at him that it was hardly worth bothering to remember the names of any of Karl's girls, he had so many different ones. 'He's rubbing your nose in it,' she said.

Wine poured, Julian asked Karl about his latest research project. Karl was on the brink of a significant breakthrough. But then, wasn't he always? The twins, he said, were working with him in Rotterdam and they looked up and nodded, then tilted their heads beneath his chin and continued their own conversation. Karl looked from one to the other in mock dismay. 'As babies they sucked each other's thumbs, you know.' They stopped their conversation and smiled.

'Sweet,' said Julian.

'They graduated from Rotterdam together and Pfizer gave them both a job in my department, lucky me!' Karl lowered his voice and leant closer to Julian's ear: 'And, yes, since I can tell you are dying to know, they do sleep every night in the same bed.'

The twins faux-punished him with sharp admonishments and synchronised pinches to his thighs, then carried on starting and finishing each other's sentences. 'Double Dutch,' Karl said with a smirk as Julia called from the kitchen that they should all sit down at the table.

The dog gives Julian's hand a lick. They share the remains of the Cheddar and he strokes its muzzle. He stares at the apple trees, at the hammock hanging forlorn and sodden and thinks: perhaps this is all there is. From now on this will be my life, remembering instead of living.

His fingers worry at a dark splodge in the fabric of the window-seat. It's a little rough there, like a cat's tongue. Mira's ice-cream. He was proved right almost as soon as they moved in. Purple velvet was not a sensible choice. But then, when was Julia ever sensible?

Michael's netsuke monkey has grown warm as a little hand in his. He returns it to the top of the bookcase. He has searched all the bookshelves in the house. Mira's picture books have been carefully removed. But here his and Julia's books remain side by side, haphazardly. Only Julia's plant books have been taken. These paperbacks that are so obviously hers – green-spined Viragos, du Mauriers, Jeanette Winterson, Bridget Jones, for fuck's sake – he hurls them, pages flying, into a cardboard box that he keeps by the porch. It is filling with a steady tide of her things. When it's full he plans to tape it up and send it to her.

Nine

Now he's edited Julia out, there's a reassuring order to the books in this, his own bookcase. Marvell, Milton, Ricks, Spenser, Virgil, Yeats. Volumes that have been investigated rather than read, spines ridged like geriatric fingernails. Faded covers remind him of the earnest student he was before he set eyes on Julia. He scans the shelves: the pleasing uniformity of Everyman editions, the Bible, Homer and Stanley Fish, his entire reading list packed into tea chests when they fled Mrs Briggs's with nothing but his unfinished degree, Julia's marital debts and his mother's wailing disappointment to accompany them to Burnt Oak.

Several of the cloth bindings have become freckled from stray grains of tea, some a little buckled. Bulging between its covers, the pages of *Paradise Lost* are swelled by his scribblings, taped-in scraps of paper, its spine broken in several places. When he pulls it from the shelf his notes stick out their tatty tongues every few pages, some flutter to the floor, his writing smaller and neater then than he could ever manage now, the computer to thank for that. This is the first copy of *Paradise Lost* he ever owned, given to him by his old friend Peace Convoy Raph, with Rubens's *Adam and Eve*, gloriously naked and unashamed, on the cover.

It was from a lecture on *Paradise Lost* that he came back to his digs to the news that Julia was pregnant. He was already making headway on his dissertation; they'd known each other only a matter of weeks. The timing couldn't have been worse and yet he remembers nothing but elation from the moment she cast her softly spoken spell of three words. He was gripped by a fierce sense of possession that had nothing to do with the baby now forming inside her. She'd done the test while he was at the lecture – '*Milton's attitude to divorce in light of his attitude to the birth of Eve*' – though even before Julia shared her news he already had many more immediate problems than *Literature, Culture and Crisis 1631–71.*

His shifts at the Crown were being cut now the summer was truly over and though this gave him back time for the mounting piles of reading, it deprived them of money they needed. Julia's wages from her job at Geldings Antiques disappeared at source, thanks to various HP and loans that Chris had set up in her name throughout their marriage and was punitively not honouring. She was left paying for his fridge, washing machine and TV, and his van and the new roof on the cottage he'd so prudently left in his mother's name. Debt was hard to divorce. Julian was cursing the mad impulse that made him splurge on the mirror in Geldings just weeks before. Soon he would be reduced to eyeing up the Co-op's bins where he knew some students went to stock up on food past its sell-by date. They barely had money for the gas meter, so kept warm in bed. Ah, yes, bed.

That morning he had left his room steeped in the smell of her. Downstairs Mrs Briggs waylaid him, brandishing a Hoover. 'I'm sick of turning a blind eye,' she said. 'That maniac beating at my front door.' Julian mumbled, took his time tucking the bottom of his trouser leg into his yellow sock. She steadied herself on his shoulder for emphasis, forcing him to look up. Her globular thyroid eyes seemed to wobble, threatening to fall like eggs from their sockets. 'I can't have men turning up here at all times of the day and night using that sort of language,' she said. 'I won't have this sort of thing going on beneath my roof.'

Only when Julian agreed to look for somewhere else did she remove her hand from his shoulder and, turning her toad's face away, she shuffled off in her slippers, dragging the Hoover behind her like a sacrifice.

He returned from his lecture hoping he'd retained something, though he'd been too distracted to make many notes. There was stuff about various sects in Milton's time, like the Ranters, Calvinists who believed that they were destined for heaven *whatever* they did. SIN IS THE PRODUCT ONLY OF THE IMAGINATION he'd written before his mind wandered to the more pressing issue of where he and Julia would live.

As he cycled back from the lecture there was drizzle. He collected the local rag and tucked it into his Crombie to keep it dry. The road was mulchy with leaves and the chain chose that moment to slip off his bike and his hands became filthy with oil. Finally he got back and was turning the pages of the soggy newspaper to the Rooms to Rent section as he climbed the stairs. The antique shop didn't open on Mondays: Julia was just the other side of the door. His heart leapt as he put his key in the lock.

She was standing at the window. An intense slant of sunlight had conspired with a break in the clouds to fall across her to the floor so that the sight of her in a blue shirt, the long brown backs of her legs and her hair loose and shining, was instantly stowed in the Dutch Master department of his brain. She remained looking out at the street, perhaps she hadn't noticed him arrive. The light hit the curve of her cheek when she turned. She leant into the sill, the shirt barely skimmed the tops of her thighs, her tan from the summer not fading now, or ever. He flew across the room and she raised her fingers to his lips, pressing

85

them flat, so for a moment he didn't know if he wanted to bite or kiss.

The pale-blue shirt was his, a fact that gave him pleasure. It still smelt of the hot iron she'd used before putting it on. She hadn't bothered with underwear and his hands found her warm back. She leant her head on his shoulder, her hair smelt of his shampoo. He slid his hands from the back of her ribcage to the front and she gasped and squirmed as he reached her breasts. 'They've become so hot and tender,' she said and he wasn't such a boy that he didn't know what this might mean.

What had he felt when she told him? Elation, yes. Fear? Maybe. However hard he tries, he can't remember exactly what went through his mind. He sees himself only from the outside, as though through the glass of a diorama or on a screen with the sound turned off. He's skinny, almost gaunt, dressed in a black V-neck that's a bit long and ragged in the hem, baggy suit trousers, yellow socks with a hole just starting at one big toe. Rakish, he likes to think, with his dark hair curling at his collar, and, unless he pushes it back, across his eyes. Scholarly, surrounded by books and untidy piles of notes, Gustave Doré's etchings Blu-tacked to his walls. Candles stuck in wine bottles, his few plates and bowls stacked by the window, a duvet with a pattern of autumn leaves on the bed. Not much more than a boy, he can see that now. Free for the first time in his life but weak against the charm of beauty's powerful glance.

There he is throwing down the newspaper, enclosing her, kissing her, unbuttoning the blue shirt, parting the cloth and kissing her belly and minutes later rising above her on the single bed, entering her cautiously and with such an exclamation of wonder and awe about the facts of life – the sudden facts of *their* life – that he made her laugh and then cry, her arms thrown back, palms to the ceiling and fingers spreading, begging him not to stop, her hair across the pillow like something unravelling.

He had not a flicker of doubt, this new blood-borne certainty snuffed out all other thought. The next day he went to Professor Mulligan's room to tell him he was dropping out.

Paul Mulligan tried to dissuade him with words that just days before would have charmed Julian's ear. 'Your work on Milton leaves me in no doubt you've got a contribution to make, well beyond degree,' Mulligan said with twinkling eye. But the rich music of books and study and far-off PhDs had overnight become only incidental. He was moving to London, he said, as Mulligan fiddled with his glasses. There would be work tutoring rich kids through A-levels.

A couple of years ago Mulligan had written to him, c/o Abraham and Leitch, on home, not college paper. He said his young nephews very much enjoyed a film about a space-age dog, Mulligan himself liked the scene where Laika appeared as a ghost on the moon. He had, he wrote in his neat script, been astonished but pleased to see Julian's name in the credits. He signed off saying: 'People say that when life gets busy, the time for study and reflection fades. I very much hope this is not true in your case.'

Julian replaces the Milton, belches. He counts the empty beer bottles, which confirm that he is quite drunk. He takes what's left in the last bottle to swallow his sleeping pill.

Though the storm has cleared, the air remains stuffy in his bedroom. It's that or the stink of the jasmine if he opens the windows. The little owls screech from the roof of the granary. He strips off and falls into bed, fishing around in his mess of bedclothes until he finds what he wants. Julia's jumper is thin and lavender-coloured, floppy from wear and thin at the elbows, long enough to just about cover her bum, and pulled on in the mornings when she went down for coffee.

A far-off vixen pierces the valley with anguished screams. The cashmere is old and soft, the ribbing a little frayed. He is furious with himself, throwing it away across the bed. He should go downstairs now and put it in the box with the rest of her junk.

His pill fails to tame his unresting thoughts – round and round they fly – and he finds himself with her jumper to his face. The smell of Julia is fading, it's hardly there now, but he clutches it to quell a pain that has started in his groin, squeezes his eyes shut. He curses the beginnings of a hard-on, and also the part of his brain that conspires continually and lasciviously to light the way to a bed containing Julia. 'In loving thou dost well, in passion not . . .' Who says that? Ah yes, Raphael to Adam, *Paradise Lost*, Book VIII. Already the taper is lit to a hotel in Paris, spicy candles burning all along the bar. It's a place he can't stop himself returning to, time and again. Julia's long swaying walk along the aisle of candles, high heels of black satin, and lips painted a shade of red called Rampant, a fact he knew because they'd got the giggles in the pharmacy in Rue Jacob choosing it. There's low-level trance music, buttoned banquettes the colour of kidneys, murmured conversations and a man in a brown corduroy suit sitting at the bar drinking alone.

Julian spotted the man moments before Julia made her entrance. He was clearly resident in the hotel, as he kept fiddling with his room key which he'd placed beside his glass. He was fiftyish, Julian guessed, with a head of cropped steel-grey curls and a large nose. He was drinking red wine and glancing around the bar from time to time, nodding almost imperceptibly along with the beat. Julian saw the man stop with his glass halfway to his lips, suddenly transfixed, and followed his eyes to the door. There she was: Julia, pushing a pin into her hair, stalling.

The white silk of her blouse shimmered as she entered. God, she was good. Venus stepping from her shell. Va-va-voom. Every head turned to watch her.

She was dressed exactly as he had asked and despite her earlier protestations was managing perfectly well in the heels and tight skirt. She paused again just inside the bar, momentarily gathering her courage, before sashaying closer. He was holding his breath. They'd had vodkas from the mini-bar upstairs before he left her to get ready, so she must've been already quite drunk. Through the sheen of her blouse her breasts bounced as she passed so close he could feel the breath of her movement but not so much as a wink of complicity. Total strangers. She settled at a table in the corner, within his sightline. Her hair was half pinned up and half tumbling. She crossed her legs and uncrossed them, ignoring his stare as she studied the cocktail list, and he found he had to keep gulping from his glass, his heart pounding then as his fist was now.

Julia. Quite the actress. Oh, yes. He hates himself and her raggedy jumper and, retrospectively, for how he felt when the man in the brown corduroy suit slid from his bar stool to Julia's table. He watched as the man reached out and took the menu from her hand. She leant forward to hear what he was saying and Julian watched the unrestrained trajectory of the man's eyes as her blouse fell away from the pointed cones of her breasts.

He was supposed to hold back until after the first cocktail and endured Julia running her fingers up and down the stem of the glass as the man spoke. He found himself wondering if that was part of her act. The man was leaning closer, almost handsome for someone of that age with his three-day stubble and evenly cropped curls. Finally she finished her drink and he was free to move in and offer them both another. Might he join them?

'Of course,' Julia smiling, welcoming him, gesturing to the banquette, the man, disgruntled, shuggling himself beside her. The man had taken off his brown corduroy jacket, loosened his tie, iron-grey question-marks peeked at the base of his neck. He turned his shoulder, did his best to block the young English interloper, twice laying his hand lingeringly on her thigh.

Julia and Julian maintained their act – that was all there was to it really, his grubby birthday wish. He would've stuck to the script but after a third margarita an impious spirit rose up inside him. He was almost laughing out loud as he leant back in his chair, calling for his bill, preparing to leave, Julia's lipsticked mouth falling open: '*Merci*,' he said, putting down a few notes and standing with a little wave. '*Amusez-vous bien . . .*'

She was soon back upstairs where he lay naked beneath the hotel sheets, pretending to snore. She pulled them back and slapped him on the bum. 'You were supposed to rescue me.' She was hopping to rid herself of the heels. 'What happened to the sudden proposal of a fuck and leading me off? I thought that was the point of your little fantasy?'

He pulled her on to the bed before she got a chance to remove anything else. 'Admit it. You wanted to fuck him,' he said, pushing up her skirt. 'Go on, admit it . . .'

Her legs around his neck, heels battering his shoulders. The beating of wings in his ears. 'You wanted to fuck him . . .'

He was thrashing hot with shame and fury at her jumper. 'Admit it, Admit it . . .' She wandered around in the mornings with nothing on underneath it. It had become stretched over the years where she'd pulled it to her thighs but was not long enough to cover her at all when she bent over to pick her pants up from the floor in that straight-legged way she had, hips so flexible she could lay her hands flat when she touched her toes.

'Admit it,' he shouts into the empty room, kicking the sheets to his feet, headboard drumming, louder, faster, one sleeve of her jumper furiously flapping. Blood pounding. 'I did. I did. I did.'

Ten

It was bound to happen sooner or later. He couldn't hide from Katie for ever. Another day of brutal sunshine. His milk growing warm on the step. She follows him into the kitchen, rattling her keys like an estate agent and clanking together the two pint bottles her arrival has made him forget. 'I keep meaning to leave a note for the milkman,' he says. Not easy to do. The second pint was Mira's.

She plunks the milk into the fridge, pulling a face at the chaos inside. He starts apologising.

'OK, OK. Now let's get a look at *you*,' she says, flinging wide the kitchen curtains, making him wince. She's wearing a brightly patterned dress of blown roses and her skin is flushed, her arms bare. The dress is cinched at her waist by a wide red patent-leather belt that catches the light as she moves.

She turns from the window, advancing on him like a bush in full flower. 'Oh Jude,' she says, reaching for him as the dog comes skittering from the garden, bouncing on his haunches and trying to lick her.

'At least someone's pleased to see me,' she says, crouching to ruffle his ears. 'Good boy, Zephon.'

'I'm afraid he's been rolling in something dead,' Julian flees to fill the kettle. 'He stinks.' Katie gets up sniffing her fingers, pulls a face. 'To be honest, that makes two of you.'

He lifts his armpit to his nose. Agrees.

'And when did you last shave?'

He turns off the tap, scrapes his hand along his jaw, which sets it itching. She comes and takes the kettle from him, runs some water over her hands and looks around for something to dry them.

'I'm so sorry,' she says. 'I can't begin to imagine what you're going through.'

He passes her a tea towel, ashamed of its grubbiness, of the mess of empty bottles and bowls pasted with half-eaten meals, of his own stink.

'Go on,' she says, drying her hands and giving him a little push to the stairs. 'Have a bath and a shave and I'll clear up a bit down here. Mum's got the boys so I can make you some breakfast and I won't make you talk if you don't want to . . .'

Water thumps into the tub conspiring with his conscience to summon a song, the beat of the claves and a female singer with a breathy voice: 'Easy, easy, easy. Loving you is easy.' He'd gone straight to the Marylebone hotel from Great Ormond Street. The song was playing in the bar; a rhythmic cow bell, watery percussion, the singer was Swedish and pronounced 'easy' as 'ici' which had made him and Katie smile.

Katie in that too-tight blue dress, her cloying sadness and hyacinth scent. Bar snacks of posh burgers. She was telling him about the humiliating end of her marriage. She might as well have been talking about the humiliating end of her blow-dry for all he was taking in. Instead of listening he was sketching on a paper napkin, the kitchen at Firdaws: lines and arrows indicating where the cupboards should be, the layout of the tiles, the places for pots and pans. On a second napkin he drew a floor plan for Mira's bedroom; her bed was to be toes to the window, shelves right the way along the wall from the door.

'It was while I was on maternity leave with Billy . . .' Katie was saying. He wanted to ask her to get Mira's room carpeted so she wouldn't have to wear slippers when she got home. Her room at the hospital was shiny lino, the whole hospital was. 'Camilla was his classroom assistant. Most original.'

He put down his pen, realised he was ravenous and stuffed his mouth with the burger. Katie was telling him she couldn't stop dwelling on all the times she'd walked into the staffroom at break and everyone fell silent.

'She had this ruby cross on a chain and they all knew he'd bought it for her.'

He thought of Mira in her hospital bed, her hand above the sheet, Julia's arm reaching across from the camp bed to meet it.

'It all started when they took a group rock climbing,' Katie continued. 'Adrian came back with a pulled ligament in his groin. *From the climbing.*'

The bartender came to clear away their leftover chips while Katie listed Adrian's sins. There were complications over the sale of the house, she and the boys would have to stay on at her mum's after the summer and she'd get whatever supply teaching she could. 'I'm not going back there,' she said, and held up her hand and a finger grown fat around her wedding ring. 'And this has got to go . . .'

He asked the bartender for some butter, the least he could do, his list and plans ready for action in her bag. The bartender brought the butter in a basket with rolls. It was soft, almost melting, when he unwrapped it. He picked it up within the foil to smear it along her ring finger and she turned her head away as though from a medical procedure as he rubbed it in. He twisted the ring back and forth until it slid from her finger sur-prisingly easily.

She stared at her finger so shiny and bare. 'Oh, I suppose that was really inappropriate of me,' she said. 'Asking you . . .'

He wiped the ring and handed it back to her. She still wore a band of paler skin. 'Think of it as no more to me than the removal of a splinter,' he said, making her stick out her lip at him: 'That's really very callous of you,' and he shrugged apologetically. She smiled without showing her dimples and picked at one of the rolls. 'I know I shouldn't be going on about this,' she said.

Ah, she meant well. In the bathroom he lathers his face. His conscience won't leave him be: it wouldn't hurt to be a little kinder to your one-time paramour, it says. Reaching for his razor, he clears the steam from the mirror and is hit by a wave of yearning so strong it makes him screw his eyes shut, but still he sees her splashing around at the opposite end, his Mira like a little elf with her hair in a topknot, watching him shave. Mira liked it when he squirted his foam on her face and she copied him shaving, using a lolly stick that had found its way to the bathroom, pulling all the right faces, jutting out her funny chin.

He squirts the foam and starts at his throat, leaning into the mirror. The bathroom is old-fashioned, unchanged since his father's, or possibly even his grandparents' time: a primrose suite that always made him think of lemon meringue pie, a brass rack across the bath with a round swivel mirror just right for resting a book. He runs more hot water, starts scraping at his face. His conscience rises around him in the steam: Remember, if it wasn't for Katie, Firdaws would have stayed lost. No one else was going to tell you it was for sale. Not even Michael. He *kept* it from you. Bristles fall like timber into the snowy waste of his throat.

It was fate that he should be the one to take Mira for her booster that day or he would never have known that Firdaws was up for sale. He'd changed tubes at – haha, you gods – the Angel Islington and that's when he saw her: Katie just ahead of him on the platform.

At first he wasn't sure; her hair was different, much blonder. She grasped a tot firmly in each hand, a bulky canvas bag strapped to her back like a camel. She hadn't yet seen him, but as he edged through the crowds he became convinced it *was* her. She scooped the younger boy on to her hip, his fat legs gripping her like a pair of nutcrackers, and as she turned to say something to him Julian clocked her smile: the one that spread more up one side of her face than the other, the double dimple in her cheek that made her unmistakably Katie, and he called out her name.

She was plumper than he remembered but still as pretty. Her bosom was back, he was glad to note. The last time he'd seen her, the grief of their break-up had shrunk her in a shocking way; the sight of her tiny breasts poking her thin T-shirt back then had made him want to throw himself at her feet and beg for forgiveness.

'Katie?' She turned, dipped her chin in disbelief. 'Julian? Jude?' She shook her children's hands at him, dimples flashing. 'What are you doing here?'

Three trains, four, filled and emptied while they talked, the air whooshing at them with gastric sighs, the boys squirming impatiently.

'Billy. Arthur.' She made them say hello. 'I got married and then I got these.' He ruffled Billy's hair while she peeked into his pack where Mira was sleeping, her head lolling against his neck.

'Ahhhhh . . .' It came out slowly.

The lips he pressed to Katie's cheek that day were those of a man who has been spared. 'You've changed your perfume,' he said, sniffing her neck. And she said: 'Well, seven years is a long time, what do you expect?'

He couldn't be late for the clinic so he scribbled down his number and slid it into her bag. The next tube was his.

'You know Firdaws is up for sale?' She said it quite casually as he climbed through the doors, and his heart missed a beat.

He was almost hysterical with excitement when he got back

to Cromwell Gardens. Freda was on her way out to deliver plants, amber beads clacking. She pulled a face at Julia, he clearly wasn't making much sense. He eased the backpack with Mira still strapped inside on to the floor while Julia went on chopping onions, her brow furrowing. 'It's almost too good to be true, this was meant to be.' He danced round and grabbed her. 'Firdaws, it's for sale.'

She studied him hard, eventually putting down the knife and wiping her streaming eyes on her sleeve. 'They told you that at the *health centre*?' He didn't answer. No point confusing things by mentioning Katie.

'You should suck bread while you do that,' he said, tearing off a crust and handing it to her.

She released Mira from the backpack. 'What are you talking about, Julian?' She swept her free hand through her hair, then smelt it. 'Damn, onions.'

'I have to get hold of the agent immediately. Mira was very brave about her injection, by the way, just one little cry,' he said as he danced towards the phone.

'Firdaws? Are you serious?' she said, stopping him in his tracks.

'Don't you see? I'll never get the chance again.'

'This is ridiculous.' She jerked her head away from him as he tried to pick some stray foliage out of her hair, perched Mira on her hip. 'Have you thought for a moment about me?' Mira started to cry. 'I can't commute from Firdaws and all my work is here. What am I supposed to do?'

'We'll sort something out,' he said.

Mira was beside him like a partner in crime as they ran away together to Waterlow Park. Mira pulling him and stumbling so she was dangling on his arm but still urgently pointing at things she needed him to explain, to look at more closely. Dogs, birds, a comic left fluttering on the pavement, a 10p piece in the gutter. In the park, on a seat with ice-cream cones and the rhodoendrons in lurid flower, he told her of Firdaws, of her bedroom that used to be his with silver stars on the curtains, the fields she would run in, the lovely dog that would be hers. He promised he'd teach her to swim in the river and show her the baby birds in their nests. A squirrel was bold enough to hop beside them to hear these wondrous tidings. Julian held his finger to his lips, telling Mira to keep still. Breaking the end of his cone, he made a little scoop of ice-cream and the squirrel took it from him, staying on beside them, politely sitting on its breechy haunches, licking its miniature cornet like a tiny neat child, while he made up and whispered the things it was saying to her in its posh schoolboy voice until Mira's explosion of giggles sent it scampering to the foot of a tree.

'You *knew*?' Before the end of the day he was standing in Michael's office, the estate agent's particulars shaking in his hand. He'd hurtled from the tube and through the elegant doors, the ignored receptionist sarcastic – 'Well, good afternoon to you too' – as he bowled past, Michael appearing on the curve of the stone stairs – 'Julian?' – and, noticing the set of his face, taking him by the sleeve and steering him into the conference room, gesturing for him to sit.

'You knew, didn't you?' Julian refusing the chair, slapping the property details on the table.

'What?' Michael standing beside him. 'Oh, I see . . .'

'Were you scared that if my mother found out about this she'd want to move back there? You'd have to retire if she persuaded you . . .' Julian said. 'What, retire to Firdaws and give up all this?' sweeping his arm to indicate the room with its gleaming mahogany, the tall windows, the trees in the square just coming into leaf.

Michael shaking his head, saying: 'How the hell do you think you'll manage it?' The receptionist popping her head around the door – 'Coffee?' – and retreating without waiting for an answer.

'I'll sell Cromwell Gardens. There's plenty more work out there, you said so yourself. Oh, and I'll postpone writing my novel.'

'Again?' Michael grimaced.

'Look, Michael, I do know it won't be easy . . .'

Michael pulled out the chair, persuaded him to sit. 'That wasn't really what I meant,' he said and clearing his throat: 'Have you thought about Julia? She seems very happy in her work. What will happen to her business if you move out there? All she's built up? Are you expecting her to just drop everything?' And Julian had been only slightly abashed to tell him that yes, that *was* what he was expecting. 'It's paradise, Julia will love it,' he said. 'I've never felt more certain of anything before in my life.'

Michael picked up the estate agent's brochure, flipped past a photograph of the Nicholsons' unpleasantly marmoreal kitchen. 'That's a hell of a lot of money for a man in your position,' he said, stabbing a finger at the page.

'It's for Mira. Don't you think she should have the chance to grow up at Firdaws? I've seen the children marching in croco-diles up the road past our flat. Grey school jumpers and matching grey faces. That's not what I want for her. And it's fate. Yes, that's right. Don't look at me like that; I'm not a total idiot, Michael. It's there, the gates are ajar, I owe it to her . . .'

They'd outgrown Cromwell Gardens and that was a fact. Back at the flat he cast a critical eye. Julia's sheets of graph paper were spread out at the table, her Caran d'Ache pencils arranged anyhow in the tin. In the alcove his desk, with everything pushed to the wall to stop Mira grabbing, his headphones lying across the pages of his half-baked script. He'd started work on that one with Mira crawling at his feet, no wonder it was taking so long.

Hardly ideal. Mira's baby room was tiny, they would have to move eventually. Not much more than a box room really, her cot beside a window with a view across their strip of lawn to Julia's greenhouse, close enough to see the leaves pressing against the glass.

The bath is growing cold around him. His conscience won't leave him be. Katie's going through a hard time too, it reminds him. You'll have to man up and go downstairs sooner or later. You've been in this bath for over an hour, it says. Look, the walls are dripping.

'That's better,' Katie says as he comes down, rubbing his hair with a towel. He's wearing a clean T-shirt and jeans. She nods her approval. There's a bowl of raspberries on the table, each one perfectly plump. She's been out into the garden to pick them; she'll have seen how lax he's been with the watering, how he just lets everything die.

She fills the silence with an update on her marital crisis, offers him eggs or pancakes. He shrugs. 'You choose.'

'Why do I always pick such rotters?' she's saying, cracking eggs into a bowl. 'First of all you and then Adrian.'

His head is pounding, she's opened all the windows, outside the buzzards scream. 'Please, Katie?'

She stands from the table, her blonde ponytail swings. The air is thick with Pledge. The worksurfaces shine, she's swept the floor, picked some sprays of jasmine for the table and dealt with the overflowing fridge and bins. She's filled the bird feeder that hangs from the lintel and the blue tits tell him off for not having done it himself. She brings him the coffee pot and scrambled eggs, sits down to butter his toast.

He pours the coffee into two mugs, and for a moment, as he reaches for the milk, it's Julia and not Katie he sees across from him at the table. Julia passing him the jug.

Katie offers him second helpings, tries to prompt him, reaches for his hands, tells him he should find someone he can talk to, makes him want to scream at the cod-psychology of it all. 'I quite understand if it can't be me,' she says. The birds chatter at the feeder. Come on. Say something. She fiddles with the end of her ponytail. He wishes she'd leave. He's overcome with tiredness.

'Can I drag you out for a walk?' she says, and at the word 'walk' Zeph jumps from his chair. 'Just to the river and back?'

He shakes his head. The birds squabble, sunlight glances from the pans. She squeezes his hands. 'Jude, I really think you should try to talk about it.'

He relieves himself of her grasp, stands and starts to pace. 'I couldn't believe she wouldn't fall in love with the place once we got here,' he says. 'Do you remember we saw you and the boys the night we moved in?'

'At the bonfire, yes,' Katie says. 'Mira wanted to play with Billy and Arthur, but you were too worried about the older children throwing fireworks.'

'And how sad Julia was? She looked like she'd been brought to her own execution.'

They had set off from Cromwell Gardens on the morning of November the fifth and it was dark by the time they reached Firdaws. One large black cloud hung above the treetops with half a moon like a coin going into its slot. He had wanted to carry Julia over the threshold, but she laughed at him, told him he'd break his back – besides she still had Mira, dozy from the journey, in her arms.

He'd arranged for the fire to be lit and for flowers. 'Doesn't it look welcoming and cosy now the furniture's all in?' he said, and she nodded. Mira was awake now and running from room to room as he led Julia around. They came to a stop in the kitchen. She had tears in her eyes: 'I can see why you want this so badly,' she said. 'I just hope you're right and there's a way we can make it work.' And she buried her face in his shirt. He held her tight. 'Thank you for letting me do this,' he said, kissing the top of her head.

On the village green an enormous bonfire was blazing, cordite sparking expectation as they made their way towards the crowd that surrounded it. Rockets squealed and golden dandelions burst above their heads and he found himself turning to watch the bright little pansy of Mira's upturned face beneath her woolly hat. Exploding showers lit her skin, her mouth and eyes were rounded with wonder and he found more pleasure in her face watching the fireworks than the fireworks themselves. He was lit up with the thought: This is it! Ecstatic. I am a father, what a thing!

The air crackled from the fire, making fireflies of cinders. He caught the smell of sausages. People turned from the flames with red cheeks. Beyond the bonfire the old trees and the church made reassuring silhouettes.

Mira, her cheeks and chin caramelised, grasped her first toffee apple in mittened hands. She hid herself in her pushchair's shadowed folds from the people who said hello: toothy old faces grinning in the firelight like pumpkins. Sweetheart. Darling. Beauty.

Julia clung to his arm and buried herself in his shoulder while he ploughed Mira's pushchair through the squelch. Children with sparklers and glowing necklaces of fluorescent tubing danced around. So many people so pleased to see Julian back where he belonged. Julia biting her lip as she turned to smile, Julian keeping up a running commentary: 'That's the younger Miss Hamlyn from the village shop . . . the bloke over there with the stick is Mr Horseman who owns the land next to our house, he's aged . . . I think that's the woman with the stables, shall I ask if there's a pony for Mira to ride?'

Mira was leaning from her carriage towards the other children, arms outstretched. As they wheeled her round the fire he could remember his own excitement as a boy on this village green, screaming along with the fireworks, toasting sausages on sticks over the embers, writing his name with a sparkler, him and the others throwing rockets on to the pavilion roof . . .

Billy and Arthur ran by, Katie grabbing at their arms. She managed to haul them to a standstill when she spotted him. 'Jude!'

'Ah, Katie. I wondered if you'd be here.' He put a hand on Julia's shoulder to pull her to a standstill, felt awkward making the introduction and embarrassed by her glower. Katie was unconcerned as she hugged him and that's when he noticed she'd changed back to the hyacinth scent of her teen years. It made him tender at first and then very cross.

He stops pacing, sits down and locks his hands behind his head. The phone is ringing. 'Leave it,' he says. Katie clears some crumbs from the table, leaning across it, scraping them with the side of her hand into a cloth.

'When we got back here from the bonfire Julia went straight to bed,' Julian tells her. 'We had a furious row because I hadn't told her about you.'

'About *me*?' Katie stops what's she's doing. 'What about me?'

'Oh, you know, about you being here.' He gives her a shrug. 'That night Mira woke up crying with a tummy ache. I think that might have been the start of it. Oh, God. We always just gave her Calpol.'

He resumes pacing, blinks back tears. He really will have to ask Katie to leave now. The phone goes on and on. 'Shall I get that?' she says, rising to her feet.

'Leave it. Let it ring.'

Eleven

Julian hears his mother calling his name. He's struggling to wake, thrashing through a gap in the murk, arms tangled and fingers webbed by slime. 'That poor dog was bursting to go outside.' She's shouting at him already as she comes up the stairs. He's late for an exam, a bus, worse, he has to find Mira, weeds slip around his legs, pulling him backwards, against the beat of his arms. Mira's face falls towards him spinning like a coin, jellyfish pulsating in her hair, he emerges into the light grasping at handfuls of air, Mira crowned with daisies. He is fully awake now, scrambling for his jeans, almost falling over them; Jenna's in his room before he's got his flies buttoned. She's fanning her hand to her face, stepping over fallen clothing in her fraying Chinese slippers. Her dress is dishevelled, her greying hair needs something doing to it.

'Mum? What are you doing here?'

'How can you sleep with the windows shut?' she says, rattling back the curtain as he picks a T-shirt from the floor and pulls it over his head. 'It smells like a hamster cage in here.'

Downstairs in the kitchen a pile of Katie's sandwiches lie uneaten on a spotted plate. He can't remember what he did about food after she left but his stomach is growling. Michael fills the doorway from the hall, dipping his head beneath the lintel, carrying their bags from the car. A couple of confused houseflies tiptoe over the suddenly clean surfaces. His mother leans forward to smell the little jug of jasmine that Katie picked, then runs around drawing curtains and opening windows. Michael grips him in a hairy hug and he mentally thanks Katie for making him take a bath.

'Your mum's been frantic with worry . . .' Michael studies Julian over the rims of his half-moons. '. . . You know we've been ringing and ringing,' he says, glancing at the phone. Yes, it's still there.

Jenna hands him a cup rattling on its saucer and the smell rises to his nostrils, Persian coffee with a fat cardamon pod floating on the top, something Julia had never taken to, so he'd got out of the habit.

'In the end we decided we'd have to set off and hope you were in,' says Jenna.

'Long way to come if I wasn't.' Julian can't help but sound petulant. He flops at the table where Michael thumps a sheaf of papers several inches thick. 'Contracts,' Michael says, stacking them. 'And a couple of proposals you might find interesting.' Julian shakes his head while his mother feeds the dog and wipes down the surfaces as if she'd never left. Next she'll be hurrying him out of the house for the school bus. She packs the fridge with Tupperware boxes from a coolbag, chatting about the things she's seen driving up through the village: the new houses at Beardon Hill, the burnt-out cricket pavilion.

'I mean, what sort of person does that for kicks?'

Michael adds printouts of every unanswered email to the pile. Homework.

'We stopped at the village shop. Miss Hamlyn-the-younger said it happened the night of the bonfire, some yob with petrol.' His mother starts shunting the broom across the floor, at all the tiny yobs that need to be swept away, while Michael tells him of TV interest in his *Restoration Dogs*; a good production company, apparently.

'They want you to write the script . . .' Michael glances over his specs again: 'I thought you might have fun with it and it'll boost the rest of the series . . .' and falters when he sees Julian's face.

'It's got to be the best thing,' Michael says, pulling out a chair and sitting beside him, laying a kindly paw across his. He gestures to the pile of papers. 'You know, to keep your mind occupied.'

Julian raises his head from his hands. Jenna, determined as ever to feed him, slides glistening flesh from a mango using the side of a wine glass as a scoop, slips the slivers into a bowl.

'Your skin is terrible,' she says, handing him the bowl. He could tell her she didn't look so hot herself, with her shapeless grey dress crumpled from sitting so long in the car, her legs slightly scaly above the terrible Chinese slippers that she wears to death.

'Eat up,' she says, pointing at the bowl. Her eye make-up has escaped into the creases around her eyes and the tip of her nose is red, one nostril glistening. In some awful way he's glad she looks so bad. The hollow cheery chatter has been getting him down. Is it any wonder he doesn't want to answer the phone? But when it occurs to him that she's been crying, he has to look away. He concentrates on the shiny moons of fruit, juice pooling on the spoon, but he imagines her tears have made the mango salty and almost can't swallow.

At the dresser he fiddles with the pottery animals: his blobby elephant, a pair of badgers.

'You were going to make something with Mira.'

'I remember. Hedgehogs,' she says, perching on the edge of the table. 'Come on, darling, eat your breakfast.'

'After you showed her that one in the garden on Christmas Eve. Isn't that right? She made you cross your heart?'

He replaces the badgers, reaches to the uppermost shelf and takes down two figurines, a clay man and his lady wife. 'Lording it up,' he says. 'Up there above all the other animals.' He lays them flat on the table. 'Actually, Mum, I don't know what to do about these.'

She looks from him to the clay figures, stands and takes him into her arms and he stifles his sobs against her bony shoulder.

'Oh, and it was such a lovely Christmas.' Her words knock against him, an empty bucket being drawn from a well as she pats his back.

'It was there when we went out to search for Santa's sleigh, it rolled into a ball when Zeph got close. She'd only seen a hedgehog in pictures before. We took it a saucer of dog food and she put a silver star from a cracker on the side, said it was his present.' She sighs and reaches a hand to the ceramic figures, says: 'And not at all greedy on Christmas Day. Just as excited about everybody else unwrapping their presents as her own.' Her voice catches and she presses her fist to her mouth.

Michael steps forward. 'Come on,' he says. 'We promised not to do this.' He lays a hand on Julian's shoulder, gives it a shake. 'Let's get out in the sunshine.'

Jenna blows her nose on Michael's spotted handkerchief while Julian tries to conjure excuses. Zeph places his paws on his knees, cocks his head to one side, an entire orphanage of pleading in his eyes.

Julian searches for his sunglasses, Jenna fetches a rug. Even the light through the window hurts his eyes. 'I think I've become agoraphobic,' he says, sitting down again, not entirely sure he hasn't. Michael hauls him back to his feet and outside.

Jenna looks away from the granary as they pass, reaches for Michael. Horseman has baled his hay, marking the route from the house to the river in green avenues, flanked by silent trees. The sky is an unrelenting brittle blue. Zeph bounds ahead, sniffing the air like a newly released prisoner, leaping on top of bales to bark at the swallows.

Clouds of small creatures rise around their feet from the baked grass and lanky weeds of the water meadows. Zeph sniffs something on the air and makes a run for it, spraying grass seed and scabby dock. Jenna points to the brambles in the hedge, the clenched fruit just starting to blush. 'Blackberries look promising this year,' she says. 'You must remember to make jam.'

They pass half a rabbit abuzz with flies and have to drag the dog away from it.

The woods lie ahead: a single silver birch nervously quivering on its own hillock marks the entrance. Jenna points to it, tells Michael it's the tree that always has mistletoe.

Julian had brought Julia and Mira to this tree to pick mistletoe at Christmas. They went early, wrapped up warm, their boots squelching, Mira muffled in scarves, a hat with knitted earflaps tied beneath her chin. She ran ahead looking for ruts and puddles with sparkling frozen crusts that she could crunch beneath her wellies, tunelessly singing a song about baby Jesus they'd taught her at nursery.

He led Julia by the hand; she'd lost her gloves but he kept hers warm in his. Her woolly hat was the same pale blue as her eyes, as the crisp and clear winter sky. She pulled it to cover her ears and gathered her hair, twisting it into the collar of her stockman's coat. The tip of her nose and her cheeks were a little scorched from the cold, she had a basket in the crook of her arm, secateurs poking out of her pocket.

He hoisted Mira on to his shoulders as the silver birch came shivering into view, its whiteness making it seem more naked than any other, stark against the dark woods, a local landmark famous for witches.

Mira was playing pat-a-cake on his head. He had to twist around to talk to her. 'See, she's a fairytale princess of a tree.'

He swung her down so she could run and curtsy. 'There's her crown jewels,' he said, pointing to its single snaggle of mistletoe, carelessly tangled and studded with pearls.

Julia was clapping her hands as Mira went lolloping around the hillock, still singing her song.

'Have you ever squished a mistletoe berry in your fingers?' he said, leaping for the branch but not quite high enough.

'Not that I remember,' said Julia. 'Should I?'

'I used to use it as glue. For glitter and stuff. When I made Christmas cards,' he said. 'It goes all stringy like semen.'

She pulled a face. 'Such a wholesome childhood.'

'The ancients worshipped it as a symbol of the testicles. That's why we kiss beneath it . . .' he said, gathering her to him at the trunk of the tree, Mira leaping at their legs. 'What about me?' she cried, her catchphrase making them laugh. 'What about me?'

He jumped again for the end of the branch, grabbed it. '. . . because of its appearance and the texture of the juice, which is, you know, a bit viscous . . .'

'Yes, I get it,' Julia said.

He brought the branch close enough for her to reach up and snip off a few pieces. He took a sprig from her basket. 'Divine male essence,' he said, holding it aloft, and, as she leant in to kiss him, he burst a berry between his finger and thumb and anointed the tip of her nose. She shrieked and leapt away. 'What about me?' Mira cried.

When they got back they stapled wishbones of mistletoe over every door. Mira raced round the house pursing her lips. She said: 'Ooh, la la!' in that saucy way she'd learnt from who-knew-where when he and Julia kissed at the door to the bathroom.

Jenna cuts into his thoughts. 'Darling, I really can't talk about any of this any more.'

'Huh?' He's not aware of saying anything out loud. 'I was just thinking about the mistletoe.'

'Please understand,' she says as they skirt the woods, passing a field of horses that trot hopefully to the gate, kicking up dust, flies feasting at their eyes. Jenna stops to talk to them, to smooth the flies away and blow into their noses. Michael fills the gap. Julian keeps walking, staring at each foot as it falls to the scuffed ground.

'I know it's hard,' Michael is saying, striding beside him. 'But you don't want to fall behind on your payments.'

His mother catches them up. 'It's too easy to lose your sorrows in the bottom of a gin bottle,' she says. 'I know what you Vale men are like. And I've seen all the empties around the back.'

If there was a door in this field he'd run at it and slam it.

'Remember your father was a drinker.'

'Oh really? I didn't know!' Thinking he'd like to just turn around, to stomp away. She bumps him with her hip and gives him a squeeze but he shakes her off. She's been wielding his potential alcoholism since the first time he came home drunk from a party. He sends a clod of dry mud and grit bouncing. It was only a matter of time before he'd be found dead behind the wheel too. His father had *chosen* the bottle over his wife and child, wasn't that what she said? He finds a stone and kicks it into the nettles, startling a bird and sending others squeaking.

'Well, at least you're not hiding the empties,' she says. 'And the place doesn't look too bad. To be honest, I was expecting it to look like a slum.'

Good boy, you've cleaned your shoes, tidied your room; he waggles his head from side to side inwardly making up words for her while she goes on.

'Are you managing any work at all?' Michael asks.

'Katie came to see me yesterday, she cleared up a bit.' He ignores Michael's question. He doesn't like to say that Katie ambushed him, let them believe he invited her round, if that helps.

'That's good,' his mother slips her arm through his. 'I'm glad you're not locking yourself away. Is she back down here for good now?' His head is thumping in the heat, the ground is stones and baked dust beneath his feet.

'For now anyway, I think. She's supply teaching. Thinks she's got a good chance of a job at Woodford Primary.'

'That's a long way for What's-his-name to have to travel to see his kids,' Jenna says, tutting.

Julian shrugs. 'What's-his-name is living in the marital home, there's not much else she can do right now.'

'Still, Penny must be over the moon to have her grandsons at home,' Jenna says, stumbling then pressing her head into his shoulder, and they amble on like this for a while, the walking wounded, his arm slung along her back.

'I remember the very first time you brought Katie home,' she says.

Julian can't help but smile. A July day, as burning hot as this one. The last school bus of the year, his hand creeping inside her skirt. Her skin very soft on her inner thighs and a little sweaty from where she'd had them pressed together and Katie staring through the bus window as though nothing was happening, her school bag clasped to her lap, gradually unsticking them and allowing his hand to wander.

'After school, one look at her and I knew it wouldn't be long before someone should talk to you about condoms.'

'Yeah, well,' he snorts, batting her away for embarrassing him. 'Raph sorted me out, you didn't need to worry.'

'You could always have asked me,' Michael says, making Julian wince. 'Instead of some stranger, some hippie.'

'Raph wasn't a stranger,' Julian says. 'He wasn't even really a hippie.'

Jenna looks thoughtful for a moment. 'He's around again, by the way,' she says. 'I couldn't believe my eyes when we passed his van on the verge. He must've been coming here for, what is it? Fifteen years now?'

Julian does the maths on his fingers. 'I think I was fifteen the first time,' he says.

'OK, almost fifteen years,' she says. 'You were a bit moody that summer and prone to wandering off for hours on your own. I never knew what you were doing. You were with him more than you were at home. You showed him our place to swim in the river and after that I felt a little like an intruder when you were there with him.'

Julian gives her a squeeze. 'I'm sorry about that, I never knew,' he says. 'But I liked him. We read a lot of the same books.'

'It's OK,' she says. 'Everyone always said you'd need to find some sort of male mentor.'

Michael clears his throat but she interrupts whatever he was about to say. 'But I didn't like that you shaved your head after the first summer he was here. It made you look quite thuggy.'

The summer of '83. Raph's van on the verge, an eyesore of slats painted bright purple and brown, terriers running around dangerously close to the fall of an axe, a shaven-headed muscular man leaning to pull against the blade, his boot to a stump of wood.

Raph was shirtless, baked brown, his tattoos flashing as he disarmed Julian with a smile that made a sunray of his face. He gestured for Julian to come over. The stubble was darkly etched over Raph's scalp. His lustrous curls would not be revealed until the following summer. His eyes had glitter.

He threw the axe so the blade stuck into the turf and wiped the sweat from his face with a red and white spotted scarf unknotted from his neck. Over his shoulder Julian could see the interior of the van, its brightly slatted shelves crammed with stuff: books, papers, pottery hanging from hooks. 'I was wondering if you could tell me the best place to swim,' Raph said as he grasped Julian's hand in greeting.

'So, he only came in August? Where did he go the rest of the year?' Michael wants to know as they walk on.

'Oh, everywhere, Devon, Dorset, Glastonbury, Wales. But with the whole convoy. He said he needed to take August for himself, that's why he came here.'

Michael clears his throat with a slight harrumph. 'Must've been a blessing for the village that the whole rabble didn't turn up. Can't see anyone around here liking that much.'

'Yes, there was always a hoo-ha whenever a bit of machinery went missing,' Jenna says. 'Can't have been nice for him every time the parish council got its knickers in a twist. And I admit it, I worried sometimes, the amount of time you spent hanging around with him. Once I came looking for you across the fields at night and there you were, like a pair of gypsies, cackling away, beers in your hands, a little fire burning. You never saw me. I remember standing there thinking it looked quite an appealing way of life, almost wishing I could join you.'

'I couldn't stand not being able to have a bath,' Michael says, slightly short of breath.

'He's the happiest person I've ever met.' Julian smiles just thinking about Raph. 'He hadn't been on the road very long when he started coming here. He only joined the Convoy when he discharged himself from the Navy – he was there at the sinking of the *Belgrano*. Did his head in . . .'

'Bloody Thatcher,' Jenna says. 'No wonder he joined the Peace Convoy.'

'Yeah, and straight away into another battle. Do you remember the state of his van after the Battle of the Beanfield?' Julian shudders to think of its leaking water tank, the glass of the door taped up with cardboard, the curling frills of metal where the crowbars had ripped through the side of the cab.

'I couldn't believe it still drove. They'd smashed every window and kicked in the doors. The Convoy was just trying to get to Stonehenge, there was no need for that. And poor Raph's face.' A livid line of proud flesh scored his cheekbone, the result of having been pulled out of his lorry through the windshield.

'I watched it on the news,' Jenna says, and grimaces. 'That bloody woman flexing her muscles. They were really laying into them all. I mean, the police just looked like uniformed hooligans. Some of the buses were on fire, smoke everywhere, and I'll never forget the sight of this pregnant woman in a white dress standing among the bean plants, begging to be allowed to leave, and terrified children running and screaming around her.'

'Raph had to have stitches,' Julian says. 'He was trying to negotiate with the police. They wanted to turn back but they'd been cornered in the field. It was like they'd been told not to let them go until they'd given them a beating and burned their homes.'

Zeph drives a pheasant from the hedge, flapping and squawking, and they stop to watch its ungainly ascent. Julian shoots at it several times with pistol fingers.

They reach the river and Jenna takes the picnic rug from Michael, shakes it out on the bank. Canada geese have been shitting everywhere. They kick sausages of green turd into the water. Dirty things, always making a nuisance of themselves, and not even decent to eat. 'Like tough, greasy fish,' Jenna tells them.

'Will you invite Katie over again while we're here?' she asks. 'She looked so pretty at Christmas, hasn't lost her figure, which, given how fat her mother . . .'

'Can't have been very pleasant for Julia to find your ex holed up down the road like that, that's what I thought,' Michael interrupts, plonking himself on to the blanket with an *oooff*. Julian turns on to his front, rests his head in his arms and wishes he'd stop. No such luck. 'And with Julia always having to go to

London. Not easy at all,' Michael says, and though his eyes are closed Julian can feel his mother trying to shush him with a look.

Michael was present the second time Julia and Katie met. It was Christmas Eve. Heralded by singing. Julia, cheeks flushed with wine, barefoot, scraping the remains of their lamb dinner into Zeph's bowl, hair escaping from a green and white paisley rag. Michael at the Christmas tree, swilling a glass of red, wearing his festive yellow waistcoat that made Julian think of a cartoon fox. Mira running to the window: It's Father Christmas! Lanterns twinkling in the lane. 'Hark the Herald Angels' getting closer. Jenna skipping across the hall in her latest pair of Chinese slippers and flinging wide the door to the raggle-taggle choir from St Gabriel's. Among the cluster of men, women and children Katie was quite something in her full-skirted coat, its fur collar like mist framing her face. Her boys, blond in bobble hats, were cherubic as a Christmas card, their faces illuminated by candles in jam jars that hung from shepherds' crooks. Michael with his hearty baritone stepped out to join them, extending his arm like Pavarotti. Behind him, in a huddle in the hall, Mira bounced up and down and Julia pressed herself to his back, hissing into his ear, 'That's Katie, isn't it?'

Jenna had eyes only for her old friend Sue, who was waving and grinning while she sang with a torch in her hand. Jenna mouthed: 'You look fantastic!' and when they finished asked if they'd come in and sing another in front of the fire. She offered to find sherry and mince pies, with only a quick look at Julian to check she wasn't overstepping the mark. 'You haven't changed one bit,' she said, clasping Sue on the threshold, and Sue came inside saying: 'Ooh, and Firdaws looks just the same. Like you never left.' Jenna reached for Julian: 'Yes, I suppose it does. Though it's his place now . . .'

Julia was standing there right next to her. 'And Julia's,' he said sternly, extending his hand. 'Mine and Julia's.'

The choir traipsed in, leaving their boots at the door, though Julian told them there was no need. Mira leapt at Billy and Arthur. The firework boys, she called them. 'Yeah, and then we went home and Granny had more rockets just for us,' Arthur boasted, wiping his nose along his sleeve, Julian wishing that Katie wasn't flushing from her fur collar to her blonde roots, and that she hadn't just called him 'Jude', making Julia raise an eyebrow. He shot from the room when his mother called to him to find the brandy butter.

Much to Julian's relief Christmas Day dawned with Katie seemingly forgotten and he and Julia stumbling together, wiping the sleep from their eyes, the cockerel not yet crowing, past the guest room and Michael and Jenna's gentle duet of snores, to Mira calling to them and cooing over her stocking. They gazed at her from the door, their grins growing ever wider as her delight became their own. Mira, surrounded by wrapping paper, pronounced every little thing perfect like a polite maiden aunt: 'Oh, I say. Just what I wanted.' Blowing a train whistle, squeaking the new duck for her bath, making the little wooden cat dance on its elasticated legs, making them laugh.

At the Christmas tree Michael beamed as Jenna routed out a largish parcel and handed it over.

'Ooh, wait until you see what she's made for you,' Michael said, rubbing his hands.

'Shhhh.' Jenna prodded him in the waistcoat. 'You'll ruin the surprise.'

Julian and Julia pushed the parcel back and forth to each other across the floor.

'You open it.'

'No, you.'

'Careful! Don't shake it!' Jenna said. 'Oh for goodness sake, one of you open it. Julian?'

'What about me?' came Mira's voice, so they placed the parcel with its sash of green satin in front of her on the floor.

'But remember it's for Mummy and Daddy,' Jenna told her as she pulled at the bow and tore off the wrapping.

Inside was a sturdy box with a lift-off lid. 'Careful now,' Jenna was hovering as Mira reached into the tissue paper and grasped two pottery figures, one in each hand. 'Ooh, don't bang them together, darling,' Jenna said. 'I'm rather proud of them.'

They were beautifully sculpted and painted, naked but for the merciful green fig leaves that Jenna had positioned at their groins. Julia went immediately to hug Jenna and was acknowledged with a peck. Jenna's attention had already been claimed by Julian, who was laughing at the knobbly knees of the male figure.

Now he sits at the riverbank and they don't want to hear about any of it. A damselfly lands on Jenna's shoulder and she keeps still so they might admire her enamelled jewel. The sun warms their backs. Zeph settles himself a little further up the slope in guarding mode.

Jenna stands and stretches her arms above her head. She walks to the brink. 'We should have brought towels.' Michael and Julian exchange panicked looks.

'She made me swim in the Serpentine on her birthday,' says Michael, looking sorry for himself.

Julian groans. 'Oh, hard luck. But you should have come here. I can't believe I forgot.'

Jenna whirls around. 'It was last week,' she says. 'And no one would expect you to remember. Not right now, anyway, I haven't got my swimsuit on.'

She plonks herself back down beside them. 'What about the time we came down here for my birthday, loads of us, and your friend Raph was swimming naked?' she says, making Julian snort. Raph didn't care. He was treading water and laughing up at them, calling out happy birthday to Jenna, raising his hand to salute her, tattoos rippling along the broad blades of his shoulders like wings.

Jenna giggles: 'Sue was all for us all ripping off our clothes and joining him.'

For a moment it feels good to picture the great marshmallow mounds of Sue flying free from the bank. 'It was the first year he came,' Julian says. 'After that he always wore trunks.'

'I'm too old to sit on this hard ground,' Michael says. 'Let's head home.'

'Do you think you might see him?' Jenna says, sticking with the subject of Raph. 'I'd love to know how he's getting on.'

'Why so keen all of a sudden? You never used to be, you used to interrogate me about him.'

'Well, of course,' she says.

Back at Firdaws Jenna sets about grilling some chops, puts water to boil, slicing apples and onions and moving around as if she'd never left. Her chopping boards are where they should be, stacked beside the glass cupboard, her knives in their usual block by the sink. As an act of faithful reconstruction Katie couldn't have done a better job.

Jenna brings plates and cutlery to the table, gestures for him to set them out. The pottery figures are where he left them: the man slightly turned on his side towards the lovely curve of the woman's long waist, smooth skin the colour of brown paper, electric-blue eyes, hair as shiny as a newly hatched conker.

The fatty smell of grilling meat fills the room. Jenna waves a spatula at him, suggests he put on some music once he's laid the table. He reaches across and picks up the clay woman. She is exquisitely proportioned, a beauty, perhaps a little more pendulous in the breasts than Julia. Her bright-blue eyes, he now sees, are quite mad.

Jenna brings the water jug to the table, starts laying out the plates herself as the chops pop and spit beneath the grill. She sees him sitting there with the figure in his hand and flies at him, making him leap to his feet.

'OK, I'll help!'

'Give it here!'

She snatches the woman from his grasp.

He tries to shout 'No!' but the word won't come quick enough as her arm arcs back and she hurls the pottery woman against the fridge, shattering it. Shattering her. Zeph is barking and Michael comes into the room with his telephone still to his ear, sees the pieces on the floor. 'What the hell?'

Twelve

Lights. Action. Shiny corridor, feet falling. Ding of lift, stomach sinking, another corridor shines, bedrails juddering, a head on the pillow the colour of tallow. Perspex tunnel, dark ribs flying, swallowing them like a whale. Someone's beeper goes off, fluorescent lighting flashes by. Mira, one hand pressed to her forehead, the space-age suck and sigh of the twin doors marked PICU.

Motionless forms adrift in seas of wires and tubing, monitors blur, waves of neon, skylines, mountains, lifelines. Machines schlip schlap, voices murmur and call, a phone rings and an alarm sounds, blip blip blip. The bings and bongs of ventilators, monitors sliding into position, tick of pump, plasters and tape hold her tubes in place. Mira's hand is limp in his. Her tiny fingers look nicotined.

One of the dials is flashing a red light and he can't get his money in the slot. He slams it with the palm of his hand. Behind him somebody else hits the jackpot with a cascading crash of metal on metal; a kidney dish falls to the floor splashing its contents. His coin won't budge and he's punching the machine with his fist. The ventilator comes to a halt, sending the alarm frantic, and Mira's eyes shoot open. He shakes her bed like a pinball machine as the nurses come running.

He wakes in a sweat. His mother is standing over him bearing a cup steaming with her cardamon coffee. 'Drink it while it's hot, darling.' She perches on the edge of his bed while he reaches for his phone to check the time. His hand won't stop trembling. 'Shit,' he says, inching himself up the pillows. He's shaking his head, trying to dispel his horrible dreams, but it's no use.

'Oh God, I keep having the same nightmare over and over again,' he says. Jenna hands him the cup and goes to the window.

'Will this ever end? I can't shake it. I keep seeing her in Intensive Care, all those tubes, her hair falling out in chunks, her scalp all yellow.' He has to shield his eyes as she draws back the curtains.

'Shhh . . .'

'I worried about her waking to find her hair all gone, what a fright she'd have to see her head like a Belisha beacon . . .'

'Julian, try not to do this.'

'And I longed for her to wake up again, I was willing her to smile hour after hour. And then I wake up here and think of all the times when she was ill and I fobbed her off with a video.'

'Will you please stop beating yourself up,' his mother says, leaning across and laying her palm on his forehead. 'You had no way of knowing what was wrong.'

'No?' His hands fly to his head.

'Stop that pulling at your hair at once!'

'You have no idea how irritable I was when she kept getting ill . . .' Jenna tries to shush him, to smooth back his hair. 'I used to just plonk her in front of the telly with cheese and biscuits until bedtime . . .'

'I used to do exactly the same with you,' she says. 'You were practically a single parent during the week.'

'I dosed her up with Calpol when I should've taken her to the doctor.' He puts the pillow over his face, buries his fists into it.

'Julian, we've been through all this a hundred times. You *did* take her to the doctor. You took her to Dr Andrews several times.'

'And every time I let him send us away.' Julian lowers the pillow, mimics the old doctor dismissing him, his smile one of great forbearance. 'Yes, children get ill, they get temperatures and tummy aches.' He crawls back beneath the covers. 'Oh, poor little thing!'

Jenna tries pulling the pillow from his face, but he clings to it, begs her to leave him be.

'Julian, please stop. Get up now and let's take that poor dog for a walk.'

'I can't do it. I just want to sleep.' Waves of despair suck back and forth beneath his ribs. His mother sits and rubs his ratcheting back, talks of one step at a time.

He needs to work, nothing else will save him. Jenna made him open his post. She read over his shoulder. There were final reminders from the builders and the building society, bad news from the bank. His accountant's calculations had been optimistic when he went to him about Firdaws: in the end the sale of Cromwell Gardens covered less than half. This year his New Year's resolution had been to work his socks off to get them out of the mess he'd got them in to.

'I'll drink to that.' Julia had crashed her glass to his as Big Ben bonged and fireworks exploded on the telly. Christ, he wanted to say, I'm doing my best. They were supposed to be at a party in London. But Mira was going down with yet another bug. The party was on a houseboat at Hampton Wick with a hog roast and dancing on the deck; Freda would be there, and William. Karl was coming with his girlfriend from Amsterdam. Jenna and Michael tried to make them go, it really was no problem to care for Mira. Mira was shivering on the sofa despite the hot-water bottle at her chest and a quilt tucked all around. 'But what about me?' She hadn't spoken but he could hear her just the same.

He went for the Calpol. Where better to see in the new year than here, he thought, looking at Julia sitting with Mira's head in her lap, gently smoothing the hair from her forehead, the scent of pine and Christmas tree sparkling, apple logs crackling in the fire.

Julia took a long silent bath behind the locked door of what he thought of as the Nicholsons' bathroom. He paused on the landing for a couple of breaths of her Christmas bath oil, grape-fruit and roses, resisted the temptation to knock so that he might come in and watch her bathe. The thought of the hide-ously out-of-place egg-shaped bath where the bed should have been and the fake marble walls made it easier to ignore his inner Bonnard. He went to check on Mira. She lay in the centre of their bed, her mouth open, steadily snoring, one arm slung across her forehead, her temperature soothed by the magic pink liquid.

Downstairs Jenna was muttering about the turkey and ham pie drying out. Eventually Julia joined them, looking more relaxed after her bath, her skin gleaming with body lotion. She was wearing her lavender jumper and jeans, some silk irises that he'd put in her Christmas stocking pinned into her hair. Jenna gasped. 'Beautiful! They match your pullover.' She pointed to the flowers and Julia reached her hand to her head and laughed: 'Oh, I used them to pin it up to stop it getting wet.' She started unclipping them and shaking her hair free.

He took the silk flowers from her while she combed her fingers through her hair. He clipped and unclipped a clasp and it gripped the skin of his thumb like a tiny plastic jaw. The silk petals had been hand-painted by a woman in the next village: delicately coloured irises with velvety black stamens, and yellow blazing throats. He'd found them at St Gabriel's Church Christmas Bazaar, sworn Mira to secrecy when she saw him buy them. 'For Mummy,' he said, putting his finger to his lips. She solemnly copied him, saying, 'Cross my heart,' making the motion at her chest which always gave him the shivers.

He stood behind Julia, pushing her hair aside to breathe the warm scent of her nape, the new grapefruit and rose body lotion and the deeper musk of her skin.

'Stop mauling me.' She jumped away from him, and he was so stricken by her glare that he dropped the irises to the floor where they stayed until Jenna picked them up and placed them high on the dresser like a fallen wreath at the feet of the ceramic man and woman.

He winces now to think of the space on the dresser, of Jenna's fury of the night before; the woman she'd so lovingly wrought lying in smithereens on the floor. It's shocking still, the violence of it. Today his mother looks calmer, her hand on his forehead is softened by cream.

Just for a change his head is thumping. He wishes Jenna would give up opening the curtains. He saves his last gulp of coffee for a paracetamol. He wishes she'd stop opening the windows too: the birds are turned up to unbearable, bickering and screaming. There's a breeze and the creepers flick V-signs at him. He rootles through the drawer of his bedside table for painkillers. Vaseline, vitamins, nail clippers, scraps of paper. He pulls out a single pipe cleaner bent around itself, greyed by fluff, no sign of the rabbits he'd made to amuse her with their felt-pen faces, a whole family of pipe-cleaner bunnies, all with names. He smiles to himself as he remembers Mira doing Baby Bunny's voice, her funny high-pitched rasp, her oddly husky chuckle, and continues rummaging for the pills. At the back of the drawer, tangled with rubber bands, he finds the packet and also a little glass canister containing half a spliff.

He holds the tube up to the light, the spliff is expertly tailored. It's been lying there since January, forgotten since his night out with Karl in Amsterdam.

'Are you a total idiot?' Julia had gone on and on about the stupidity of coming through customs at Heathrow with it still in his coat pocket. He was dancing around with cheeriness, simply couldn't keep still. A whistle-stop trip to his Dutch publishers had been a great success. Her fury only made him laugh. 'I completely forgot I had it. Honestly. Karl and I had a smoke in the hotel and after that I didn't think of it again.'

She was making such a thing of it. He had to keep asking her to listen, hopping with impatience to tell her a particular piece of good news: 'Now, if you just shut up for one moment . . .'

She brought steaming toad-in-the-hole from the oven, the oven glove on her slender arm making him recall the leather gauntlet she'd worn for the hawk. 'Listen to me,' he said.

He had a yo-yo for Mira from Amsterdam, one that lit up when it was spun. She was back to normal, just a little snotty, and instantly upset that she couldn't manage the yo-yo herself. She was too short for the string and he stood her on the kitchen chair and put his hand around hers so they could make it spin and spark together. Julia stopped being cross about his new career as an international drug smuggler. She was heating onion gravy for the toad-in-the-hole. 'I think I've sorted out a place for you to stay in London. With Karl's dad . . .' She stopped stirring, a hand to her forehead. 'Oh, God,' she said.

A full seven months this half-smoked spliff has been lying here. A sudden impulse makes him slide it from the tube. He sniffs it, rubs away the charcoal from the burnt end. He finds a lighter and takes it to the window, leans out. Just lighting it makes him cough so hard that his eyes water. He takes two more drags, holds the smoke in his lungs for as long as he can hold off the coughing fit and grinds it out on the window ledge, his throat burning.

He has no idea why he did that but immediately feels calmer.

Leaning out further, he can see the glint of the river across Horseman's fields, someone trotting by on a skewbald pony with swinging tail, leaves shimmering in the breeze. A crow catches his eye and he watches it marching back and forth along the fence, coming to a standstill to make officious notes beneath its wing. He still has a headache but at least the thumps have become rhythmic.

He relights the joint and puts it out again after a single puff. At least being stoned might give him the munchies. His mother's meals keep coming at him, as though from a magic porridge pot.

Eat. Eat. Eat. The pounding of Jenna's wooden spoon to the skin of a pomegranate, jewels as bright as a baby's lips falling on to lamb and spiced lentils, arriving before him in a bowl, steaming, heaped on a bed of rice. She was putting cream in his porridge and buttering his toast until it dripped, making Michael's slavering eyes follow it to his mouth. Eat. Eat. Eat.

There would be talking, endless talking, the plates would keep coming, the pitch of Jenna's voice growing ever higher, Michael's like a hammer to his brain, and no sign that they were leaving any time soon.

Oh, but that last small toke was a terrible mistake. He finds himself stumbling around the room, sure there's a packet of biscuits somewhere, but of course there are no biscuits and all roads lead inexorably to the tangled undergrowth and the lavender jumper that lies beneath his bed. He listens at the bedroom door, regrets it has no lock. Grasping the jumper, he gets back beneath the covers and curls himself around it.

Julia was wearing this jumper the morning he left for Amsterdam. Bending for her knickers, still so sleepy, barely mumbling as he leapt up and grabbed her.

'I wish you weren't going,' she said.

'I can't get out of it,' he said, grabbing her hips and pushing himself against her from behind.

'Mira's about to burst through that door.' She was laughing, only half pushing him away.

He released her and they sat side by side on the bed. 'I feel bad leaving with her so under the weather but I promised I'd be there. It's the only day the Dutch can get everyone together.'

Michael was driving him to the airport; the roads would be slippery so they'd have to leave plenty of time. He checked his watch, still early enough: 'Time for a quickie?' As was their habit, this took place, hiding from a possible Mira, on the well-worn bit of carpet between the bed and the wall. Afterwards Julia brought coffee and marmalade toast while he threw a few things in a bag.

'I must get to London as soon as you're back,' she said, handing him his cup. 'At least for a couple of days. Freda's doing her nut.'

'It's only one night. You'll barely have time to miss me.'

She stopped chewing. 'Is Rotterdam far from Amsterdam?'

'It's just over an hour away.'

'Will you see Karl?'

'He's meeting me for dinner,' he said and though she had turned away he sensed she was scowling.

His Dutch publisher was generous. The suite he was given at the Dylan Hotel made him yearn for Julia: behind sliding doors a king-size bed in a beamed alcove, the arrangement of cushions suggestive of soft play.

Julian's meeting had gone well; he liked his Dutch publisher even more in the flesh than he had on the phone. The first *Fletch le Bone* spin-off was to be their lead title. He was introduced to the translator, who dressed rather like Fletch in a Columbo-style mac and had a tic that made it appear he was constantly winking. The film of *Fletch le Bone I* had been a huge hit in Holland. Julian felt his eyes flashing with guilders. Karl, arriving at the Dylan, found him in excellent spirits.

Karl had noticeably lost more hair, his suit was familiarly rumpled. 'This is going down well,' he said when Julian passed him a beer from the mini-bar. 'The traffic out of Rotterdam was awful.' He explained something of the work he was doing on a new anti-psychotic while they drank. 'We're getting close,' he said. 'It could become the protocol for Capgras.'

'What's that?'

'You've never heard of it? No? Well, simply put, it's a delusional disorder where the patient is convinced that a close family member has been replaced by an identical-looking imposter.'

Julian shuddered. 'It reminds me of a recurring dream I had as a boy: me on the doorstep at Firdaws, pointing to a portait of my father, but my mother's face is furious and she's trying to push me away, denying that we've ever met . . .'

'It's an awful syndrome,' Karl said. 'Very hard on the spouse. Sometimes the patient forms a whole new relationship with the "imposter", which is completely separate from before. The worst is when they decide they hate them and try to get rid. There was a gruesome case where a man beheaded his father to prove that he was a robot. He said he wanted to take the batteries out.'

Julian opened a couple more beers, handed one to Karl. 'Hey,' Karl said, taking a swig. 'You should phone down to the concierge for a spliff. When in Amsterdam . . .'

'I can't do that!'

'Of course you can, in fact you must, you're only here for one night.'

'No, I meant, you know, just call down to the concierge for it.'

'Honestly, they won't bat an eyelid. It's a good hotel.'

The spliff arrived in its glass canister on a silver tray alongside a single stem of Singapore orchid. It was extra long and beautifully tapered. The room-service waiter placed the tray with its floral garnish on the table, said: 'Enjoy.'

After the smoke they ambled along by the canal. Karl was in a good mood too, one arm around Julian's shoulder, insisting they take a wander through De Wallen, though Julian was suddenly so ravenous all he could think about was the restaurant his publisher had recommended. Meatballs and noodles was the thing to order.

The lights bounced on the black water, rippling golden, blue and orange, a fuzzy drizzle felt refreshing on his face. He grinned at Karl. 'I'm really quite stoned.' He was chuckling at the slightest thing. 'Julia doesn't really go for it so I haven't in a while.'

'How *is* Julia?'

'She spent most of her marriage to that git out of her brains on the stuff, poor girl. It was the only way she could tolerate him.'

'Is she taking to country life?'

Julian struggled to put up the umbrella he'd taken from the hotel foyer. 'Good job I brought this,' he said.

They stopped at a bridge and Karl took it from him and held it over their heads. They looked down into the water. 'Thousands of bikes a year get dredged from these canals. People are such idiots,' Karl said. 'So, Julia?'

'Ah, yes. Julia. She's a bit knackered, to tell you the truth. Her business with Freda has taken off which is great except that it's too far for her to keep travelling in and out of London from Firdaws. Ah. It's a nightmare . . .' Julian tailed off, turned up his collar. He took the umbrella from Karl. 'Come on, I'm taller.'

'OK, take it, but let's walk fast to keep warm.' Karl's face was lit by a passing boat. His thick brows seemed even more comedic since his hair had thinned.

'I've fucked up,' Julian said with a sigh. 'I got carried away by the thought of living at Firdaws again . . .'

'I've heard it's heaven on earth,' Karl said, teasing a smile out of him.

'Yes, well, you should come and stay when you're next in England, that is, if I manage to hang on to it that long. Oh Christ, I think the dope has made me maudlin.'

They walked on through streets that were gradually filling with people.

'We're basically broke and the distance from London makes it impossible for Julia. She has to stay three nights a week at her brother's and the wife's a bitch. And it's not as though her business brings in that much, her petrol practically wipes out her share, but, you know, every little helps . . .'

'Oh dear. What's to be done?' Karl said.

'I don't know. I've got plenty of script work and a book I actually *want* to write, but I'm alone with Mira all week; it's difficult to get much done and right now the budget's too tight for extra childcare.'

'You're alone with Mira?' Karl took a step away from him, said: 'You mean, Julia just buggers off?'

Julian nodded. 'I hadn't realised how important her work is to her.'

'Wouldn't it be better for you and the child if Julia got gardening jobs closer to home?'

'I tried that. There was a good one going in the glasshouses at Harbinger Hall, not too far from Firdaws. My mum knows the owner.' Julian made a cutting motion at his throat. 'Didn't go down too well when I suggested it.'

Nearby a church bell was sounding the hour, tyres hissed on the wet cobbles, the clamour of swearing and bicycle bells was starting to echo around his head. The reflections on the water were whirling and he was glad when Karl broke off at an alleyway. They were in a tunnel, graffiti rising high on the walls, throngs of people pushing by, the lights doing nothing to ease his sense of mild tripping.

They emerged into a wider street where neon signs clashed

against the famous red windows. A girl rolled her hips at them through the glass, her tiny bra and pants gleaming like an advert for washing powder, such was their bright whiteness against her skin. Further windows were lit red the length of the street, turning the puddles flamingo pink. 'Oh God, it's like a human vending machine,' Julian said.

A stag party ran past, pushing each other and howling, women hung from doorways to chat, another gyrated behind her window on all fours, her backside rotating like a spinning top from the tiny pinnacle of the waistband of her thong. Julian was determined not to be stirred by anything he saw. 'It's true what they say, isn't it? That most of these women have been trafficked?'

'I'm afraid so, but everyone comes to see it,' Karl said.

'I just want something to eat,' Julian said and a man with an accent threw back his head and pointed to a teenager in a window – 'Eat that' – and made lapping motions towards her with his tongue.

'We'll get out of here if you like, but first you should at least step inside the Oude Kerk. It's Amsterdam's oldest building. It's just up there.' Karl was steering him towards the square. 'We'll go now, if you're absolutely sure you don't want to watch live couples having sex,' he said, reading from a flashing sign above their heads. 'Come,' Karl tugged at his sleeve. 'Rembrandt used to pray there.' And they threaded their way through the Japanese tourists and various hustlers, turning down blowjobs and girl-on-girl action as they went.

Julian was too hungry for anything but a cursory tour of the ancient church that rose from the heart of the red-light district, from Pandaemonium. Here it was: Mulciber's temple pressed right up against God's. A bronze hand that was set into the cobbles groped a single bronze breast. 'An unknown sculptor,' Karl told him, and then inside, something of the church's history. Before the Reformation it had been the hub for beggars and pedlars and gossip. Karl translated a text above a screen of ornate brass: 'The false practices gradually introduced into God's church were here undone in the year of seventy eight.' The false practices, Karl said, were mainly homelessness. 'The Calvinists weren't having any of that, oh, no.' There was something else about Catholics still coming each year to celebrate the 'Miracle of Amsterdam' when someone was supposed to have vomited up the Host, though Julian wasn't sure he didn't make that bit up.

Karl shepherded him to a water taxi and they looked back at the church looming large at the flaming centre of sin. Red and sulphur lights blazed across the black water and reflected the writhing throngs as demons chained to the burning lake.

They found the restaurant. The speciality of the house was overrated, the noodles claggy, the meatballs oozing grease, but Julian, ravenous from the grass, tucked in with a vigour that Karl found amusing. He talked while Julian ate. He was excited about his work on the Capgras drug. 'Imagine the difference it could make,' he said. 'Hundreds of thousands of people lifted out of confusion, more than I could ever help if I'd become a doctor.'

Julian laughed to find Karl still making excuses for going into research. It seemed the world, or at least his doctor father, would forever wag a finger at this decision. Julian remembered Heino Lieberman as kindly, with mischievous eyes. It was hard to imagine he had ever been angry with his son. They once stopped off from university, some gig or other at the Town and Country. Karl's parents lived right by Great Ormond Street Hospital, a convenient resting place for him and Karl that night. They passed the entrance to the hospital on their way back from the gig. 'Up there's where my dad mends hearts,' Karl said, resting his hand to his own as they passed.

The Liebermans' flat was above a florist. It was spacious and warm with red runners to several floors. Heino and Ellie were a handsome couple, he with the eyebrows and she, Karl's twitching smile.

Karl's meatballs and noodles remained mostly untouched. He was still talking about his Capgras research and it occurred to Julian that it had been years since he'd seen him without a girl-friend. He paused with the fork to his mouth to ask after the last girl. Birgitte? Sofie? What *was* her name?

Karl pulled a face and changed the subject. 'Moving to Connecticut couldn't have come at a worse moment.'

'Connecticut?'

'Yes, I told you, you weren't listening. I'm being drafted back to my original research, but now funding is coming out of America. So, the deal is I go and run it from there.'

Julian stopped with the glass halfway to his lips, horrified. 'But we'll see you even less than we do now,' he said.

Karl clapped him on the shoulder. 'Well, for better or worse, I'll be constantly back and forth. Since mum died my dad has become a bit more needy.'

'I'm so sorry about your mum,' Julian said. 'I thought she was lovely that time I met her.' He remembered the night Ellie died and Karl ringing Cromwell Gardens from the hospital: Julia in the kitchen handing him the phone, a heavy sigh, her hand to her belly. The baby due any day. Karl's ratcheting sobs.

'It was a horrible way to die. I'm sorry I wasn't much of a shoulder to cry on at the time,' Julian said and Karl waved away the apology.

'It's just my dad's going to be a bit of a long-distance problem, from now on. From Connecticut, I mean.'

'Isn't there any way you can do this work in London?'

'No. And, well, there are other good reasons for me to go.' Karl tapped his nose, and Julian thought: Aha, so a woman *is* involved.

'Father won't have the word "carer" mentioned in his presence. To be honest it hasn't got that bad, but since Mum died he sleepwalks and I can't have him wandering out into the street, so I need to work out some sort of rota of people to stay overnight at Lamb's Conduit Street. I've got the weekends sorted because my cousin's daughter Claudine wants to be in London with her boyfriend, but she has to be back at York from Tuesday to Friday.'

Julian put down his glass and tugged Karl's arm.

'You're looking for someone to stay overnight three nights a week? Is that it?' His voice was rising with excitement. 'Midweek, right?' He couldn't imagine why Karl hadn't thought of it already. It was the obvious solution: Julia.

Julian still hasn't managed to get out of bed and his mum is back. 'Julian, are you OK?' He hears her sniff as she enters. 'Have you been smoking dope?'

'Get out, get out!' And, for once, she goes. He groans into his pillow, grinds himself into the jumper that Julia had shed like an old skin. Who was she, this monster? Perhaps he was suffering from Capgras himself. Karl should have offered him the cure. He sees Julia rising in all her fury from her sea of blankets and sheets. He sees the unknown lace strap of her imposter's nightgown, wide at her shoulder where her wild hair snakes, and the words that fall from the black hole of her mouth make no sense to him.

Thirteen

Julia's room at Heino Lieberman's was beside the sitting room. The sash windows that looked on to Lamb's Conduit Street rattled whenever an ambulance went by and from the bathroom across the hall you could see down into the florist's yard.

The flat was arranged on three floors. Once you came up the stairs beside the flower shop and through the front door, it had the air of a slightly grand townhouse, with china push plates on the doors and red Turkish runners up the stairs, pictures and books lining the walls. The light was muted by voiles at the tall windows to the street, but there were plenty of lamps. The smell of the place was somehow familiar to Julian: lavender, face powder, old paper, wax, lint, peppermint. Something like the inside of his mother's handbag and strongest where he stood with Julia and Heino in the doorway of what was to be Julia's room.

'The bed was put in for Ellie when she could no longer manage the stairs. Before that it was her music room, with the piano for her students,' Heino said, leaning on his stick and momentarily closing his eyes. Julia reached for his hand.

'Come,' Heino led her inside like a bride to the altar. The light was gentle, the wallpaper sprigged with violets, there was a sheen to a bronze satin eiderdown, lace-edged linen folded over on a queen-size bed. Beside the window, a small day bed where Ellie's nurse had sometimes slept, sheets neatly stacked at one end. Heino waved his stick at it. 'Bring your little daughter, won't you? She will be able to sleep there,' he said.

Heino was much as Julian remembered him from his visit with Karl, though a little more bent over, and the stick was new. It was of dark polished wood, a single carved snake winding towards the handle. Heino followed his eyes. 'My Aesculapian staff,' he said, waving the handle at him. 'The God of medicine and healing. Karl had it made for me and I've rather taken to it.' His way of speaking was precise, his German accent slight and most detectable in the word 'God', which he pronounced 'Got'.

Heino motioned to the sitting room. 'Make yourselves comfortable while I fetch the coffee.' Julia perched on the edge of a winged armchair, looking around. Some of the paintings were surprisingly modern, above the fireplace a large abstract of orange and green, towering bookcases, a baby grand piano in the corner. Julian sat on a sofa and leant across to a sepia photograph in a small leather frame on a side table. A distinguished-looking couple stood shoulder to shoulder.

'I remember now,' Julian said, holding it so Julia could see. The man had a walrus moustache and lavish eyebrows, his wife a face as neat as a mouse, a froth of lace at her collar.

'These are Heino's grandparents. They didn't make it out of Germany, neither did his father. Heino and his siblings came to London on the Kindertransport . . .' He stopped talking as Heino brought the coffee in its tall bone-china pot, the cups and saucers clattering, and Julia jumped up to take the tray from him.

'Thank you, my dear,' he said, reclaiming his stick and levering himself into his chair.

Karl had warned them that his father might be a little taciturn but he was grace itself, eyes intent on Julia, resting his white cup of black coffee on his knee.

'Tell me again what it is you do, my dear,' he asked her. 'Karl mentioned something about indoor gardens, but I couldn't really follow.'

Julia told him about Arbour: 'I design outside spaces for the indoors. Mainly in offices.'

'And the plants do well?' he enquired in such a doctorly fashion that Julian snorted.

'It's astonishing how much success you can have, even with trees, if you get the irrigation and light right. And Freda, my partner, is a brilliant plantswoman. We try to run everything from timers and we remove anything the moment it's sickly.'

Heino was finding it impossible not to stare at her, a feeling Julian knew all too well. His coffee remained untouched. 'I would like to see one of your gardens,' he said. She leant across and told him he was welcome to come along in the van anytime.

'Your wife is very beautiful,' he said, good manners demanding that he turn his attention to Julian, who at that moment had been caught by a portrait on the piano. He nodded to it. 'Yours too, Heino. I thought so, very much, when I met her.'

Julia followed their gaze to the silver frame and she jumped, seemingly startled by the sight of Karl's mother. Ellie was young and lovely, with a graceful curve of neck and upswept hair.

Julia got to her feet, walked to the piano. 'We must go, now, I'm afraid,' she announced, tapping her wrist, though she never wore a watch. 'We need to get the next train back or we'll miss Mira's bedtime.'

She became brisk, arranging her return for after the weekend. 'Let me get you keys,' Heino said, and she offered him her arm when he bowed forward to stand. 'No, it's OK,' he said, smiling up at her. 'Not such an old cripple yet.' He tapped his way to his desk, took the keys with their leather fobs from a drawer and handed a set to each of them.

It's a mighty mental effort for Julian to shut the door on Lamb's Conduit Street – he doesn't want to think for another moment about her there. He's still a little stoned from those few puffs on the joint, and hungry. He comes downstairs to an empty house. There's a note on the kitchen table from his mother; they've gone shopping in Woodford and then on to Sue's for lunch. She's left him courgette soup, which he slurps lukewarm from the pan. Zeph nudges him with his nose and there's solace in stroking his silky ears. The air is a little cooler today: there is even a breeze. It would be a good day for striking out across to the Mill to see Raph, but he's halted by the sudden peace of finding himself alone. Even the birds sound less harried, something's singing a syrupy song.

He thinks of a battered tin coffee pot that looked more ancient than its owner, enamelled brown inside from the constant brew. This coffee pot suspended from a tripod that straddled a fire and Raph waiting on the step of his lorry with a china mug in his hand. In repose he looked troubled, but when he smiled his eyes disappeared into the friendliest crinkles.

In the heat of the day Raph went shirtless and shoeless, his combat shorts hanging low, their baggy pockets weighted down with tools and tricks. His muscular body was brown as ancient terracotta, etched with the fine blue-black of his tattoos. A gracefully drawn dove dipped her wings over one bicep, an olive branch in her mouth, and, more intriguingly, a series of tiny interlocking hearts spread from the left side of his chest, across his shoulder and down, like hundreds of petals falling from his heart, each with a man's name at its centre. He refused to tell Julian who they were. Some were hard to read with the dips between his muscles as he moved about. His back was covered by a mighty pair of wings, every feather exquisitely inked, so they rippled as he moved.

The wings were first, Raph told him. Just before he joined the

Royal Navy he'd met an artist, a girl from the Slade, who could only get work in a tattoo parlour. The wings were her goodbye present to him.

When he left the forces, Nell, the girl who gave him his wings, became his wife. The hearts were Nell's second goodbye present, just before he took to the road. The mysterious names were inked in tiny script: Matias, Tomas, Santiago, Juancho, Marcelo, Felipe, Kiko, Ricardo.

How lovely they were, those long summer nights: the words and the silences, the sunsets and the stars. Raph sitting on his step teaching him card tricks and to roll a coin across his knuckles, to light a fire without matches, to trust the universe.

He stands at the small bookcase to consult with the netsuke monkey, resists the lure of the window seat. Perhaps today you'll do some work, the monkey says.

But his thoughts have stuck with Raph. The last time he saw him was the night Firdaws was lost.

'You're young. There will be other places,' Raph said then, as they sat, poking sticks and making sparks of the embers.

He must have gone on about Julia in too much detail. He remembers Raph holding up his hands to make him stop: 'OK. She's fabulous to look at and hot in the sack. I get it.'

And Raph shaking his head at him, saying: 'I thought you were meant to be working for your finals, huh? I'm not sure you should let this animal lust rule your mind like this.'

'Of course it's not just sex,' Julian said.

They stayed talking like that long after the fire died. When it was time to leave Raph laid a hand on his shoulder. 'Your love for this Julia coming at the same time as losing your family home, that's heavy,' he said. 'But be strong my friend, live happy and love well. There's plenty out there for you to learn, not all of it at university. But looking at the state you're in, I'd say be careful with this Julia. Especially if she's as beautiful as you say.

But, you know, keep your wits about you, study hard, write your book.'

Julian looks again at his scraps of paper, at the sea of his desk choppy with Post-its. He had started scribbling this thing the moment he returned from that moonless flit, had continued with it until sunrise and then all the way back on the train to Julia, safe, he hoped, from the ire of her husband behind Mrs Briggs's sturdy front door.

He rereads a couple of the Post-its, sits down with his head in his hands. Some scraps have fallen from the bookshelves, a couple of sheets of old notes from between the pages of the Milton. They are yellowing, folded in two, the perforations from where they'd been torn from a jotter grown brittle, his tiny script. A few words, a couple of sentences, catch his eye. A small jolt turns to a wave of recognition as he reads.

He remembers sketching it out at Mrs Briggs's, the gin bottle beside him egging him on, a ring-bound notebook that he'd taken to carrying around in his pocket since the idea had taken grip in the maelstrom of meeting Julia and losing Firdaws.

The pages are lined with tiny writing in a variety of pencil and pens, he evidently hadn't been as fetishistic about his writing implements in his student days. The plot hadn't wavered over years of thwarted good intentions. His Eve was a feminist who argued long and energetically with her Adam in their bower, a flat above a fruit market. He'd sketched her out arriving on her bicycle in her black and white hooped tights and don't-fuck-with-me boots: 'her basket overspilling with bunches of marigolds, bright as her hair, and crammed with vegetables from the market . . .'

Marigolds as bright as her hair. Well, that could be changed. It made him snort. But this was it. The thing that he'd been attempting before Mira became ill. The falcon. The obscuring clouds. And for the briefest beat of a wing all the pieces fall back into place.

Fourteen

Easter had been a time of illness and short tempers, with no time for Julian to do anything much with the book that was stubbornly rising, this scattering of Post-its on his desk the only proof he had ever started. One night he rose from his bed with the title being whispered in his ear and crept downstairs to his desk, still dreaming as he wrote it down. Afterwards, sleep-walking back up the stairs, he had stumbled on the landing and woken Mira.

He was waking in the mornings with whole scenes writing themselves but no time to get them down. There was the script for *Fletch le Bone II* to finish and Julia had already done what she could by taking Mira to London with her for a few days: Mira liked sleeping on Heino's little day bed in Lamb's Conduit Street, but not all the trailing around in the van, especially not a man in an office who shouted at her for dropping fistfuls of gravel into his executive loo.

Now Mira was ill. While she slept off her fevers, he wrote. On the days when she was better he got no work done at all. The days and nights until Julia's return stretched before him like a junkyard for broken deadlines.

Most of the meals he prepared for Mira ended up in the dog. Several times she pleaded with him to take her to the village to feed the ducks or to be clucked over by the Miss Hamlyns in the village shop where she eyed the Easter eggs, finally choosing one for Julia with Maltesers inside. She was tearful and wanted to sit curled into him on the window seat, with her rabbit hot-water bottle on her tummy. He read to her while she dozed, with his script already in overtime and thoughts of his book penetrating almost every waking hour.

Eventually they went to Dr Andrews who felt her tummy, said that it was probably constipation and sent them home with some powder for her orange juice. He took her walking by the river so the roses would bloom in her cheeks but still she looked wan. He carried her on his back and she nodded off with her head on his shoulder, while the words he wanted to write blazed briefly and disappeared like smuts on the breeze.

It was on one of these walks that he ran into Katie's mother. Penny Webster stopped him to chat, stroking Mira's sleepy cheek. 'Katie will be in Horton soon. She's bringing Billy and Arthur, so there'll be someone for this little one to play with,' she said.

Back at Firdaws, Julia exploded: 'What, just Katie? No husband?' She stared into Julian's eyes until he found himself staunching a flush of unearned guilt. It rose unbidden from who knew where as she mocked: 'Oh Jude, Ju-ju, Jooo-ooood.'

'Stop it,' he said. 'Do you have to?'

But yes, it appeared she did have to.

There had been a letter once, on blue paper, Katie's writing on the matching blue envelope. He remembers Julia reading it, cross-legged on his bed at Mrs Briggs's, naked but for his dressing gown, which had become separated from its belt. Julia's pregnancy was showing almost immediately with a dark line that ran from her navel to her pubic hair, her slim ribcage was out-proportioned by the new and astonishing swell of her breasts. Katie's letter was shaking in her hands. 'Well, that is really very unpleasant,' was all she said, abruptly gathering the dressing gown around her and reaching for his lighter. Sheet by sheet she burned the pages of that letter, holding each by its corner until there were only three tiny blue triangles in his ashtray, the rest of it curling ash. She cried for a bit but refused to let him know what Katie had written. Whatever it was was enough to turn Julia hostile whenever Katie was around.

On Good Friday Julia returned from London early. It didn't help that he hadn't heard her van pull up. It was bright and there was actual warmth in the sun for the first time that year. He was lying in the hammock with Mira and Billy, a canopy of apple blossom between them and the sky. Katie and Arthur were making daisy chains close enough to listen while he told them a Fletch le Bone adventure. He knew how it looked.

But still he stayed put as her shadow fell over them. *When the cat's away the mice will play* on repeat in his head, so it was hard to work out if he wasn't secretly punishing her for going away. 'Very cosy,' Julia said, turning tail as Katie stumbled to her feet, brushing daisies from her lap.

They didn't speak until Katie and the boys were gone and Mira was settled. He brought tea for them to drink in bed, found her sitting at the dressing table in her white shirt and pants. 'So now she's breaking up with her husband. Is that it?'

He shrugged, tired of the conversation already. 'They're having problems. He's a shagger.'

'Oh, what timing. She's going to be here all the time, I suppose. That's nice for you.'

'You have nothing to be jealous about,' he said, watching in the mirror as she attacked her tangles with a brush. He was weakened by the sight, wishing they could get this row over with and get on with being naked. Lady Lilith's hair crackled, her cheeks ablaze.

She tugged at a knot, grimaced. 'I knew you'd think it's all about jealousy,' she said.

'Hardly surprising, the way you behave around her.' He reached out to touch her. She'd been away for three nights, it was hard not to leap at her.

She drew away. 'I will never forgive her for what she wrote. It's not me being jealous.' She threw the hairbrush on the bed and abruptly changed to a subject of equal fury. 'And what about this place? I suppose you're going ahead with the builders?'

'What?'

The men were due to start work demolishing the kitchen and the Nicholsons' bathroom the following week.

'This is getting silly, your priorities are all wrong,' Julia said, but he'd gone ahead and paid the builders half up front. She was right, a bit of help over the nursery-school holidays would have been a more sensible use of the money.

Mira started running a temperature almost the moment Julia left for London. He laid cold flannels across her head and wondered if Dr Andrews was right, that she really was starting to sicken for her mother during these midweek absences.

But the next day Mira was better, though still talking about tummy ache and being picky about her food. She was dangling a sausage for Zeph.

Mary Poppins, where are you? Hello, Nurse Matilda? Mrs Doubtfire? The phone was ringing but not a moment to answer it as he tried to commit his waking thoughts to paper. He'd dreamt an entire scene. Julia and Raph, a sunlit road. Julia walking along the verge, her mouth and hands stained by berries from the Pick Your Own at Horton Farm. She has brought a basket of fruit, has selected the juiciest berries. The strawberries so sweet he could taste them as he woke. He could still see her: face upturned and gently mocking, the sun glancing from golden callipers that Raph was pressing to her features to demonstrate Fibonacci perfection. The phone stopped ringing.

Mira was down to her last pair of pants, he had to get the

washing on. Zeph leapt for the sausage. 'Stop it, Mira!' he snapped. 'It'll be your fault if he gets your finger.'

'Horrible sausage,' she said when he insisted she at least try it. 'And Dadoo, you're a horrible sausage too!' she added, pushing her plate away and glaring at him.

Outside there was the honking of a car horn. Through the window he saw Katie at the wheel: Lady Madonna in dimples and fur, a vision emerging from her mum's white Volvo. In the back Billy and Arthur bouncing in their seats. He ran to the door with Mira in tow. Katie came across the grass smiling lopsidedly at them, the fur collar of her coat lending a glamour to her jeans and wellies.

'There are lambs at Tiggy's Farm Park that you can feed with a bottle. Does Mira want to come? I've got a spare car seat . . .'

He thanked his lucky stars Julia had already departed as Mira threw herself at Katie and the boys. Without looking back at him, she pulled on her wellies and clambered across Billy's legs and into the seat between them.

'Well, that's decided then,' he said, laughing, and Katie came in with him to grab Mira's coat.

'I'll take her back to ours for lunch and a play afterwards if that's OK with you,' she said.

'To tell you the truth, that'd be more than OK, Katie.' He ran both hands through his hair, making it stick up. 'I'm not getting any work done at all.'

She looked at him as though he were simple. 'You should have said something. I've got stuff going on for the boys all the time we're down here. They're running me ragged, but I'm very happy for Mira to come over and play if you need to write.'

'Really? Oh, Katie, you've no idea.' He was looking beyond her, to a squeal from the back of the car, Mira leaning over to tickle Billy.

She grinned at him, full-on dimples.

'Are you sure? I'm late with about a hundred things and Julia isn't back until Friday to take over with Little Miss Oh Majesty Who Must Be Obeyed over there.'

'Why don't you let me take her off your hands?'

He could've kissed her – to be honest he did, right there at the front door of Firdaws, with the children watching, lifting her up to deliver it and then another when he put her down and saw that he'd made her blush.

Mira loved Billy and Arthur, her 'naughty boys', and with almost insulting alacrity waited at the door each morning with her haversack packed and ready for Katie's arrival. While Mira was gone he worked like a maniac, getting himself back on track with the wretched *Fletch le Bone II*. He even found time for the other thing, which was emerging as surely as the cyclamens that were pushing up shoots around the apple trees where he swung her.

Tuber. Tumour. His book. The secret things had all been swelling and growing.

The alien land of his desk testifies to how he squandered the time he could've spent with her, swarming as it is with messages to himself from a previous dimension, from the time before they knew she was ill. He starts peeling the Post-its, slowly, deliberately, screwing each one into a ball to aim at the wastepaper basket.

Zeph barks at the sound of voices and Julian follows him to the porch. Jenna and Michael are approaching across the fields, hand in hand, the sun low through the branches behind them so he has to shield his eyes. His mother picks through the stubble, nimble as a cat, Michael less so, in fact, he notices as they get closer, Michael is hobbling.

He points to his leg and then at Jenna: 'She made me walk all the way back from Sue's because she thinks I'm too drunk to drive.'

Jenna ignores him and starts talking of lamb and couscous. Julian could stick his fingers in his ears as they follow him inside and she wails about okra and red shallots. 'They're all still in the car. We left the shopping!' She gives Michael a light cuff around the ear as punishment. 'I told you not to let her open the second bottle,' she says. Michael tries to pinch her bum, but she skips away. They're both flushed in the face, as much from Sue's wine as the walk home. Jenna looks at him expectantly. 'The shopping? Julian, would you?'

He forces himself to do the right thing, sticks out his hand with a sigh.

'Give me the keys if you've locked the car.' The phone rings and Jenna springs to answer it, no matter how many times he's asked her to leave it.

She covers the mouthpiece. 'It's William,' she says. 'Again.'

He shakes his head at her.

'Don't you think you should speak to him? He's a good friend to keep calling.'

'I'm off to get your shopping from Sue's. Tell him I'll call him back.'

'OK,' she says and mouths after him. 'But you never do.'

Michael steps forward: 'Here, give me the phone.'

William? A good friend? William with his Clark Kent specs and button-down collars, and his rocket-fuelled ascent up the editorial ladder at Random House. William and his endless ill-fated romances. William: some godfather he'd turned out to be, stupid Larkin poem and then what? Mira might just as well not exist for all the attention he ever paid her. He never once visited her in hospital, but he was all over the phone now.

Since the naming party William had met Mira only once. It was at Cromwell Gardens, the first time Julia poppered her in to the terrifying baby bouncer with its inadequate-looking clamp on the doorframe. It still makes Julian chuckle to think of the look on Mira's face as she boinged about, surprised by the power of her own tippy-toes, her expression growing so earnest anyone would've thought it was her *job* to bounce. He and Julia got the giggles watching her, but William just stood with a bottle of champagne about to pop, looking from them to Mira and not really getting it.

They drank William's champagne and ate at the table in the bay of their plum-coloured sitting room. Julia had cooked osso bucco in honour of this rare visit and William told them all about his latest minx, while they ate with Mira passed between their laps and William trying to look interested in her latest achievements: the pot she could bash with a spoon, her sophisticated tastes, a piece of marrow bone grasped in her tiny greasy fist. They put Mira to bed between the main course and pudding and William feigned barfing when Julian changed her nappy on the sofa and Julia admonished him with a poke to the stomach. 'Stop it! You'll give her a complex.'

Though Julia found William easy company, laughing often in his presence, she was soon ushering them both out of the flat for what William irritatingly insisted on calling a 'boys' night out'. She couldn't stop yawning. 'Go on,' she said, heading for bed with her book and a hot cup of tea. He yearned for her to say: *Oh, don't go. Stay here with me.*

'Go on,' she said. 'You haven't been out once since Mira was born.'

Surprisingly soon they were in a strip club and William was calling for cocktails, shouting above the music: 'You don't have to tell Julia.' The girls had shaved pudenda. A redhead in a smattering of sequins and elastic slithered to their table. William gulping and nodding. The girl dancing to Madonna, mouthing the words as though in some insane ecstasy. 'Crazy for you . . . touch me once and you'll know it's true . . .' Her skin so white it was almost blue, thin as milk, her veins showing through. The unfastening of ribbons and slippery stuff sliding away. Grinding and pulsing to the beat, freshly plucked chicken skin juddering and slightly shiny just inches from his face.

The road from the village is clear and Julian takes the hump-back bridge at speed, as he has done ever since he passed his test. It's more habit these days than thrillseeking. Still he feels the bounce in his stomach the moment his tyres leave the tarmac.

He slows his car at Deadman's Curve – everyone in the village calls it that, but not in front of Jenna. Jenna never takes this road, but Julian often finds himself here. There's a rolling view all the way down into the valley, a rocky wall to sit on, clumped with moss. Not many cars pass. The land slopes away, hedges, trees, and down below the river snakes through its water meadows. He often pulls over and tries to imagine what was going through his father's mind as he lost control. People said it was lucky Jenna and the baby weren't in the car: perhaps that's what Maxwell was thinking as his wheels left the ground.

Julian had caught himself helplessly praying on the day Mira was admitted to the hospital, begging his father not to let her die. Wedged into every space beneath the stained-glass windows of the hospital chapel, a crowd of totemic soft toys witnessed this folly. Alleluia! In great gold letters at the font, a vase with coral-red gladioli, a picture of a baby propped at its base. He prayed to his dad. Who else was there to pray to?

Apparently it was icy the night it happened, and black. No view for Maxwell as he left this earth. His car tumbled three times, they said, nose to tail. He was already dead when they cut him from the wreckage and when they opened the boot a sea of broken glass spilled out from all the empties he'd been hiding in there.

Julian starts the car. Jenna will be needing her ingredients, only cooking keeps her sane.

Of course Sue is waiting for him when he gets to Michael's car parked outside her cottage. No chance he could smuggle out the shopping like a burglar. She stands with her front door already open, a butcher's apron askew across her uncontainable bosom. 'Oh Julian, you sweet boy.' She sweeps him into a suffocating hug and he braces himself for her tears. He's noticed it's always him left doing the comforting.

'Tea? I'd offer you a glass of wine,' she says, patting her eyes and blowing her nose with a tissue from her apron pocket. 'But I'm afraid we finished my last bottle.'

He starts switching the supermarket bags from the boot of Michael's sleek car into his own. 'It's OK,' he says. 'I'd better get this lot back to Firdaws.' Judging by the amount of shopping, it doesn't appear his mother and Michael are planning to be anywhere else anytime soon.

Sue pats escaped straggles of hair towards her blonded bun, licks her lips. 'Jenna told me what she's cooking, shame I'm on a diet.'

'But you're not fat,' he says, unconvincingly.

As a boy, one of the high points for Julian at his mother's river parties was Sue, stripped to her bra and pants, with all her delicious-looking pink flesh spilling out. She embraces him again, says: 'Oh, it is always lovely to see you back where you belong,' as his face grows warm at the memory.

Sue fills the silence. 'Your Peace Convoy mate is back, I've noticed. Have you seen him?' And he remembers Sue once telling Jenna she had the hots for Raph.

'Your mum was saying she thought you should go and spend some time with him, and I thought, well, that's a turn-up for the books.'

Julian opens his car door. 'I'll probably catch him in the next two days or he'll be gone. He never stays beyond the last day of August.' He's behind the wheel, ready to go.

'He doesn't get any less handsome with the years,' Sue calls as he starts his ignition.

He hadn't wanted to share Raph with anyone, that was the thing. A couple of men in the village sometimes stopped at Raph's fire and he would find them chatting there, folded back on their haunches on their way to or from the pubs in Woodford. Julian was tongue-tied when the men were there, a boy who shouldn't be drinking beer, but mostly it had been just the two of them on those August nights: a fire, a sky, man to man.

He turns to the rutted road of his father's final failure to return home.

He puts his foot down, gathering speed up the hill, here comes the bend, he's pointing the car at the wall but his foot slams to the brake and he swerves. He pulls over, his hands shaking on the wheel.

Dusk falls, the moon not yet risen. He stares into the void. Jenna will have to wait for her shallots because he needs to pee. His trainers scrunch against loose stones and grit as he clambers over the wall and drops on to the grass. The birds have given up for the day, all but a few shadowy night-timers who call from the trees. Julian unbuttons his jeans and pees into hawthorn and dark nettles while above his head his father's Fiat takes flight across the sky, a glittering constellation shattering in its wake.

Fifteen

Julian and Julia stalling at the entrance of the Byzantine chapel at Great Ormond Street, the gleaming gold hush of it, PAX in a mosaic beneath their feet and the very notion of peace a shattered dream. PAX: what was this? Some sort of imperative? An impossible promise in exchange for obedience?

He tried to speak as he followed Julia, but his mouth was so dry that nothing but nonsense would come. She shushed him and knelt to pray. Around them, spinning, the overwhelming goldness, even the air, a simulacra of heaven trapped inside a Fabergé egg or the brass workings of an ornate clock. He didn't know whether to sit at the carved pew beside her or keep moving.

In the end he knelt. Prayed to his dead father. Our father. My father. They both started crying again; she, silently, hidden by the kinking curtain of her hair, and he with racking sobs. The chapel was just somewhere to go, that was all, while upstairs in the Lion Ward the medical staff worked to stabilise Mira's blood pressure, and then, oh God, oh father, and then.

At Firdaws he drags the shopping from the boot, glad to be home. But now there are voices, he stops on his way through and listens, the polythene of Jenna's shopping bags cutting into his fingers. There's pealing laughter. Katie's, if he's not mistaken.

The kitchen is ablaze. Jenna doesn't appear to have sobered up, she is barefoot, and a bit jingly, her bracelets and her voice. They have put on some music: Leonard Cohen. Jenna sings along to 'Closing Time', muddling the words. Katie jollies by her side.

'Swift and brave with the knife like this.' His mother is teaching her to make her special kebabs, slicing lamb fillet as thin as leaves while through the open windows he smells the charcoal that Michael is preparing for the grill.

'You see, you slice almost through but not quite, so it stays in one long piece like a book of many pages . . .'

'Crikey,' Katie says as Jenna's knife flashes, 'that's surgical.'

Jenna slits the meat, a cut for each line of the song. '. . . And it's one for the devil and one for Christ.'

Zeph's toenails clatter on the tiles as he tears himself away from the meaty doings to throw himself at Julian. Julian holds out the shopping bags as Katie advances. She is dressed entirely – T-shirt dress and some sort of wraparound-cardigan thing – in a bright emerald green that matches her eyeshadow. Her kiss falls awkwardly between his cheek and mouth.

It occurs to Julian to make an excuse – bed being the only one that springs to mind – but Katie silences him. 'It is so lovely to see your mum again,' taking up her knife by Jenna's side and eyeing him over her shoulder. 'And very nice of you to invite me.'

They have their backs to him as they slice the meat, Jenna's shoulders slightly raised, a scheming pigeon in her crumpled grey dress beside Katie's resplendent green cockatoo as she shows her how to weave a skewer through the meat. The green fabric is pulled tight as Katie shakes her tailfeathers.

Jenna points to a tray piled with plates and cutlery: 'Why don't you make yourself useful and take this stuff outside?' She gestures through the window, a look that says she cannot contain her excitement a moment longer. 'I think Michael has a proposal for you.'

The hurricane lamps are lit. Michael has a striped tea towel tucked into his waistband and his sleeves rolled up. The night is spattered with stars.

'That was good of you to get the shopping,' he says, turning hot lumps of charcoal and nodding towards the kitchen. 'She's got herself set on preparing quite a feast tonight.' He puts down his metal prongs and rubs his stomach. 'Lucky us!'

He wipes his hands across the tea towel, looks at Julian over his specs. 'Your mother wants me to talk to you about Firdaws. She's had an idea . . .' But Julian interrupts him before he goes any further and makes a run for the kitchen.

Safe in the pantry he overhears Jenna and Katie.

His mum, what was becoming a well-worn theme: 'I never thought she was that pretty, if I'm honest . . .'

'Oh Jenna, you're wrong. She's stunning.'

'Icy eyes,' Jenna says as he walks in with a bottle of elder-flower. 'Glaciers,' she adds sotto voce with a small shiver.

He waves the cordial bottle at her. 'Perhaps not too much wine tonight, huh?' Mixes it in a glass jug with sparkling water, hacks apart lemons. Bubbles cascade to the surface, but all he can see is Julia in the plastic chair by Mira's hospital bed reading her *The Ugly Duckling* for the umpteenth time. 'I'm a very fine swan indeed.' And the tears in her eyes because when she was little her mother used to say: 'See, there's hope even for you, Julia . . .'

'Julia never believed she was beautiful,' he says as he clanks the ice into the jug. Jenna and Katie carry on slicing the meat, their heads so close he'd like to bang them together.

'Oh, come on,' Katie has a blush coming.

He picks up the jug. 'If you'd ever been around her mother, you'd understand why.'

Outside Michael places the grill over his bed of embers, wipes his brow with the tea towel and holds out his glass. 'I've had a very interesting conversation with William,' he says.

Julian pours him some elderflower, plonks the jug on the table and himself into one of the slatted seats.

'He wants to make an offer for the book you spoke to him about before Mira got ill . . .' Julian picks at the bread while Michael waits, spatula in hand.

'I told him he'd have to speak to you direct, of course. But I've given it some thought, and though the advance wouldn't be huge, and we'd have to sort out what to do about Firdaws, I've a feeling it might not be a bad thing. You know, writing your book might even help a little to make sense of what's happened . . .'

'Right. I'm getting a proper drink, do you want one?' Julian launches himself from his chair and bumps straight into Katie carrying the lamb to the grill. Zeph almost gets his dearest wish, but Michael makes a surprisingly agile leap and a save just before it hits the ground.

A bottle of red wine and the smell of cooking meat soothes them all. The thin strips of kebab almost melt in the mouth, the okra is sweet. Katie regales them with stories of Billy and Arthur. No one mentions Mira. Jenna brings a brown earthenware bowl to the table. Saffron rice pudding with almonds and pistachios. 'Your favourite,' she says to Michael as she lifts the lid and releases a cloud of fragrant steam.

Julian pats his groaning stomach. 'I'll just take myself off for a little smoke.'

He rolls his cigarette and falls into the hammock, swinging himself with one leg to the ground as he smokes. Their voices carry across the grass. He stares through the leaves at the sky. Bats flicker. He tries to relax his eyes and not search for shooting stars. If you try too hard you never see one. There is only one thing to wish for. He softens his gaze. The ropes sing and there it is, sizzling through time. One flare of magic and things are unsaid, knowledge unlearned, the lock back on Pandora's box. He closes his eyes and wishes, can almost believe it is true: Julia waiting for him, reading in the kitchen chair, Mira upstairs, her white rabbit, her thumb and one of its ears resting on her bottom lip. He opens his eyes to find Katie staring down at him.

'May I join you?'

'You don't smoke . . .'

'No, I meant in the hammock.' She doesn't wait for his answer but slips off her pumps and levers herself in with her head at his feet and her legs stretched beside him. He leaves his leg trailing the ground but stops swinging. She wriggles to get comfortable and he feels the fabric grow taut beneath them and the knots creak against the trunks of the trees.

'Your mum really doesn't want to talk about Mira, does she? I was just telling her about that game she used to play with Billy and Arthur . . .'

'Bad Rabbits,' he says. 'I think it was Beatrix Potter-inspired. I always had to be Mr McGregor.'

'Yep, that one; it's all they ever wanted to play, but every time I mention Mira's name she changes the subject.'

'Tell me about it.' He shifts his weight so he has one arm and shoulder hanging Chatterton-style from the side of the hammock.

'It must be hard for you,' she says.

'Yes.' He screws his eyes over the final drag of his cigarette and flicks it into the bushes.

'We had so much fun with her over the Easter hols. I can honestly say she and the boys couldn't have had a lovelier time.'

'Yeah, I feel bad now, fobbing her off on you.'

'Oh come on,' Katie says. 'I offered. She was bright as a button, so much more articulate than my boys. And then the following week you were all gone and she was in Great Ormond Street, and I was searching my brain for any sort of sign I'd missed. I'm sure it's awful to have to think about. But what I've never pieced together is ... if you don't mind talking about this ... but how did she end up in hospital so suddenly like that? Did I miss something?'

'I was an idiot is what happened,' he says and laughs bitterly and for too long until she prods him with her foot to make him stop. 'It was the day the builders had arrived to start knocking out the kitchen.' He reaches for her foot and gives it a grateful squeeze and she curls her toes around his fingers as he continues. 'It was a nightmare, the whole day. Mira had been awake every hour through the night complaining of tummy ache. I gave up putting her back to bed in her own room and let her sleep in mine. I couldn't stop her crying. She wanted Mummy, she said.'

SO DO I! he'd found himself roaring into her face at four o'clock in the morning, but he's too ashamed to tell Katie that bit.

'She was pale and whiny and the men had started upstairs, demolishing the bathroom. I was trying to pack the kitchen into boxes, plaster falling from the shaking ceiling, banging, banging, Radio One blaring.

'I'd been planning to drop her at nursery and spend the day writing in Woodford Library, but she was floppy and the Calpol hadn't brought down her temperature, so we were both stuck here while it went on. The egg-shaped bath had to be sawn in two to get it out, you can imagine the noise that made. Dust flew everywhere, making her cough, so I moved a camping stove into the sitting room, though she wasn't interested in any of the food I cooked for her. Karl called while I was boiling some rice. He sounded stressed, said he had to talk to me. He seemed so wretched I wondered if something had happened to Heino. But we were interrupted by Mira screaming outside and I dropped the phone and ran to her. She was burning with fever – she kept pointing at the ground, though no words would come. Eventually she managed: "A t-t-t-oad. It kept looking at me," and burst into hot tears. I carried her indoors and when she was calmer called Karl back.

'He said what he wanted to tell me wasn't the sort of thing we could talk about on the phone. He insisted on seeing me, on coming down. But by then I just wanted to get away from the builders. I wasn't getting any work done anyway.

'I tucked her up with a beaker of warm banana Nesquik in front of the *Teletubbies* and tried to work. I screwed some of those yellow ear-plugs from an old airplane bag into my ears. Obviously that was no use, because she could barely hear the television over the banging and in the end I decided I might as well take her to London.'

'So, that's when you took off? You went to meet Karl?' Katie has allowed him to talk uninterrupted all this time. It's getting a little chilly, he's almost glad to have the warmth of her beside him in the hammock.

'Yes, I did. Screaming all the way in the back of the car. I know now that she was in agony, but shit for brains here just kept on driving. I even turned the music up.'

'She'd only managed milky things that day. She complained that the seatbelt hurt her and I kept having to pull over to adjust it. In the end I made the straps so loose they'd have been useless in an accident. At some point she stopped screaming and fell asleep with her cheek lolling on her shoulder. She woke up moaning as we pulled off the motorway: pale, curdy sick was pouring from her mouth. I gave her extra Calpol in the lay-by and cleaned her up as best I could. She just looked at me and said: "Sorry, Dadoo . . ." '

Katie manoeuvres herself around so that they face the same way. She holds his head to her chest as the hammock rocks, enfolds him. 'Oh Mira,' he moans her name aloud.

Karl shouted up the stairs to his father as Julian stumbled from the car, Mira screaming in his arms.

'Christ, she's started up again. Where's Julia?'

Karl led the way into the flat, Mira's cries piercing the hallway, Julia running, taking her from him, kissing her hot, vomit-flecked face: 'Sweetness, whatever's the matter?'

Heino came in leaning on his stick, shaking his head when they told him it was tummy ache. 'I think I'd better take a look at her,' he said.

Mira quietened in Julia's arms. She moaned when she laid her on the couch, her knees tucked into her belly. Heino motioned for Julia to pull up Mira's sweatshirt. 'May I?' She flinched when he put his stethoscope to her chest. He pressed the dome of her tummy with his knobbly hands, snapped the stethoscope from his ears and turned to Karl. 'You feel, tell me if I'm wrong.' He looked at Julia while Karl put his hands on Mira's belly. Heino grasped Julia's elbow. 'You need to get this child to A and E,' he said. 'It's always better to be certain.'

They were seen almost immediately at the Paediatric Casualty Department at UCH. Mira was in a cubicle and the pressure sleeve already on her arm by the time Karl got back from parking the car. Her blood pressure was 150/100. Calls were being made. Karl knelt before Julia, held her shoulders to calm her, looked into her eyes: 'They know what they're doing,' he said.

They were transferred by ambulance to Great Ormond Street. There were more blood tests – it was almost worse when Mira didn't scream at the needle than when she did. X-rays. Scans. Mira awake for very little of it, he and Julia hearts pounding as they followed her hospital bed along corridors and through doors, to and from the lift, back and forth to the ward. Julia turned her face to his shoulder as a tiny hairy baby was wheeled past, a nurse leaning over the cot gently squeezing air into its mouth from a ridged plastic tube.

Mira was hooked up to a drip, nurses around her bed, tearfully resisting as they tried to insert the canula, then floppy again. Karl said he'd wait with her while they followed Esther Fry, their consultant, to the parents' interview room along the corridor. Esther Fry sat with her clipboard of notes on her knee. They perched on stiff blue chairs while she passed Julia the box of tissues, corkscrew curls bobbing as she spoke with brisk confidence. 'Once we've brought down her blood pressure, we can talk about the next stage.'

'What next stage?' Julian started pulling at his hair, and Julia had to grip his hands to make him stop; he could feel hers shaking.

'We should have done something sooner . . .' Julia said. There were so many things to beat themselves up about. 'We used to laugh at her pot belly.'

Esther Fry flapped the sheaf of notes at them: 'This sort of tumour can be very hard to diagnose in the early stages. She's here now and that's the main thing. You're in the right place.'

Tumour. There, it was said.

'Please just tell me that she won't die,' Julia said, asking for both of them.

'The main thing is she's comfortable now. She's lightly sedated and we'll be administering the Nifedipine to bring down her blood pressure. Everything else we can talk about tomorrow.'

'Doctor, please . . .'

'Call me Esther.' She gave them her kindest smile. 'This will be the worst day, from now on it'll get better.' And over the weeks to come they would repeat her words to each other, *from now on it'll get better.*

'First she will need to have a biopsy and a port fitted to her chest.' Esther Fry pointed to a spot beneath her own collarbone and the thought of so tender a part of Mira being pierced made his palms sweat. 'The port will remain under the skin and drugs will be administered through it.' Again Esther Fry tapped the place on her chest where Mira would be cut, he could see lilac veins beneath her skin. 'It's a straightforward operation and it means we won't have to keep pricking her.'

Esther Fry produced some leaflets and laid them on the table. They'd have to make choices, though choices were the last thing they felt capable of making. 'If the scans show that the tumour is contained within the kidney, you can be part of a randomised clinical trial comparing the US approach, where immediate removal of her left kidney would straight away rectify her blood pressure, or the European approach of starting with four to six weeks of chemotherapy to shrink the tumour with reduced danger of it rupturing and spreading during the operation.'

Julian was overcome with weakness. 'Let's ask Karl,' he suggested. 'Or, better, his dad. I'm sure Heino must know what's best.'

They found themselves hovering at the door of the chapel. Inside a choir of golden angels soundlessly played their instruments around the star-spangled dome. His eyes blurred; there was nothing but glitter, PAX at their feet and, within, a great eagle spreading his gilded wings at the lectern. He knelt and prayed to his father to send him a sign that Mira would recover. He looked around the walls at the huddles of soft toys parents had placed there: teddy bears, Tiggers, rabbits, love-torn monkeys, a little felt mouse with a bright-red nose and flowers embroidered across its ears. Julia pointed, whispered: 'I can't stand it. These must have belonged to children who have died here.'

'Stop,' said Julian. They clung together until they heard somebody cough behind them. It was Karl holding Mira's rabbit. He'd been back to Lamb's Conduit Street to fetch it; Mira never slept without it. The rabbit was wearing Mira's own baby dress, the one with her name in red appliqué.

'Mira will be all right,' he was saying. Julia pointed to the toys and started to sob. Karl had his arm around her. 'I expect the parents put them here as an offering to God to keep their little ones safe,' he said, pulling her close. 'In fact, I'm sure of it.'

Sixteen

Katie strokes Julian's hair as they lie together in the hammock. 'Poor Jude, you're exhausted.'

'I think you're right,' he says. 'Let's call it a night.'

The mist drifts from the river. They cross the grass, she's shivering, so he puts his arm around her shoulder and gives her a squeeze. Michael and Jenna have cleared up the supper things and slipped away to bed unnoticed while he's been talking at her in the hammock.

She curls in the chair beside the Rayburn and he pulls the dog blanket around her. He thinks a brandy will warm them both up, whether or not she'll be sober enough to drive herself home doesn't cross his mind. He hands her the glass and she looks up at him, the yellow speckles of her eyes like grains of pollen. Her green eye stuff is still in place but her mascara has smudged into black rings. Her dress has twisted around and as she adjusts it he sees, with a stab of pity, that her bra is green to match the rest of her outfit. She raises an eyebrow.

'Oooh, look at you, Cassandra,' he says, embarrassed to have been caught looking.

'What?'

'Don't pretend. Like in *I Capture the Castle* when the Mortmains dye all their clothes green? Remember?'

The pollen dances in her eyes. Oh yes, she remembers.

They came across the burial mound racing on their bikes through the bluebell woods after school. *I Capture the Castle* was Katie's favourite book, even that it was their set text for GCSE didn't spoil it for her.

The grassy mound was fringed by white wood anemones and bluebells and home to clumps of primroses, chocolate-raisin rabbit droppings, maybe even a shy scattering of violets. Their bikes lay in the bluebells. 'It's perfect,' she said. 'We have to do it here.' The scent of bluebells was intoxicating, her dimples flashed. Through the trees you could see across the river to the west. 'Look, we'll be able to watch the sun setting,' she said.

There was a crumbling bit of wall at the foot of the mound where once had been a boundary, so they loosened some large stones and set them in a circle for their fire. She crouched down, grinning at him through her fringe. 'What is it we need? Salt, herbs, a bottle of the vicar's wine . . .'

The sun was set, their offerings made, the vicar's wine drunk. Her hastily gathered garlands were askew, her naked skin was strewn with petals. A sweet peaty smell mingled with squashed bluebells, their crushed stems sticky beneath his knees.

'The rite of midsummer exactly as they did it in the book . . . oh, I still love that book.' Katie gives a little shiver at the memory and smiles up at him.

He snorts: 'I don't remember the rite of midsummer in the book ending with a bonk, also, it wasn't midsummer, it was bloody chilly.'

'Oh, bonk off, Jude. That's a horrible word for it. Why do you have to spoil things?' He's horrified to see that her eyes are welling.

'Well, you looked very pretty covered in my floral tributes,' he says. 'Oh, stop it, Katie. You're doing it again.'

She sniffs. 'Doing *what* again?' Stands, pulls her dress straight and folds the dog blanket.

'You know what I'm talking about,' he says over his shoulder. *Why* was she following him up the stairs?

'I do not.'

He stops on the landing, at the door to Mira's room, turns and spells it out: 'Trying to seduce me, that's what.'

'Oh, you know me, I just want to *bonk*.' She grins at him. 'Jude, I'm *teasing*,' and because she gets him laughing with that great big grin of hers, he almost reaches down and turns the handle, momentarily his bedroom and not Mira's, such is the slip in time. He stops and presses his hands to her shoulders.

'Then stop teasing, Katie. It's not fair.'

She holds his stare, at first bemused and then affronted, trying to shrug him off. He rests his arm on the doorjamb above her head, attempts to keep any trace of nastiness from his voice.

'Like at the hotel.'

'The hotel? Oh, I was out of my mind. And I was drunk,' she says and bats his arm out of the way.

'Yeah, well you're drunk now. Too drunk to drive home tonight, anyway.' He spins her round and marches her along the corridor to the dark side of the house: 'You can take any room you like down there.'

He flees to his own room, kicking aside piles of discarded clothing from the floor, opens the window and sticks his head out. For once the jasmine doesn't affront him. He takes a few deep breaths and lets a breeze ruffle his hair.

Before long he hears the door open behind him.

'All the lights are fused down that end. I can't see a thing, but as far as I can tell there isn't any bedding, not even pillows.'

'I suppose you'll have to sleep in here then,' he says, turning reluctantly from the window. She's beside his bed fiddling with the lamp. 'I hope it's not too smelly,' he says. 'Perhaps I'd better see if there are any clean sheets.'

'It's OK.' She follows his eyes to the wreck of his unmade bed then dims the lamp and joins him at the window.

He points to his bedside table. 'I just need my pill from there and I'll be up to the attic,' he says, but she's pulling him close, whispering in his ear.

He lies back on his pillow, an arm wedged behind his head. By the window Katie manages to wiggle herself out of her bra – 'sorry, it digs in too much' – producing it in one long strip of green lace from the armhole of her dress. 'Ta-dah! Oh, don't look so worried. I'll sleep in the rest of my clothes.' She moulds herself to his side, tugs his arm out from behind his head and wraps it around herself. He can do nothing but stare at the ceiling. Something inside him is swelling, overflowing, filling him up. He shuts his eyes. There's nothing but milky yearning and for a moment he can make himself believe it: falling towards him in the dip of the bed. Soft, sweet skin, limbs thrown across his chest and groin. His love, his child, folded around him like warm risen dough. He groans and Katie shushes him, runs a finger along his lips. He almost cries out their names.

'Will you try to forgive me?' Katie says, propping herself on one elbow.

'For what?'

'For Marylebone. The way I behaved in the hotel.'

He doesn't answer. Her hair tickles his neck.

'God's sake, I couldn't very well *not* see you to your room,' he says, pulling his arm away from her and propping it back behind his head. He had wanted to see her safe. *That was all there was to it.*

'Sshhh.' She's leaning over him stroking his chest, though he wishes she wouldn't. 'It was a terrible time for us all. There's no need to be so hard on yourself,' she says. 'Just try to go to sleep and I'll hold you in my arms.'

It had been past two in the morning when they staggered into Katie's room on the third floor of that Marylebone hotel. The barman had left them downstairs with a bottle of whisky, the list for the builders and decorators at Firdaws was taking shape. Katie got straight to it, made a couple of calls from the foyer: the plasterer was booked and she'd found someone who knew about architectural salvage who might be able to turn up a vintage Rayburn. He felt warm towards her, of course he did.

His plans for Firdaws were folded into the zip pocket of her handbag. Instead of returning her kiss goodnight, he folded her in his arms and laid his cheek across the top of her head. She made him feel a bit calmer, *that was all*.

He stood in the bar with his hand raised in silent salute to her departing rump and felt a wave of amusement and affection as she tottered out in her too-tight dress, but really that was all. He grabbed his jacket to leave and there it was: her bag still hanging by its chain from the back of her chair. He snatched it up and ran with it to the lift, but the doors were already closing. He took the stairs two by two, was out of breath when he met her coming out on the third floor. She sashayed along the corridor, her room key dangling from one finger and a wiggle to her walk while he trotted along by her side thrusting the bag at her, trying to get her to take it and stop play-acting.

She was so drunk it took her two or three goes to get the card into the slot on the wall. Various lamps came on, dimly, around the room. He placed her bag on a table, turned to find her stumbling towards the bed. She had her back to him, hips swinging. 'Unzip me, Jude.' She wriggled this way and that within her stretchy dress, her waist a stem above the bulb of her boom-di-boom bum. The covers on the bed were folded back, a single chocolate in mint-green foil on her pillow. Floorboards creaked confessionally beneath a thick covering of carpet. Through the wall he heard the clank of the departing lift. His hand rose briefly, only briefly, towards the top of the zip that snaked through the valley from her nape to her tail. No sooner had his hand moved than he snatched the thought back and stepped right away from her. 'Stop, Katie. You mustn't do this.'

He'd already decided, even before his phone began to ring. *That was crucial.*

Katie rocked back on to the bed, kicking off her shoes. 'Lighten up, Jude,' she said. 'I'm nearly thirty and can manage to put myself to bed perfectly well thank you very much.' But she had stopped existing. His phone was ringing. The screen showed it was Julia.

'Julia, what's up?'

'Where the fucking hell are you?' And her voice started to shake: 'Mira, Mira,' and it was hard to make out what she was trying to tell him between sobs. He heard the words 'Intensive Care'. Katie was oblivious, back on her feet, swaying to music only she could hear, spraying herself with a cloud of perfume that made him cough.

He listens to the screeching of the little owls and the flush of the lavatory and Michael stumbling back to bed. Katie's eyelids flicker, her bottom lip has fallen sideways. He manages to extricate his arm, inch by slow inch, and she moans softly as he levers her to Julia's side of the bed. The way her dress has twisted around he can see the full curve of one breast hanging free of the green fabric, the faint silvery trails of stretch marks. He pulls the quilt to her shoulders, rolls over and quietly slides open his drawer and removes his pills, is thankful for a glass of stale water.

The attic-room door yawns on its hinges, a bare bulb makes a pale pool of the bed. The boards are creaky and dangerous with splinters. There's never been much up here, never was, just the bed and a wooden table on which he sets down his tumbler, a cane-seated chair and beneath the eaves a pile of suitcases and travel bags, boxes of old toot. He sits at the table fiddling with a bowl of random knick-knacks, takes out a forgotten pipe, a brass padlock, a jade egg. The pipe was his father's, those are his toothmarks on the stem. He sniffs at the bowl, can still detect the charcoal of its burnt edge, the tobacco so faint as to be little more than memory. He holds the egg towards the window. It is beautifully smooth, pale green with an orange glow at its centre, like an embryo in stone. 'You can't possibly give your mother that!' Julia had said. They were in a funny little shop in Hay-on-Wye. He thought it the sort of egg from which a phoenix might hatch under the right conditions, if placed in a fire of cedar pencil shavings and gum arabic, for example. 'But it's beautiful. Look how the light makes it flame. And feel, it's lovely and smooth in the hand.'

He remembers her laughter: 'Don't you know what it is?' Him shaking his head.

'It's a concubine's egg. You know? For strengthening their fannies.'

The pillow feels gritty and he remembers how cluster flies plague this attic. He tries not to dwell on the crazed slow buzz of their hibernation and the crispy rasp of their bodies. The desiccated commas of stray legs separate him from sleep. He gets up, shakes out the pillow, brushes down the sheets, slots himself back in.

Before too long he feels himself drifting, but still ugly creatures cling to the surface, battling the inevitable, ushering him along the dark, ribbed tunnel, on and on until he emerges in a blaze of fluorescence, shapes burnt into his retina, pulsing lights, the pale-green whirligig of a ventilator tube, the white gloss of bedrails, and on and on, through the shining corridors of the hospital, heart braced, bursting the seal of the doors marked PICU with a hiss.

Mira was laid high on a bed, metal rails raised all around, unconscious and naked with heart-monitor dots on her chest, so much tape holding everything in place that he couldn't see her face. The nurse: 'Kiss your little girl, she'll know you're here, even though she's asleep.'

Julia wept into his jacket. 'Where the hell have you been? I've been trying to get hold of you for hours. Feel her tummy. It's like a drum.' Tubes were taped to Mira's nose and mouth, a line to her port, a bag of fluid protruded from the bed that was yellow like her skin. When he put his hand to her head strands of her fine soft hair came away in his palm. Somewhere a phone was ringing, drowning out the thin wail of a baby. There were the soft sounds of shushing and whispering and nurses' shoes. The ward had been dimmed because it was the middle of the night and parents sat like penitents at the head of beds in haloes of light from the monitors. Each time a bin lid rattled shut they jumped out of their skins.

'They're keeping her unconscious. Her liver's been poisoned,' Julia said, and they clung to each other as a doctor arrived; not Esther Fry, but a Mr Goolden with bloodshot blue eyes that Julian searched for signs of reassurance.

In the doctors' room Mr Goolden explained the diagnosis as they craned towards him from their seats. 'It's a rare reaction. Combined Vincristine and Actinomycin D is standard,' he said, pulling three tissues from the box and handing them to Julia. 'Your daughter's unlucky.'

Julian found himself pivoting to his feet. He thought of Esther Fry, her curls bobbing: 'This will be the worst day . . .' A surge of despair made him grab Mr Goolden by the shoulders. 'Luck?' He wasn't certain he hadn't roared the word. He was amazed to see his own knuckles shining beneath his skin, white as the doctor's coat.

'There's plenty we can do,' Goolden said, gently easing him back into his chair. 'She has every chance of pulling through.'

After the doctor left for his rounds, they found themselves once again at the hospital chapel, though Julian would soon have to go out for a smoke. Julia chose the window closest to the chapel door. She wedged Mira's rabbit amongst the other toys on the ledge. From the stained glass above it, saintly Eunice offered her book, her golden slipper resting on an emerald footstool. The rabbit's ears were worn from where they'd been sucked and one flopped over its eye, its head lolled to the bodice of Mira's baby dress, her name appliquéd in red felt. Folds of white silk fell from the sill. Julia knelt and prayed. Julian thought the toys looked about as blessed with luck as tatty prizes at a fairground shooting range.

Seventeen

The curtainless attic is no match for the dawn, which is not at all sweet, with foul morning breath and raucous chorus. Julian sits with his feet to the bare boards, his head in his hands. The sun pokes fiery fingers at the dimpled glass, the flies already buzzing. There's a drop of last night's water in the tumbler. He swallows it and stretches in the only part of the room that will allow it and picks up the brass padlock from the floor. It's heart-shaped, a little green around the lock. Bits of polish have caught in the engraving and he runs his thumbnail into the curlicues of a pair of entwined Js.

He pockets it, creeps down the attic stairs cursing each groaning board. He hears Michael's steady snores as he passes the guest room, the sound of water in the pipes is magnified as he eyes the door to his own room, willing Katie not to wake.

He would like to gag the dog when it shoots through the back door and starts barking at a crow. He checks his pocket for tobacco and takes his coffee to the porch. He rubs the padlock to a shine as if a genie might appear, turns the key. The hinge is smoothly oiled. It was the sweetest thing. Julia and him on the Pont des Arts as they walked arm in arm to the Louvre. They were lovers. It was his birthday, his twenty-fifth. The sun was shining. A Bateau Mouche slid along the river, brightly dressed passengers waving like flowers.

In the centre of the bridge they stopped for him to open his present. She bit the corner of her lip as tissue paper fluttered to the boards.

'Goodness!' He was astonished to see it again, that she'd even noticed he liked it or remembered. He was turning the heart-shaped padlock over in his hands, twisting the filigree brass key, grinning and springing the catch. 'How did you know?'

'I came by it years ago. When we first met,' she said. 'But there was never a right moment to give it to you.' She hefted her canvas bag on to her shoulder. 'Also, I liked hoarding it, knowing that one day you would have it.' She smiled back at him. 'Like a lovely secret,' she said. A saxophonist busked the opening bars of Pachelbel's Canon. A breeze caught a few ribbons tied to the bridge, and Julia adjusted a rag she had wound around her hair. Even in Paris she looked ready to dig a garden in her floppy brown top and rolled-up chinos. He felt a childish stab of dis-appointment that she hadn't dressed up for his birthday. He pulled the rag from her head, mussed up her hair. 'My birthday,' he said when she objected. And that's how it started.

They weren't so used to being apart in those pre-Firdaws days. His sap was high after the nights spent alone in his swanky Paris hotel that smelt of cinnamon, its draped-black bed and suede-ef-fect walls.

In the rush of leaving London he'd forgotten all sorts of things: a plumber who was due to mend the boiler and that he'd prom-ised Karl dinner.

He had been about to shout to Julia to let her know about Karl but the phone immediately rang again. It was the French animator Claude De'Ath, the great man himself, and of course Julian was prepared to drop everything to work with him in Paris. In the panic of packing and Julia coming in from the greenhouse and growing a little tearful that he was leaving, he forgot to cancel Karl.

He only remembered their date the next morning while walking with Claude De'Ath through the Tuileries, his schoolboy French stretched to its limits by the director's vision for his film. They stopped to watch the toy boats at the fountain and Julian excused himself. Karl's number clicked straight through to the answering service and he remembered that he had been only passing through London on his way to a conference in Brighton. He was about to leave a message when a dark-brown rat crossed his path within kicking distance. It was fat, with the confidence of a cat. He shook his head at it and it wandered into the bushes.

He told Julia about the rat as they walked along the bridge, making her shudder. 'Its tail was like a fat worm dragging along behind it.' He decided ('My birthday') that they should kiss again to the strains of a nylon-strung guitar, though she, desperate for the *Mona Lisa*, said she'd heard better on the underground.

He started listing all the things that a 'my birthday' should entail. 'Café crème in St Germain, freshly baked madeleines, French news-stands and billboards with underclad French girls, baguette and a cold slab of unsalted butter, oysters on a bed of ice, preferably one with a pearl at its heart, the hotel room and my tongue . . .' She interrupted him, laughing and shushing him and pulling him to the side of the bridge.

'Put your padlock here.' She poked him and pointed to the wire meshing. 'Let's do it.' She gave his arm a shake. 'Go on, quick. Lock it here now and throw the key to the Seine.'

'What? Why?' he said, keeping his fingers closed around the lock.

'Oh, I don't know. I feel superstitious, that's all,' she said.

'OK, but let me own it a bit longer.' He was already sad to think of it gone. 'But in return, and as it's my birthday, I get everything my own way.' He lit up at the thought of a dare, said:

'We'll have half an hour with your Giaconda but then it's pastis and shopping.'

The Mona Lisa smiled, the pastis made them heady, the boutique was expensive.

'This one, really, must I?' She emerged from the changing room in the clothes he'd chosen. 'I'm not sure I can even walk in this skirt, it's like being hobbled.' The skirt was incongruous with her loafers, the blouse as soft as emulsion. It was almost impossible to keep sitting on the hard chair beside the mirror as the shop assistant came back with the very high heels in her size.

'Julian . . .' she made an imploring face.

'My birthday,' he said, laughing. 'You agreed.'

She was unsteady on the shoes at first, wobbling from foot to foot as she walked towards the mirror, as unlike herself as he'd ever seen her, and somehow more naked. He made her squeak by pinching her through the silky blouse: 'That top is a little bit see-through, by the way . . .' She batted him away as he went on: '. . . and tonight no bra.' The shop assistant pretended not to hear or speak English.

Lunch was in the Rue Bucci in a restaurant with Belle Époque ceramic frescoes, goddesses and water lilies, flowing robes, baguette that was almost nutty it was so good. There were two dozen oysters raised on their silver sacrificial bed and Julia got the giggles doing quivering stung-oyster squeals as he dropped Tabasco on to their flesh.

The insides of her wrists were stained with lipstick, a dozen fading gashes. Her chin was cupped in her hands and lately he'd been noticing little creases around her eyes when she frowned. He raised his glass to her and she wrinkled her nose – the scattering of freckles across its bridge would give her the look of a girl at any age. He wished she'd wear her hair loose more often. He pulled the padlock from his pocket, put it on the table between them. 'So. How did you know I loved it?'

'Oh, I've been meaning to give it to you for ages. Since my last day at the shop when Mr Gelding asked me if there was anything I wanted . . .'

'Woah, that was quite a risk for Mr Gelding.'

'To be honest, I'd been hoping he might give me some sort of bonus, I'd worked there so long. And I didn't have the wit to ask for something that we could sell.' She looked quite depressed at the memory.

'With what we were trying to live on that would've been fair enough . . .' he said.

'I remembered catching you once, reflected in the glass at the front of the shop. I was with a customer and I saw you pick it up from the tray, look around to check if I was watching you and then you lifted it towards your pocket. It really made me catch my breath and just as your fingers were about to disappear, you put it back.'

'Really?' He choked on a mouthful of wine. 'I can't remember that at all.'

'If you'd stolen it, we had no future together, that's what I told myself at the time. So that's what I asked for and Mr Gelding was happy enough. I wanted to give it to you straight away, I even had it engraved in the High Street. But then . . . Oh God, Julian, it was awful. Back at Mrs Briggs's the day you chucked your course. I'd been in your room all day, feeding the gas meter with coins, with all the coins we had. I had the padlock in my bag, ready to give you. I thought it would cheer you up. I waited for you, surrounded by your books and notes, your desk thick with them, your atrocious scrawl, reams of what would now, because of me, not be completed. You came bounding back into the room. You looked like a boy. You even had a bit of acne.'

'I did not! Julia, I can't bear this.'

'You were so thin and your elbow stuck right through a hole in your jumper. And there I was, about to be an old bag of thirty, pregnant, brainless and broke. I felt like I'd already trapped you. The last thing I could give you was a lock.'

He leant across and kissed the tip of her nose. It made his heart ache to think of her so anxious and frightened. He pictures his room at Mrs Briggs's, its terrible stained mattress, its worn sticky carpet, the taste of blood on Julia's lower lip, she'd been chewing it so much. The hotel room that was waiting for them had chocolate-dipped strawberries in a crystal dish, dark folds around the bed. He picked up the padlock. If she completed his dare, he had promised her to go back and lock it to the bridge in the morning. The shopping bags were on the banquette beside her. Every time he glanced across he smiled to himself, though it took the rest of the bottle to believe she would go through with it.

But she did it, just for him. He would never forget the man in the brown corduroy suit nor the sight of her flailing about on that bed with its rumpled dark coverings, her heels drumming his shoulders and her face contorting in an uncontrolled scream as she came back at him, straight into his face: 'I did. I did. I did.'

In the morning she was too hungover for the Pont des Arts.

'It's OK,' he lied, concealing the padlock in his sponge bag. 'I have to cross the river to meet De'Ath. I'll do it en route.' On his return they headed out to a café and, hiding from the weak sunshine behind dark glasses, passed a shop selling baby things. Her arm was in the crook of his elbow, he felt the subtlest tug as she slowed her stride and on impulse he turned and pulled her inside. They'd never done such a thing before. The assistant wrapped the white silk christening dress in layers of tissue paper as though it might break.

Alone in the porch he drains the last of his coffee, rolls his second cigarette of the morning. He turns the key in the padlock one last time and on his way to the kitchen for a refill hurls it into the box of Julia's junk. Let her know he broke his promise.

What does he care now? Things keep turning up around the house: bits of paper with her writing on, her swimsuit, stretched and faded as an old skin, a jar of Clarins cream he'd made the mistake of unscrewing and sniffing before chucking in. The box is almost full. He must remember to buy some packing tape.

A hand on his shoulder makes him jump. Katie has scrubbed away her panda eyes. If she's hungover she's managing to disguise it beneath pink cheeks, her hair brushed back into a ponytail, the mintiness of her breath suggesting she's helped herself to his toothbrush. She lifts his hand and presses it to her forehead. 'I need paracetamol,' she says, and flops down beside him. She is drenched in hyacinths.

She dangles her pumps from the end of her toes. 'I don't remember much about last night. I hope you didn't take advantage of me.'

'Stop it,' he says, and she digs him in the ribs with her elbow.

'I hope I'm not still drunk,' she says, yawning. 'I'll need to get my act together before I face the inquisition back at the Mill. I'll have to tell the boys my car wouldn't start.'

'Perhaps if you left now there's a chance they might still be asleep?' he replies and she ignores him, says she's gasping for coffee.

'I woke up thinking about our conversation last night and now I can't get it out of my head.'

He feels himself prickle. 'Do we have to go there again?'

'What? Oh, I see. No, not the hotel. I meant, about Mira at the hospital. I keep thinking if I had to stare day after day at Billy or Arthur unconscious . . .'

He holds out an arm and she snuggles in, her head on his chest. 'Just awful.'

'The worst of it is that you've got so long to sit there and regret every crappy thing you've done. We'd been dreading the chemo and the op, but as you saw when you visited, we'd sort of got into the routine of her being kept in. I mean, it was better that than have a sudden emergency with her blood pressure. You know there wasn't a single night that one of us didn't stay? And then, after what happened with her liver, there was no hope of getting her out until after the operation and only then if she got the all-clear.'

He sees Mira propped against her Disney pillows, the day she got off the ventilator, coming back to the world crying, soundlessly at first, her lips making the shapes but her vocal cords silenced by the path of the tube. Angry, silent tears. Leaning over her, him and Julia, trying to kiss them away and soothe, her cries becoming thin rasps, the ventilator gone. As they wheeled her bed back to Lion Ward he thought she'd never been so beautiful as now she'd lost her hair. Her wide lovely eyes and lashes, the smooth dome of her head vulnerable as an egg.

'Oh, God. Katie, stop me now. Let's talk about something else. Anything.'

They hear Jenna call from the kitchen. 'Is anyone else up and about on this beautiful day?' He stands and offers Katie a hand.

She follows him inside, says: 'OK. I'll tell you. I think I'm about to accept the permanent job at Woodford Primary.'

'Good God, you're staying on at your mum's? What does Adrian think about that?'

She made a gesture of brushing so much dust from her hands. 'Well, there's always the train. I expect he'll have them for half the holidays, but we'll see . . .' She looks spiteful, enough that Julian shivers. '. . . He should've thought about that before he got his cock out.'

Jenna is already chopping things in the kitchen. Michael is squeezing oranges. He stops what he's doing and glances at Katie, raises an eyebrow at Julian, who replies with an irritable shake of his head. Jenna asks if anyone's remembered to feed the dog.

Katie is resting her cheek to his back with her hands around his waist as he heats the milk. 'Just one coffee and I'll be off,' she says.

He hears a car pulling up, the slam of a door. Michael leaps to attention, Zeph barking. Julian disentangles himself from Katie as his mother thrusts bowls at them. Her special breakfast: baked slices of last night's pudding topped with glistening fruits and nuts. Michael returns from the front hall, his face a little rueful, and behind him William.

William fills the doorway in his this-is-what-wc-wear-to-the-country coat, all flappy pockets and plaid lining, slinging down his luggage and throwing wide his arms. 'Aw, mate,' enclosing Julian in a voluminous waxed-cotton hug.

'William, *what* are you doing here?'

William doesn't get a chance to explain as Katie advances with the coffee pot. 'This is Katie,' Julian says, as she hands him a cup. William shoots him a look and for the second time that morning he has to shake his head in denial. William releases him with another slap on the back. 'Mate, it's good to see you,' he says and turns to give Katie the onceover, visibly approves, and then to everyone: 'Christ, have you lot not heard the news?'

Michael shakes his head. 'What news?' Jenna stops chopping fruit.

William pulls out a chair and slumps at the table: 'Terrible news,' he says, looking slowly from face to face. 'It's been confirmed. She's dead.'

Eighteen

Jenna thrusting a bowl at him: Eat, eat, eat. The TV news blaring. The Prime Minister is standing outside a church wringing his hands. 'Questions will need to be answered,' he says. Katie, her elbows to the back of the sofa, stares at the TV in wide-eyed shock, William, though they've only just met, appears to have his arm around her waist. There's footage of mangled metal in the tunnel. 'Oh, just so sad,' Jenna says, dabbing the corner of her eye with her sleeve.

Julian has to shout to make himself heard: 'What are you all doing here?' and Michael steers him away to his study, pulling the door shut behind them.

'Julian, don't take it out on everyone else. It was me. I said William should come . . .'

'But, why?'

Julian knocks over the waste-paper basket, scattering his purge of balled-up notes, and leans on his desk, the glass surface clear now of that clutter. He keeps his back to Michael, attempting to reel in his temper, failing, and thumping his desk so hard the pens jump in their pot. 'Can't you see? I want to be alone!'

Michael lays a hand on his shoulder: 'Calm down,' tries to turn him around, but Julian shrugs him off.

'If you're alone you'll need to be getting on with something.

William is here to talk to you about the book. And now seems like a good time, while I'm still here,' Michael says. 'As you know, I'm very keen you should do it – it's the book you've always wanted to write and right now you need something to pull you out of yourself.'

Michael hitches himself on to the corner of Julian's desk, legs swinging: 'Now's your chance. Take it,' he says.

He silences Julian's objections with a raised hand: 'I know life hasn't turned out the way you thought it would, but you're still young.' He pauses to wave at the sea of screwed-up paper. 'It's not the end of your story, nor is it your only story. You've been given many gifts, a great imagination, the ability to write.'

'Please stop.'

Michael takes a momentous breath: 'I couldn't be prouder of you if I was your father.' There. He's never said such a thing before. Julian looks up and hopes it's the light glancing off his half-moons and not his eyes glistening. He stares beyond him to the window. Michael takes another big breath and continues: 'You've had happiness and now you have sadness. But, believe me, there will be happiness again.' Julian shakes his head. Michael lays his hand on the side of his face and leaves it there, which feels strange because they never do that. 'There will be different versions of happiness.' Again Julian shakes his head, but Michael's hand is still on his cheek and he's still talking: 'I know your loss feels unbearable right now, I know all around you seems like hell, but perhaps by writing you'll find some kind of a paradise within,' and he coughs self-consciously. 'Sorry about that Milton, my bad paraphrasing, but you get the drift. Let me take on Firdaws for a couple of years while you give it a go. What do you think?'

The problem is Julian isn't thinking at all. While Michael is talking a wasp busies itself against the window, its incessant buzzing making these wise words come and go. Julian's limbs grow heavy and his throat starts to close. The wasp hurls itself at the glass. Julian is struggling to swallow. From the sitting room he hears the others calling, sirens on the TV. Michael pats him on the cheek and he feels the warmth of his kindness burn through his skin: 'So. What do you think? Call it a convalescence if you like. Your mother and I wanted to talk to you about it last night but we couldn't because you had . . .' and he rolls his eyes towards the other room. 'Um, company.'

Julian leaps away from him, as though he's been stung: 'Oh, stop it! I didn't invite Katie. You did. Or Mum did. And nothing happened. I don't know what you think you're all doing here, but I wish to God you'd leave me alone.'

Michael stubbornly shuffles himself deeper on to the desk. 'Sit down a moment, Julian,' and then less sternly: 'Please. Let's take a look at all your possible futures . . .' He spreads his hands, palms up, open like a book.

'Do we have to?'

'Well, I could stand back while you do nothing but drink yourself stupid, not even bothering to wash properly, while your mother brings you little meals on trays and cries herself to sleep at night. Is that what you want? To let sadness rule your life? If it is I will still take on the Firdaws debt for you, I care enough to find a way to do that for you, but I'm not sure this is a good picture of your future. Tell me, what do you think?'

The wasp at the window ricochets from the glass, heading straight for Julian. Buzzing crazes his ears. He runs for the door. Faces loom, leaning over him, people patting him, touching him. Their demands coming at him like flashbulbs exploding. He battles his way out of the house, gasping for air. He outruns Michael and looks down to find Zeph bounding along at his side. His headache is blinding, every leaf and blade of grass the shatterings of a mirror, dust glitters with the fall of his feet on the gritty earth. Light stripes the rails of Horseman's fence, the sun beating hard enough to make the creosote melt. Hot tar and hay dust fills his nostrils.

He passes the younger Miss Hamlyn by Horseman's barn, her black Labrador runs bottom-sniffing rings around Zeph. 'Julian!' she calls to him with her thin quaver, waving at him with her stick. Her grey hair is in curlers, squashed beneath a pale-blue net.

'Come and see this,' she says, leaving him little option, though his heart is still pounding. 'Look under here, how many ripe figs there are.' She pokes her stick among the branches, unzipping the sound of angry buzzing. 'Oh, but so many wasps,' she says, batting her hands. The smell of the hot fruit has never pleased him, something too much like tom-cat pee. Where she parts the branch he can see a pair of figs hanging like purple testicles and he's already starting to scoot off, but she's rushing with him, saying what a shame it is that no one gets to eat those delicious-looking figs, her little legs working hard, two strides to his one. She stops him on the path with a hand on his elbow, says: 'Let me catch my breath.' She stands for a moment readjusting the net around her curlers, blinks a couple of times. A cloud passes across her face, the tremor of a sudden realisation, she even grows a little pale: 'I had to come out here to get away from the radio. My sister is glued to it.' Her hand flutters at her chest and she reaches to steady herself against him.

Julian is momentarily puzzled. What could Miss Hamlyn the Elder possibly be listening to that would drive her younger sister from the shop? *The Archers Omnibus*? Jazz? Hip-hop?

'Oh, my goodness,' she says. 'You mean you haven't heard? Oh, that poor woman.' And to Julian's horror a tear leaves a trail on her chalky cheek.

He's past her now and he calls over his shoulder to where she stands motionless with her stick: 'I've got to get out of here. If I get stung I go into shock.'

He's running again and the dog couldn't be happier, the ostrich feather of its tail streaming. The track is rutted from a tractor, his feet fall between hard ridges. At the stone bridge he passes a woman with a child throwing bread to the swans. What does the death of some princess have to do with him? With anything?

He searches his mind for clues as he runs: he must have missed something. Snatched meals in the hospital canteen, Julia never saying very much. It seemed, by then, that she did most of her talking to Oscar's mum, Becky, who had torn at her fingernails so viciously in PICU the nail beds had to be covered by plasters. Julia scowling when he showed her Katie's photographs of the reclaimed Rayburn for Firdaws, and the one of Mira's new bedroom, her dinosaur lamp beside her bed and silver stars at the window. All the days she shot out to work almost as soon as he arrived. Julia running out of the playroom to be sick.

The nurses had to keep telling them to eat. 'Even if it's only chocolate or cake,' they said. It was difficult to swallow. 'Of course it is,' they said. 'We know how you feel, there's a lump in your throat that won't go away.' They ushered them to go out, but Julia never wanted to. 'Look, she's sleeping now,' they said. 'We'll be here looking after her.' But she just shook her head.

He remembers Mira with Oscar, the pair of them on their knees over the train set – he was Thomas and she was Percy, her hair coming back in dandelion tufts. The way the sparse down met the nape of her neck gave her the appearance of a newborn and a pain straight to his heart. Through the port to Mira's heart six more weeks of Vincristine before she could have the operation.

She was on and off the nasal feed, she had to get the calories from somewhere. Heino was visiting the first time the nurse allowed Julia to set it up unaided. He sat beside the bed smoothing Mira's forehead in a grandfatherly fashion and Mira took his cane because she liked to look at the carving of the snake. Julia leant across and attached a plastic syringe to the tube that came up from her stomach and was taped from her nose across her cheek. With a smile to reassure her, Julia withdrew the plunger, drawing out a minuscule amount of yellow liquid – this part never stopped making his own stomach heave, the taste of his own juices rising in his throat. Julia was less squeamish. She tested the little pool of yellow liquid with pH paper, holding it to the light to watch it bloom. It showed acid and they all sighed with relief. The tube was where it should be – there were nightmare accounts from other hospitals of patients killed by feeding tubes mistakenly pushed into the airways and not the stomach. Julia ran the pump to flush the system and attached the line to the bottle of creamy liquid food. 'Very good,' Heino said, and nodded at her. 'I think this hospital should hire you immediately.' As Mira closed her eyes Heino leant across the bed and enclosed her in his arms, his old brown cheek beside her young pale one on the pillow. Days felt like weeks. The outside world stopped.

Polling Day had passed them by. The whole election had. Tony Blair was now in power. Julian joined Julia and Becky in the Parents' Room, huddled together, so close their heads touched. There was only space on the stiff little sofa for two. They looked up when he entered and carried on with their conversation, Julia's shoulder set against him. Becky was trying to say something but had to keep blowing her nose in a tissue. His back creaked as he lowered himself into the chair beside the TV, twisting his head around to distract himself from their misery.

From the look of it the whole nation was rejoicing. The Blair children stood, all three awkwardly shod in trainers, on the doorstep of number 10. The girl's hands were clenched together, a white baseball cap doing little to hide her anxiety, poor thing. The boys, arms hanging helplessly by their sides, had unfortunate haircuts that only drew attention to the fact they'd inherited their father's ears. Cherie, their mother, sleekly groomed in tailored burnt orange, and Tony Blair waving, his white cuff and proper cufflink, his face turned to the sky in benediction. The children looked like they were at a separate occasion, earthbound and clumsy, unblessed, a different species.

'We were just talking about that poor woman down in PICU,' Becky said and Julian struggled to follow their conversation.

Tears wobbled at the rims of Julia's eyes: 'Those terrible cries, I never want to hear anyone in that much pain again,' she said. He knelt beside the sofa so she could weep on his shoulder and felt like an insensitive pig when he noticed that Becky was crying too but had no one to comfort her. Now as then he can't bring to mind the woman whose child died, has no memory of the noises she made as she threw herself to the floor. He has blanked her out. Every nerve cell was thrumming to the tune of one thing: Mira.

The pumps and IV tubes doled out the hours in droplets. He watched the rise and fall of her chest: if his concentration failed, her heart might stop. His eyes twitched from monitor to monitor, his ear tuned to every breath and click. Her feed might choke her. Her ventilator fail. Maybe she would open her eyes, or talk in her sleep, or grip his fingers. There's only a hole where the flailing woman should be.

Mira was well enough to be bad-tempered when the day of her operation arrived. She'd been crying and whining non-stop since five in the morning; she wanted her breakfast and nothing they said would convince her they weren't starving her by choice. His palms were so wet he had to keep wiping them on a cloth while the surgeon and the nurses filed out to meet them. Mira clung to Julia, her arms monkey-locked around her neck. A visiting clown flatfooted by, a woman one with a fluorescent green wig.

Mira refused to honk her red nose and turned away from the stickers she gave her. The anaesthetist shook Julian's damp hand and gave the usual reassuring patter, but Julian could make little sense, the clown had unnerved him. He worried it would give Mira disturbing dreams.

The anaesthetist told them he preferred not to use a mask, showed him the black hose secreted in his palm. He said that he would simply place his hand over her mouth while she sat on Julian's lap.

Julian felt horrible, like a double agent, as he held on and tried to restrain her thrashing at the man's hand, fighting for her life. It took two nurses to keep her still and both had earned scratches.

'It's good that she's a fighter,' one said, rubbing her hand, as Mira lay betrayed and lifeless in his arms, still wearing her own dress, the anaesthetist stopping to stroke the top of her head, the nurse taking her from him to lay his sleeping beauty on the trolley.

Behind the closed steel doors of the operating theatre the surgeon's knife, a morning slot. Time came and went. Blurred. Morning slot. Mourning slot. Julia kneeling in the chapel, refusing to come with him. He walked alone out of the hospital, anything to make the hours pass. A woman was feeding pigeons in the square: the whirr of their wings the soundtrack to a bad omen. Sirens blared and buses made the ground judder.

He wandered into the nearest convenience store to try and distract himself from what they were doing to Mira in the operating theatre. Time was elastic. Esther Fry, Nurse Emma, the one with kind eyes in PICU, Mr Goolden, Martin the anaesthetist. He heard them all say the dreaded words as he scanned the aisles, looking for a magic potion, a panacea, not hot dogs in tins. He picked up and put down several packets, tubs from the cold section. What was it all for? None of it seemed edible. The shelves were stacked high above his head. He reached for a bottle of Mira's favourite pear juice and a bright-blue glass bottle fell and smashed on the floor at his feet. He looked down at his shoes, the pale-tan brogues that he liked more than any others, and inwardly sobbed when he saw the dark splashes across the leather. Another bad sign. The hospital voices continued floating around him, offering their deepest sympathy.

In front of him a check-out boy in a plaid shirt stood gaping like a goldfish. Another, no more quick-witted, joined his side. Towards them a woman in a wheelchair headed determinedly for the puddle of blue glass. Still the gawpers did nothing, except to ask: 'How did it happen?' He grabbed the handles of the wheelchair, steering its occupant swiftly away from the broken glass, along the aisle and down the ramp at the door. It could've been Mira in her pushchair. But then the woman was croaking at him: 'Let me go, you idiot. I haven't paid for my shopping.'

He takes the footpath out to the Mill. He can't remember the last time he ran anywhere. He stops at a kissing gate, leans against it panting. Zeph whines at him to come through, a corsage of goosegrass, burrs and buttercups stuck to his ruff.

He has to trespass through Lordy's fields to go unobserved past Katie's house. She'll be home by now, her boys will be leaping at her, pinching her flesh. He sneaks like a fugitive with his head bent beneath the line of Lordy's brutally trimmed hedges and manages to tear his T-shirt on barbed wire climbing out on to the road. The sun flashes on to the tarmac, turning it tacky beneath his shoes. He keeps Zeph to heel though there's no traffic about today, not even tractors. He passes three people walking from church. They all want to stop and talk about the dead princess and he wonders if he should start affecting some sort of distress.

Up ahead on the verge Raph's van hoves into view, the familiar purple and brown slats. He's suddenly very thirsty. His tongue is furry. There's no sign of Raph, not even the charcoal bed of his fire. He tries the door of the van, but it's locked. He hears a shout and turns to see a plump woman in jeans striding towards him along the verge, waving an arm. 'What do you want?' She scowls at him from pink cheeks, her hair is tied back in a rough ponytail of grey-blonde that could do with a wash. She has the newspapers clutched to her chest, the dead princess splashed across the front. He sees teeth, jewels, a blue dress with a modicum of royal cleavage. Now there's movement behind him. The door of the van bursts opens and Raph lollops down the steps and clumps him on the back.

There it is: that well-worn smile. There, an arm around his shoulders, a hug: 'Well, well, Julian, here you are.'

Raph is stouter than Julian remembers, a definite belly showing through his thin T-shirt, his curls grizzled and flattened beneath an incongruous green cap with a leaping fish and *Tunbridge Wells Anglers* embroidered in yellow.

The woman stands beside him. 'This is my wife,' Raph says as she thrusts the newspapers at him. 'This is Nell.'

He grasps Julian's hand between both of his, eyes glittering from the sunburst of his smile. 'It's good to see you . . .' And to Nell: 'This is the boy I told you about. Julian. The . . . man, how old are you now?'

'I'll be thirty next year. And you? Still travelling, I see . . .'

'I left the Convoy, we just come in August for our holidays . . .' Raph reaches an arm to pull Nell into their conversation: 'Don't we, love.' She smiles up at him, her fat pink cheeks now cherubic.

Raph whistles through his teeth. 'But you. Nearly thirty, you say, that makes me feel ancient. Just before you disappeared you were crazy about a woman. A *married* older woman, if I remember right . . .'

'Julia.'

Nell interrupts: 'It's in all the papers. I feel quite shaken . . .'

It's strange. Raph doesn't light a fire, but Nell brings out a camping stove and boils a kettle with a whistling spout. She stirs honey into herbal tea for Raph who, for some reason, she keeps calling Kevin. Raph folds out three floral deckchairs and Nell passes him a tin of Ambrosia rice pudding and a can opener. She catches the look on Julian's face. 'Bland's the best we can do for Kev's ulcer.'

'I reckon they bumped her off, don't you?' says Raph, blowing on his tea. Nell climbs into the van for the radio news and he turns to Julian, wincing as he swallows a glug of too-hot camomile. 'So then, this Julia. Did you marry her?'

Nell pokes her head out at them: 'Ugh, how bloody gothic can this get? The bodyguard is alive but they're saying he's lost his tongue.'

Julian struggles for words: 'No. But we . . .' and his body starts to shake and there's nothing Raph or Nell with her soft enfolding arms can do to make him stop. 'We had a child. A girl. Mira.'

A couple of pages from Nell's papers have scattered along the verge. The dead princess turns her face to the grass. Nell soaks a towel in lavender. She lays it on his face. Breathe.

Nineteen

In the end is the beginning. Julian is at the river. A metallic strip of brightness runs the course, hemmed by ragged shadows. Michael's words come back to him, the warmth of his hand on his cheek. 'Now's your chance. Take it.'

He stands on the bank looking down. The broad glassy sheen covers hidden currents. Jenna's snake swims into his mind, her hand making the shape of its head rising up from the water, her long swaying wrist pointing it at him until he saw its eyes scintillating and heard its hiss.

There's not a cloud in the sky, the river shimmers with pearl and the concentric ripples of tiny insects, the sun beats the crown of his head. He finds his breath. The words are forming, writing themselves. He yanks his T-shirt straight over his head and rids himself of his trainers and jeans. He strides to the edge, the grass springy beneath his feet, and a sudden surge of energy sends him knifing into the water.

He is powerful. His arms break open the river like wings through air. In the end is where he'll find the beginning. It's effortless. The current is practically carrying him along. The darkness of the tunnel of thorns doesn't bother him. Weeds slip by; he feels their caresses on his stomach, their fingers slipping from his legs.

Snakes and Ladders. Hours and hours of it to help Mira pass the time. Her test results were taking for ever, but everything looked good. The histology report. No anaplasia. With each shake of the dice Mira was hitting nothing but ladders, her stitches healing well. Esther Fry stopped on her rounds to study Mira's notes, corkscrew curls bobbing as she scanned the pages. 'It looks like someone will be going home soon. Just a few more days,' she said, and his spirits rose as she grinned at him and he noticed for the first time that she was really quite pretty.

He set off to Firdaws. At last it was time to prepare for Mira's homecoming. He broke every speed limit to hit Woodford before the shops shut, making a list as he drove. Food, loo paper, baby shampoo, the stuff for the bath that stopped her skin itching. He wanted flowers for the table. Katie had called to say that he should get lightbulbs because the electrician had blown every fuse in the place rewiring Mira's room.

The mist was rising from the river, a cold wind bit at him from around the house as he dragged the shopping from the car. He was stooped over from the drive with a throbbing pain in his neck, dog tired and aching all over.

It felt cold in the house and the fire someone – probably Katie – had laid in the inglenook sent only a plume of sour smoke up the chimney. He couldn't face going out for dry wood. In the kitchen it took a mighty effort to heft open the lid of the Rayburn. Sweat started to bubble his forehead though he was shiveringly cold. It took everything he had to bend his creaking joints to open the bottom door and riddle the ashes.

He thought maybe he was dying. He crawled up the stairs and fell into bed in his clothes and that was the last he remembered. He woke with his throat too sore to shout and Katie watching him, her legs curled beneath her in the bedroom chair.

'There you are,' she said as he tried to piece together fevered fragments: the shame of Katie helping him out of his clothes

('Don't worry, Jude, nothing I haven't seen before.'). Katie easing him up the pillow to spoon some sickly syrup into his mouth, a few sips of warm water with honey and lemon, smoothing his brow with a cool flannel that dripped down his neck and made him shiver and ache.

'Do you think you could manage some soup?' Behind her through a gap in the curtains an evening sky was melting into dusk. This didn't make sense.

He hauled himself upright. 'How long have I been lying here? What time is it?'

'You had a hell of a temperature when I found you. I wasn't expecting anyone to be here.' She stood from the chair, smoothing her dress. 'I only came to bring lightbulbs because I knew you'd forget. I nearly jumped out of my skin when I heard you groan.'

He was rubbing sleep from his eyes. Her dress was blue with white piping around the collar, her hair scraped back from her face. He'd been confused, woken several times with his heart banging, thinking he was in Lion Ward and she was a nurse.

She sat on the side of his bed, her green eyes were shining. 'I unplugged the phone up here so you wouldn't be disturbed.'

'But how long have I been here?'

'You've slept through two days. Julia's been calling but I didn't want to wake you.'

He threw back the covers. 'What did she say? Has Mira been discharged?' He was out of bed, hands madly scratching a scalp made itchy from dry sweat and frustration, and with his hair on end was pulling a clean shirt from its hanger.

'Stop, Julian. Don't be an idiot. You're probably infectious.'

His pyjama bottoms were tangled around his feet, reducing him to a frantic sackrace.

Katie blocked his path: 'Julia said you weren't to come.'

He ignored her and found clean jeans in the drawer, his hands shaking with relief, not sickness. He swept past her and ran downstairs, found his shoes and Heino's keys, got in his car and drove.

Lamb's Conduit Street was quiet when he arrived. Streetlamps, shadows, a lone pulsing orange light to warn of the repair work to the pavement. He climbed the stairs from the street and slipped inside, careful not to wake the old man. His heart was beating with joy, the tock of the grandfather clock in the hall the only other sound. In the sitting room a lamp glowed dimly beside the piano, its lid raised for a ghost. He pulled off his shoes, tiptoed over. The light glanced from the lone silver frame and he searched for Karl in his mother's portrait, found him unmistakably in her smile. Her dark hair swept back and a gown of black velvet exposed the graceful slope of her shoulders, and from her neck a small gold sun hung on its fine chain. Her name was engraved along the bottom of the frame, her full name, not its diminutive. His heart missed a beat: Eliana. He extinguished the lamp. The door to Julia's room was ajar.

Slowly, quietly, he pushed it wide. It was darker than the sitting room and his eyes were slow to adjust. There was a whistling snore as he padded in his socks to the window to pull the curtain and let a slice of streetlight into the room.

He turned. The light fell like a knife.

Julia, hair spread across her pillow, lay facing the curve of Mira's back, one arm held her in its crook, the other . . . Light glanced from the edges of their limbs. There were shoulders, elbows, hands. Mira enclosed between them. Safe, cocooned. Them.

He let the curtain drop. Karl didn't stir, his chin rested on the top of Mira's head. Mira's hand lay like a starfish on his shoulder. Together, they slept on.

Whatever noise came out of Julian's mouth was enough to

wake Julia, he couldn't be sure he wouldn't be sick. Karl murmured something as Julia rose from the bed, her Medusa hair twisting across the lace straps of that unknown nightgown and the words that fell from her mouth turned him to stone.

LAMB'S CONDUIT STREET

August 2002

Twenty

Mira's eyes are closed, her hair sways back and forth across her face like weeds. Her thin slippery limbs are silvered by reflections. She lies quite still. Julia perches with a towel, staring down through the water until she can stand it no more.

'Mira! Sweetie! Come up!'

Mira remains cruelly motionless, light dappling her skin. Julia sits on the edge of the laundry bin hating every second. Mira's holding her nose with one hand, the other floats palm upturned and Julia is in no doubt that she's all too aware of the effect she's having. Mira's chest is veined with blue, her eyelids too, minute silver bubbles cling to her skin.

She should never have shown her that picture at the Tate, tragic heroines are right up Mira's street. Julia throws her shadow between the light and the water, holding out the towel: 'Come on, Ophelia.' Mira emerges with a great squeak of skin on enamel, water streaming, wiping her eyes on the edge of the towel and taking exaggerated breaths of air.

'I thought I told you not to get your hair wet.' Julia stems a wave of irritation and exhaustion. 'It's already past your bedtime and Heino won't have a hairdryer . . .' Mira smiles and dunks herself back beneath the water. She'd stay in the bath all night if Julia would let her.

A siren rises above the rumble of traffic. It screams along the street and, though Julia covers her ears with the towel, shoots straight through to her marrow. Blue lights flash from the mirror, blue pulses race across the bathwater and scatter from the taps. She pulls at Mira's arm, forcing her to surface.

She snaps more than she means to, probably the jet-lag to blame: 'Irritating child! You might as well give it a wash now it's wet.' She squirts shampoo into Mira's upturned hands.

Julia is jumpy at every ambulance. Soon she will stop noticing, but right now the proximity to the hospital is giving her the jitters. Karl's absence isn't helping: she could do with his steadying arm and feels a flash of frustration that he didn't manage to finish at the lab in time for his flight.

Mira is working up a crazy lather and pulling faces at herself in the mirror, craning to admire her foamy pagoda of hair.

Julia tries not to think about Karl: he'll be back at work, maybe on a lunchbreak. He'll have to get away from whatever it is he's up to if he's to call before bedtime. She checks the time, pictures him at the Clamshack in town, a favourite of his, frothing bunches of sea-lavender hanging from white rafters, cold white wine in cloudy glasses. There he is with the keys to his Dodge on the table, leaning across to say something to his companion . . .

'Mommy, Mommy . . .' The bathroom door bursts open and Ruth skips in, a plump putto on dainty feet who's sweetly got herself ready for bed. Julia can't help but kiss her. Ruth is wearing a faded cotton nightie of Mira's that ends in a frill at her ankles, her hair is a rumpled mass of wild-child curls.

'Tell her to get out!' Mira grasps furious knees to her chest. 'I said go away.' She splashes an armful of water at Ruth.

'Mira, don't get her wet!' Julia feels a pang for the days when she could bathe them together, the bubbles and the squirty ducks. Ruth buries her face in Julia's lap and Julia tries threading her fingers through her younger daughter's frizzy ringlets without pulling. Ruth's hair is as wilful as her own. Mira's had a lucky escape. Hers pours in thick wet ribbons all the way down the hostile curve of back that she now turns to them.

Ruth braves looking up. 'My baby hedgehog' Julia calls her. 'Grandfather says he'll read us a story if we don't take too long,' says Ruth as Mira splashes more water at her. 'Tell her, Mommy, tell her to get out.'

Julia gives Ruth a squeeze, if she squeezed her as hard as she'd like to it would hurt her. She could bite the very flesh of this child. Ruth's eyes are round as chocolate buttons, her eyebrows set at an angle, comically, just like her father's. 'You and Heino have your story downstairs,' Julia says, nuzzling Ruth's cheek and shooting a look at Mira. 'Madam's going to be stuck up here while I try to find a way to dry her hair.'

'Shut the door, stupid,' Mira yells after her.

The phone is ringing. Julia hands Mira the towel: 'Come on you, out,' and runs to her bedroom to answer it. Catches it in time. On the other end of the line Karl keeps clearing his throat. A gruff apology: 'I know it's letting you down. I'm sorry,' and Julia sinks to the bed.

'Letting me down? That's putting it mildly.'

She tries to insist that he change his mind, her fist clenched around the bone-handled receiver. 'It's my father's funeral, for Christ's sake,' she says. Tears spring to her eyes. She can see their clothes hanging ready in the wardrobe. His suit, her wool dress with the pleats, the girls' black dresses and cardigans bought especially. He was supposed to be solidly, unimpeachably, at her side, completing the picture in the Borsalino hat she'd put on the hall table for him.

He's talking about his team, something to do with FDA trials, three years' work reaching fruition. She hates the way he says 'my team'; she'd like to hear him say 'my family' like that. 'It's a critical moment for my team . . .'

'Oh, when isn't it?'

'I can't just up and leave,' he says.

There's something enraging about the thought of them there all together in their crisp white coats: eager young Peter, Merlin – yes, really – and of course Sofie van doo-dah with the long slim limbs and bleached smile.

'Just another few days and I'll be with you. I promise.'

'But you promised already.' She hates herself for wheedling. She pictures him in his beloved lab, now he's back from whatever he did about lunch, his white coat open and his tie loose and crooked. She hears a voice calling his name in the background, then say: 'Oops, sorry.' A woman's voice, oh, of course, that would be Sofie, who else? She imagines his eyes following Sofie's slim calves towards a microscope, the phone clamped between his shoulder and ear. 'I doubt I'll manage a flight until after the weekend.' He's probably already looking into his blasted microscope he's so keen to get her off the line. 'Vernow's a long way for you to drive alone. Maybe Freda could give you a lift?' As though a driver was all that was missing.

She imagines him gesturing to Sofie that he won't be long, doing that winding-motion thing with his finger. 'It's not as though I really knew your father,' he says and that feels better, to be full of fury: she's about to smash the receiver down, can already see herself doing it, but Ruth runs in, eyes shining.

'I heard the phone downstairs. Is it Daddy?'

She thrusts the receiver at Ruth, hears Mira's splashing in the bathroom and shouts: 'Are you still in there? Get out now!'

Ruth is telling Karl about the story Heino was reading her, about the tiger who drank all the water in the taps. 'Mommy's gonna take us to the zoo tomorrow,' she says.

She pulls Ruth close, and loudly so she hopes Karl will hear:

'It was at the zoo that Daddy first kissed Mummy, you know.' Ruth raises her eyebrows and makes kissing noises at him down the line, chatters on.

Something like heat had swept her into Karl's arms for that kiss. One moment the tiger, pacing up and down, forlorn and humiliated, the next there she was, sandwiched between him and the glass, letting him kiss her, kissing him right back.

Now Ruth is complaining about her sister: 'She took my Annie doll and said it was hers and now she won't give it back.' Julia sits cuddling her with one ear close enough to the receiver to hear the buzz of Karl's platitudes. It's a shame the girls don't get on so well now. She thinks of Ruth in her hand-me-down OshKoshes and Mira with neat plaits standing on the school steps in her too-big uniform, about to cross the threshold for the first time. She used to have to prise them apart – their arms held fast like a pair of cuddle bears with velcroed paws. But Mira's been in a foul mood since they got to London and poor little Ruthie is bearing the brunt.

Outside another siren anxiously screams, a busy night at the hospital. It's gone alarmingly quiet in the bathroom. She hopes Mira isn't doing an Ophelia again.

She cuts through a cloud of steam towards the bath. Mira bursts up through the surface, water cascading down her skinny front. 'Thirty Mississippi.' She stands panting, triumphant, the lovely S-shaped torso of a girl gymnast, holding out her arms for a towel. She is a lithe little thing, with bony knees and a neat peachy bum, still a little tanned from their holiday, at her waist the pale deckle-edged line of her scar.

Mira catches her looking and Julia quells a shiver. How much *does* she remember? She reaches a finger to the scar.

Julia knows it's not good to dwell, but still she wonders. When they talk about the hospital is it really Karl Mira sees beside her bed and not Julian? It would appear that Julian has been removed as efficiently as her kidney. Mira's in the clear now. Just a routine annual check-up around her birthday.

But what of Julian?

It's easier not to think about Julian when they're all at home in Old Mystic, an ocean between them.

She sees him when their love was new. His jumper through at the elbow, hair flopping across his eyes so he has to keep combing it back with his fingers, crouched in his socks before the put-put of the gas heater, his blue china coffee cup, his big-knuckled wrists and hands.

She'd felt dirty on the train going back to him after her encounter with Karl at the zoo. Her lips felt bruised by his kiss, the dung smells seemed to cling to her clothing and hair. When she reached Julian's digs she managed to jump the rota and was so intent on scrubbing herself that she almost forgot to tell him that she'd been offered the horticultural job which had been the purpose of her trip. He had good news too, he told her. His stepfather had offered him a position at Abraham and Leitch. It was a boring enough job so he'd have plenty of head space for his own book in the evenings, especially now he'd dropped his dissertation.

The wool of Julian's dressing gown was a homecoming embrace. She put it on straight after the hot bath, had a thing about wearing his clothes. His jumpers seemed the softest. She liked his shirts freshly ironed against her skin and still smelling faintly of him, their collars frayed by his good strong jaw, the scrape of his stubble. He called her to where he crouched by the fire and pulled open the folds of his dressing gown to lay his cheek against her belly. She cradled his head, soothing her conscience by stroking his hair as he crooned to the baby who was not yet lost. Sometimes just the thought of Julian can make her eyes well. She's noticed it happens most when Karl has made her angry.

She holds out the towel: 'Jump to it!' He's made her angry tonight, no doubt about it, and she shakes it impatiently as Mira steps from the bath.

Twenty-one

Julia wakes early to the sounds of the yard below, someone slamming the lid on a bin, whistling. It takes a moment to remember where she is. The face that chastises her from the bathroom mirror is never pleasant and especially not after a restless night and a regrettable 4am call to Karl. She looks extra gaunt with shadows beneath her eyes and at the corners of her mouth that even the Touche Éclat (bought in a fit of boredom on the plane from JFK) would do nothing to disguise.

She dresses quietly, grey jeans turned up at the ankle, a clean white shirt. It's the height of summer but the English weather is in its usual turmoil so she ties a cardigan round her waist and slips her feet into old suede loafers that won't give her blisters. All she has to do is run her hands through her hair now it's so short. Karl and the girls were appalled when she first came home with it lopped. Sometimes she still misses having something to hide behind but forty had been a good cut-off point.

She slips down the stairs on the balls of her feet hoping the girls will sleep on so she'll have a little time to herself before the onslaught. In two days she must make the long journey to Vernow with them squabbling and no Karl there to share the driving and broker peace. The funeral will be straddled by a night either side with her mother at her flat in Vernow's only tower block. Confined between the furiously bare walls, Gwen will have her nerves wound tight as cheese wire within minutes.

Karl had spluttered out his tea when she told him the cremation would be in Vernow. 'Inferno?' 'Yes, yes,' she said, handing him a piece from the kitchen roll. Karl had never been to Vernow, had not seen the smoke from the chimney on the way out of town. He only met her parents in London, just once before their wedding. Gwen flew out to Connecticut after Ruth was born, but not Geoffrey. She can't remember if she'd even invited him. Well, too late now. She was strangely blank about his death, didn't really mind Karl snickering about the circles of hell of her hometown.

She managed to make herself think about her dad on the plane over, forced herself to pick through the rubble for a nugget or two, almost succeeding – a distant memory of him pushing her on a swing, the closest she came to crying. In the end she was sadder about the relationship she'd never had with him than the one they had. Nothing worse than a drinker being given charge of a pub. Always the booze to blame, never him.

The girls arrive in the kitchen together, sleepy and bad-tempered. Mira fusses about her breakfast. Julia offers her everything in the cupboard but still she whines and says all she wants is juice. Julia's own mother would have slapped her if she'd behaved like that. Or starved her as punishment.

'Do I hear the voices of angels?' Heino's walking has deteriorated now, especially first thing; he's bent right over his stick and it takes him a while to reach the table, his head nodding where it emerges from his shirt and tie. Mira ignores him, she's too busy sulking about the tiny triangle of toast she's been told to eat before she gets down. Julia gestures at Ruth bent over her second bowl of Sugar Puffs, sighs at Heino as she says: 'It's so much easier with a child who loves her food.' Ruth grins at him over her spoon.

He lowers himself into his place at the head of the table. She feels comforted by him in a way she never was by her own father. 'Ah, Mira's being picky again? You mustn't worry,' he says. 'Children will eat when they're hungry.'

He lifts the coffee pot and winks at Mira. 'And if all they want is mashed potato it doesn't matter, it's all calories.'

His hand shakes as he pours coffee into Julia's cup and some sloshes into the saucer. 'So clumsy,' he says, rattling it across the table to her. 'Comes of being so old.'

She strokes the back of his hand, the tendons blue and tough as knotted string. She looks into his reassuring eyes. 'You never age, Heino. You're exactly the same as when I first knew you.'

He raises an eyebrow when he smiles back. His widower's hump makes him look more like a tortoise than ever. 'Well, if I'm still of use to some people all is not lost.'

Ruth climbs around to his side, plants a milky kiss on his cheek, looks solemnly into his eyes: 'Daddy's not coming today.'

He tousles her hair and calls her 'Ragamuffin' and tuts when Julia tells him that Karl probably won't manage to get away until after the weekend.

'It's this contraception project we've all been hearing endlessly about. Human trials could start next year if he can get all the data for the research admin meeting next week . . . My dad's timing couldn't be worse, really.'

'Tsk!' Heino bats his napkin at her, scattering the table with crumbs. 'Always the same, like a dog with a bone once he's got his teeth into something,' he says. 'That's too bad, he should be at the funeral with you.'

Julia bites her lip. Her heart sinks, not at the thought of the funeral but of the two merciless days and nights with Gwen, who will not stint on insinuation. She can hear her already, tightening the wire: 'Not here with his family? Now, what could be more important?'

The girls are argumentative as she gathers what they need for their trip to the zoo. She insists they bring their anoraks. Outside the threat of rain and surprisingly chilly gusts surge into the footwell of the car, making her shivery despite her cardigan. She hasn't mastered all the mysterious buttons on Heino's dashboard so she impatiently flicks switches and turns dials, trying to make the cold fan stop. This English summer isn't doing much to court fond memories, it seems unable to make up its mind what to do. The combination of sharp winds and city dust and pollen has set Mira's eyes streaming and Julia wonders if she should pull over at a chemist for Piriton. She checks her in the rear-view mirror. Mira, head lolling to the window, is lost in her audio-book, red headphones clamped firmly over her ears. Perhaps her eyes are a little pink, it's never any use telling her not to rub them. Ruth, happily crunching crisps, pulls a monkey grin when she notices her mother watching her in the mirror.

Mira is dressed in an army-green top, a great favourite of hers, though Julia has tried to lose it many times. The colour is unflattering, seems to throw an unhealthy tinge to her face. It looks even worse right now because she's scowling.

Once upon a time there had been delights at London Zoo. Julia was sure there had been animal rides, the chafe of leather against bare thighs, high up on a hump, the almost fairground thrill of the camel's toppling gait. But now it appeared there was nothing to ride and the chimpanzees no longer threw tea parties. Nothing she promised them was materialising, not even the heart-wrenching horror of the elephants remained. She stood before the grey concrete carbuncle and grasped the girls' hands, trying to make them see the unhappy ghosts of the elephants that had stood there. Casson's idea of suitable housing could've won a prize for its cold lack of empathy: a great lump that spoke of imperialism beyond the sad lot of the elephants and rhinos imprisoned there. A couple of years before, an elephant had trampled a keeper to death, earning them all a passport to Whipsnade Park instead. The news had made the *Connecticut Post*. She mutters on about it as the girls shake themselves free of her ancient doomy memories, running off to look at some sort of bearded pigs hopelessly truffling in the mud.

Mira and Ruth regard the whole place as nothing more than a potential pet showroom. Mira can't immediately see why they shouldn't keep penguins in the bath. Ruth grows tearful when she says: 'No, not even a marmoset.' After that they trudge rather than skip and she misses Karl, who would have livened things up, taken them into the bug room that she's just steered them right past. He wouldn't wander around the place so listlessly, he'd have stories of evolution and arcane facts, he'd tell them about the baboons' bottoms and make them laugh.

The tigers have ugly names: Reika and Lumpur. One has draped itself across some boards and has more in common with a moth-eaten rug than its splendidly muscled cousin they'd seen on the TV. Its mate paces up and down right in front of them along a well-worn track, barely bothering to lift the weight of its own head and tail. A little boy keeps banging on the glass and shouting 'Lion, lion' no matter how many times he's corrected by his father. Every time the tiger turns, it lets out a cry of anguish, somewhere between a snarl and a groan, its white whiskers drooping. Julia feels ashamed to even be looking.

'Is this where Daddy kissed you?' Ruth says.

Karl had been waiting for her right here, as arranged. A grey November day almost thirteen years ago and so cold she'd been glad her coat had a collar she could turn to the wind. He sprang to his feet when he saw her, wringing his hands, not much in the way of conversational foreplay, asking her to forgive him for what he was about to say. His shoulders were painfully apologetic as he spoke. 'You see there's something about Julian that makes me feel protective.'

She tried to laugh off whatever was coming: 'It's that little-boy-lost thing he has . . .' but Karl was looking grave.

'He's a sensitive soul. You do realise he's only twenty-one, I suppose?' She was biting her lip as he went on. Honestly, to hear him you'd have thought she was some kind of Jezebel. Why did he find it so hard to understand that age had nothing to do with it, that she and Julian were in love?

'It's madness for him to bail before finals. You know he's been awarded the Milton Society scholarship? Yes? He's worked so bloody hard. And now . . .' He gestured at her stomach.

She glared at him, turned to walk away. '*He* can stay on and finish, it's only me that *has* to get out of town.' Karl put his hand to her shoulder and she had a momentary flash of her husband Chris, his contorted face, right close up, spittle caught in the cracks at the sides of his mouth, and felt a swelling indignation as Karl went on. She didn't need to justify herself to this do-gooder. The stuff that was going on with her husband and the threats he'd made to her were none of his business.

'Wherever you go Julian will follow, you know that as well as I do, and he's worked so hard,' Karl was saying. 'Can't you just wait a bit before you *get out of town*?' He pulled a face at '*get out of town*', imitating her like she was Mae West.

Her hand itched to slap him as she replied, 'Ever heard of free will, Karl?'

'What?' He took a step closer and she felt herself flinch. He laid a hand on her belly, the other hard against the back of her head. Her eyes were shut as he pulled her to him, a deep and shaming pain at her groin.

It was the longest kiss she'd ever known; they might never have stopped, but when they did they groaned Julian's name in unison. She started retreating, but immediately he came after her and pulled her back into his arms. She was shaking and he shushed her, gently stroking hair from her face, making the ache unbearable as she reached to kiss again, but he turned his face. His lips were to her ear: 'You see, Julia, this proves it. You're anyone's.'

She battled herself from his grip. She was flooding with shame, had to get as far from him as she could. He was wiping his mouth with the back of his hand as she stumbled. 'Are you even sure it's his?' he said. She found her feet, but he grabbed her again by the arm: 'Don't do this, Julia. Don't pin a baby on him, not now.' The tiger had come to a standstill behind him, its eye glinted at her panic. 'Have a heart,' Karl called after her.

She hurries the girls past the spot, almost expecting something to be different in the air, a vibration or a haunting. Karl had no science to explain it, the sudden unwarranted attraction and the force of the current that made him betray his friend. 'The thing is, right at that moment I hated you,' she said when they talked about it. And he always came straight back at her: 'I hated you too.'

Twenty-two

The route to Freda's is relentlessly gloomy with nothing to point out to the kids who are still smarting at her refusal to buy them anything from the zoo. Brent Cross, Asda, the Colindale Retail Park, Mecca Bingo. Mira's audiobook has ended; she pulls the headphones from her ears, has a brief spat with Ruth, rising to an indignant wail: 'That's not fair. She's finished both packets of crisps.'

'Calm down,' Julia tells her. 'It won't be too long in the car before we're at Freda's. I'm sure she'll feed you.'

'Who's Freda?' Mira asks.

She starts to explain, for about the third time since breakfast. 'Before we moved to America . . .'

'Yes, when I was in your tummy,' Ruth chimes in.

'No, even before that, Ruthie. Here in London Freda and I used to work together making gardens. She was – *is* – my best friend and, as I keep telling you, Mira, she's your godmother. You were with us all the time. Do you really not remember her at all?'

Mira only shrugs and yawns. Julia watches as she rootles around in her knapsack for another cassette. Mira listens to the same stories over and over. She seems to have very few memories of her life before Connecticut. Sometimes she talks about the hospital, but it's mainly the things they've told her.

Mira finds the tape and slots it in, pauses with the headphones in her hand: 'Was Freda Daddy's friend, or just yours?'

Julia has to concentrate; a burst of rain spatters the windscreen and she edges cautiously forward, feels herself skating dangerously close to thin ice. 'Freda and I made gardens for people in offices, we had a little white van which I'd painted with flowers,' she says. 'You used to come with us sometimes. There was a bench seat for you in the back with the plants, and you played in the greenhouse while we worked.' She falters, wishes she had Karl's steadying hand to lead her away from dangerous ground.

Giving Mira's question a swerve has made her feel sneaky. Mira is inscrutable, headphones clamped once again on her ears, with her head to the window staring out at the grey streets.

There was never meant to be any sort of secret; she and Karl discussed it early on, imagined they'd have to arrange some sort of contact. What they hadn't foreseen was Julian's unbroken silence. Nor Jenna's voice on the telephone, cold and nasty, setting her free as efficiently as surgical steel. 'You go to Firdaws, clear out every trace. Do you hear me? You and the child. It's what he wants.' And then, once they got to the States, it drifted, and within the clapboard walls of their new life in Old Mystic a simpler version of the truth floated in and settled. Mira stopped asking, Ruthie was born, it was natural that both girls should call Karl Daddy. They put away Mira's baby photographs, skated over details, decided to wait.

Julia takes a detour almost without thinking: after all, it is on the way. Burnt Oak hasn't changed much: still the streets of halal meat, Greggs, Pennywise, the oriental supermarket where she and Julian bought mystery vegetables and food in bright packets.

'I lived here when I first came to London,' she tells the girls.

'With Daddy?' Ruth immediately wants to know.

'No, before. Right down there, at the top of that building with the tree in front. Brrr.' She's shivers involuntarily. 'It was very cold up there. The winters were snowy and we only had the one gas heater.' And then checks herself for the 'we', feels herself edging ever closer to the cracking ice. 'I used to wear my gloves indoors.'

She pulls away in the wrong gear and almost stalls. She remembers their arrival, the biting cold inside and out. They'd fled from Mrs Briggs's in a hailstorm, with one white vanload between them. She was four months pregnant and Julian wouldn't allow her to carry a thing. She went up to see what could be done about a cup of tea while Julian and his stepfather, lovely, wise old Michael, humped boxes from the freezing streets and up the stairs.

It was a decent-sized room, L-shaped, so they planned to put the baby's cot in the short side and hang a curtain across. The windows looked out at the street through grubby nets at the front and to the back across some scrubby gardens towards a Nissen hut. It would all look a bit more cheerful once the trees were in leaf.

Julian had been efficient with the packing, so she quickly found everything she needed: kettle, mugs, even a fresh carton of milk and Hobnobs in one box that he'd thoughtfully – adorably – marked in red felt tip 'EXTREMELY URGENT UNPACK FIRST'.

He came stumbling through the door with boxes falling, his arms and hair across his face so it was a wonder he could see. He dropped them on the floor, spilling books from one that had split. The kettle started to boil. He was going through stuff, muttering.

He came bounding across the floor unfurling a bolt of cloth she hadn't seen before: blue silk, gold-spangled. 'For our bed.' It glittered with sequins and gold stars. He laid it at her feet. 'I got it from Pete the hippie. You know, the guy in the head shop?'

She knelt to brush her hand across it, to smooth it. 'So glamorous,' she said.

'"Heavens' embroidered cloths . . ."' he told her with a pleased grin. She looked blank. 'Do you know the poem?' She shook her head, stood up.

'It's Yeats,' he said, and cleared his throat. Though she never told him, she hated it when he quoted poetry at her, it always made her grow hot and rooted to the spot. He made a Sir Galahad flourish as though expecting her to step on to the quilt as he recited. '". . . I have spread my dreams under your feet; Tread softly because you tread on my dreams."' He held a courtly hand to her and the responsibility of not trampling his dreams made her feel instantly clumsy.

It's a relief to get to Freda's – easily recognisable from the lemon trees at the yellow front door, three in glazed pots each side of the step, with glossy leaves and the scent of their flowers in the air. Julia stoops to inhale the waxy white blossoms and slides her hand down the trunk to the line of the graft. She runs a finger back and forth around the ridge of the enjoined scion and stock. Every inch of Freda's front garden is bursting with plants, standing in pots, or sprawling, tangling their limbs. Ruth runs in and out between them, a plump little savage released from the car. 'George, George, George of the jungle,' she sings out from between the leaves, and Mira scowls at her as Freda throws open her door with a whoop of delight.

Julia and Freda hug, tears springing to their eyes. 'Julia, your hair!' Freda says. 'And Mira! You're all grown up!' Mira squirms and Ruth presses forward to get a closer look at this Tango-haired woman who hasn't even noticed her yet. 'And Ruth too! Goodness, you were no more than a babe in your mother's arms,' Freda says, scooping her up.

The girls perk up immediately in Freda's bright-pink kitchen. They're sitting on high stools at the counter talking over each other to answer Freda's questions about the zoo while she clops about in her funny boots sorting out tea and toasted buns, squeezing fresh orange juice. The glass doors to the garden are ajar, potted palms throw handprints across the room and two giant urns spill branches of plumbago trembling with baby-blue blooms. Freda's feet are pushed into her customary tough leather work boots, her dress is of a pretty blue and grey floral print. She wears her big boots without laces so the tongues flap around as she moves. She has a leather tool belt buckled around the dress and a metal blade glints in its holster. She laughs easily, her strings of amber beads catch the light and her hair is dyed the colour of tangerines. Mira and Ruth can't take their eyes off her, and she soon has them shouting to be heard.

She pushes a plate of toasted buns towards Julia. 'Your girls have American accents!' Julia tries not to pull a face but the strain of Karl's absence has got to her. Freda widens her eyes, puts down the butter knife. 'Julia, are you all right?' Julia is horrified to find herself suddenly close to tears, staring at the plants, the mass of stems and leaves swimming. In her kitchen in Connecticut a single aloe vera waits like a lone specimen on the smooth white surfaces. She can't find the words, the paradise palms blur into a flock of peacocks' tails, splendidly fanned, and now the girls are both staring at her. Freda wraps her in her arms and rocks her like a child.

Together they walk arm in arm to the glasshouses around the corner. Inside, Freda stops now and then to snip off a stem or adjust a tie. It's a familiar, steamy, verdant cloud of nostalgia, the heavenly scent a hundred times stronger than jasmine. Julia feels the brush of ferns on her arms, breathes the warmth of ripening sap, rich earth and, lingering above all else, the sweet citrus flowers.

'It's much easier these days,' Freda is telling her. 'I have two young lads to help me with the installations and after that I leave it to them to zip around town and do all the maintenance. They're good boys.'

Mira and Ruth race up and down the tiled paths. Ruth stops at a calamondin orange, its branches gently dipping with fruit. 'Can I pick one?' she asks.

Mira is transfixed by some fuchsias with pale-pink buds the shape of dancers *en pointe*. Freda has to call to her twice to come and choose an orange to take back to the house.

The girls nestle down among Freda's cushions and throws, some children's television presenters are doing something with splat guns that's making them laugh. Clashing roses and African prints, furry tiger rugs, cut-up sweet oranges within reach. Marcel, Freda's tabby cat, purrs on Mira's lap while Ruth leans across to nubble him under the chin.

As they leave the room, Julia hears Mira growl, turns in time to witness her sharp elbow: 'Stop stroking him like that, Ruthie,' she says. 'He only likes me, his eyes are cross every time you touch him.' And Julia has to quell the urge to march in and slap her.

In the greenhouse Freda's citrus orchard spreads before them. The trees are at their peak, flowering and fruiting, but still Mira's bad mood hangs heavy. Julia sighs and Freda asks her what's wrong. 'It's starting to really get to me,' Julia says. 'Mira's been awful since we got back, rude to me, foul to Ruthie.'

'Jet-lag?'

'Maybe. And maybe she's missing Karl. I certainly am.' She explains to Freda about his delay. 'It's the holy grail of pharmaceutical research,' she says and grows a little sarcastic: 'You know, Karl and his team are well up in the race to put an end to this planet's overpopulation.'

'Huh,' Freda snorts. 'As if handing the contraceptive pill to the men will make a jot of difference.'

Freda pulls down branches heavy with lemons, picks a dozen

or so and sets them aside for lemonade. 'I'll have to start making marmalade if I don't get this lot out somewhere soon.'

Julia walks among the trees answering Freda's questions about their new home in Old Mystic. It's an original captain's house, overlooking the estuary, the girls' school is a Big Yellow Bus ride away, they wake to the call of geese and yet Karl can be ready for action at Pfizer within thirty minutes. The Captain O'Shea House will, sadly for them, never come on the market. 'I suppose for that reason I lost heart quite early on whenever the grass needed cutting or the garden was full of weeds.' She tries to make light of her inactivity, but Freda lays a concerned hand on her arm.

At home there is only that single crown of aloe vera on the kitchen windowsill, put there by Karl in case of burns, and a few Phalaenopsis orchids that she keeps in their bedroom, and shamefully neglects for months on end.

'Being among all this again is making me quite jealous,' she says.

'Everyone wants architectural plants now,' Freda says, frowning. 'I might have to sell off some of these big trees to make space.'

Julia knows them all: Meyer lemons, Amalfi oranges, Persian limes, some taller than her but, oh, somehow like old friends. She runs her finger around the graft scar of a ponderosa tree and Freda nods, reading her thoughts. 'They're entirely yours, from that first batch of rootstock – it was a good one,' she says. 'We haven't lost a single tree, everything still healthy and, as you can see, fruiting like mad.'

Freda adds some oranges to her pile. 'There's a specialist nursery in Sussex that might give me a reasonable price, so you could find yourself with a little cheque soon.'

'Oh Freda, no need for that.' Julia would never stop feeling guilty about the way she left. 'I couldn't possibly accept a share. And anyway, wouldn't it be a shame to let them go?'

Freda piles the fruit into a bucket, shrugs and says: 'I've cut right down on new projects since you quit. It's not as much fun as it used to be. It needed your flair.'

Julia crouches on the path and rootles her fingers through the woodchips at the base of a tree. 'Look, this one's got some suckers coming through from the rootstock, right here.' Freda passes her the secateurs from her belt: 'Go on, I can tell you're dying to.'

Julia holds the pale-green whip between her fingers. The blades are satisfyingly sharp and in one slice the rogue spear of the original thorn tree has been banished. She rocks back on her heels and Freda squats beside her, packing earth around the base of a neighbouring kumquat.

'I really am worried about Mira,' Julia says, handing back the snips. 'Does she look OK to you?'

Freda pockets them. 'She looks absolutely gorgeous. They both do.'

'Well, I wish she was a bit more bonny. Next to Ruthie . . .'

'Pft, you mustn't worry. Different body types. I mean, look at me next to you.' Freda grasps a roll of her own flesh through the flowering fabric of her dress, laughs as she says: 'Ruth's a little chubby thing, but at least she might grow out of it, unlike me.'

Julia shakes her head. 'It's not Mira's skinniness. You know? Recently she seems to have lost her appetite for everything, not only food. All she wants to do is listen to tapes of the same old stories she's heard a hundred times before. She doesn't want to be cuddled, doesn't want to play. She's hardly spoken a word since we arrived in Lamb's Conduit Street, except to snap at poor Ruthie. It's not like her to be so silent. You know, I can't help wondering what's preoccupying her.'

'Oh dear.' Freda stops what she's doing, lays a hand on Julia's arm. 'Do you think it's being back at the flat? The hospital right there? I take it you and Karl still haven't talked to her about Julian?'

Julia replies with another shake of her head. 'I think we've left it too late,' she says.

'Tell me,' says Freda as they leave the glasshouse, running back because she's forgotten the bucket. 'Have you got anything happening tomorrow?'

Julia has nothing much planned. 'I'll probably have to drive the girls to see their cousins, but that's about it.'

Freda's eyes sparkle. 'It's an interesting space, three glass apexes – which can be vented, according to the architect – long thin windows looking down into the foyer from the offices, plenty of light for trees.'

'Freda, what are you talking about?'

Freda grins at her. 'A beautiful glass atrium at the centre of a building in the City, a green space for the workers to mingle. The tender is due with the architect by Friday. Do you fancy having a go at drawing something up? Yes?'

'Yes!'

Julia can barely contain her excitement as she drives away. She and Ruthie sing along to the radio. The traffic is bad so she takes a back route she used many times before, along Holly Hill and up the side of Waterlow Park. It's dangerously close to Cromwell Gardens. Mira becomes transfixed by a squirrel she's spotted running along a branch while they stop to let the traffic pass. She's still listening to a story on earphones so her voice comes out loud.

'I had a toy pram once, it had a wheel that squeaked and Dad . . . put some oil on it and it didn't squeak any more. And I had a doll called Wee-Ro-Ro. Isn't that a strange name?' Julia remembers the doll, which Mira had eccentrically named Wheelbarrow, and the pram, her second birthday present from Granny Jenna. But as she replays Mira's voice, she can't discern if it was Daddy or *Dadoo* who fixed the wheel. In the rear-view she sees her rubbing her eyes and then with some relief remembers her allergy.

They return to Lamb's Conduit Street with bulging carrier bags of Freda's oranges and lemons. Mira is outraged at being asked to carry one up to the door and swings it angrily as she stomps up the stairs. The bag splits and the fruit spills and bounces past Ruth's feet, some oranges roll into the street. Mira stands looking pale with the broken bag in her hands but doesn't offer to help.

Heino is already in bed but through his door Julia can hear the radio he'll keep on all night. Ruthie thoughtfully arranges the fruit in a large wooden bowl on the table.

With the girls finally settled on the top floor, Julia pours herself a large glass of white wine and spreads out the architect's drawings on the kitchen table. She visualises the flow of people between trees, paths, stone benches, some grouped planting to give a feeling of privacy. She gulps at the wine, checks Heino's calendar on its string beside the telephone. His great-niece Claudine is due back in the morning. She's already said she'd like to spend some time with the girls and the whole place is clean and tidy due to her own insomnia, so there won't be much else she'll have to do ... Freda knew she wouldn't be able to resist – '*I was thinking perhaps a lemon-orchard sort of a vibe ...*' – and Mira and Ruthie adore Claudine.

Julia pours herself a second glass, a third, and her thoughts drift inevitably to Karl in Connecticut. The phone on the wall mocks her with its silence. She checks her watch; still only five in the afternoon over there, so he'll be at the lab. She rarely calls him at work but really, after a day like today, she ought to talk to him about Mira.

It's no use waiting, sometimes the family has to come before the team. She calls his direct line but it goes unanswered and after a while clicks to the main switchboard. 'I'm sorry, Mrs

Lieberman, but Karl isn't working here this afternoon.' At the table she empties the remains of the bottle into her glass. She's starting to feel tipsy, enough that she can blame the booze for the paranoia of her actions.

Everything blurs a little as she pulls up the high stool that Heino keeps beside the phone. She props herself against it. She dials the main number, hoping for a different switchboard girl, but unfortunately it sounds like the same one and she sinks further into the mire because although it's ridiculous, she puts on an American accent. 'May I speak directly to Miss Sofie van der Zeller, please?' The line bleeps as the receptionist tries to put her through, then she's back with the heart-sinking news that 'Miss van der Zeller is not at work today.' Julia drops the phone into its cradle and the disgust she feels is mainly at herself for being so suspicious and untrusting. There's no need to link the two absences in such an unpleasant way.

She checks the front door, the sitting room, before heading unsteadily for the stairs. Heino has lit Ellie's lamp in the corner, the piano lid is raised. He'll have stopped there a moment, wishing her portrait a silent and lingering goodnight before climbing to their room. It's so touching, the constancy of his devotion. Heino goes alone to concerts and sits with his eyes shut so he can imagine she's there beside him. He confesses that he goes to bed earlier and earlier because he dreams of Ellie every night.

Julia remembers how distressed Heino had been when she first came here. She used to hear him pacing up and down through the ceiling. Nowadays he keeps the radio on all night; the World Service seems to settle him. The room below his is now Claudine's. Julia looks across at it. The door is ajar though she's certain it was shut when she first came in. She catches a glimpse of the faded violet wallpaper, the soft bronze sheen of Ellie's eiderdown. She has not been able to take a step inside since that shameful night, shudders to even touch the china door-knob. She sees him again, Julian, standing at the foot of the bed, stone-grey and motionless, his hair sticking up from his head like a thornbush, staring and mouthing, completely silent.

She pulls the door shut with a click but the memories won't stay behind it. A sudden impulse sends her back to the kitchen and, before she can change her mind, to the phone. She dials and the mouthpiece seems to amplify her breathing back at her. She makes herself hold her nerve while the old Firdaws number clicks through. She has no idea what she'll say to him if he answers.

Twenty-three

Claudine has arrived in the night. From the top of the stairs Julia sees her bags piled up in the hall, her leather jacket slung over the the banister. The door to that bedroom is closed and Julia offers a little prayer that Claudine won't sleep in too late. She's told Freda she'll be with her by lunchtime and can't leave the girls with Heino on the one day he needs to be at the hospital. Her heart sinks a little as she remembers Claudine sleeping in very late every day during the part of her gap year she spent with them in Connecticut.

Still, she's hardly sprightly and ready to go herself this morning, needs this time alone to let her hangover subside. Stupid to drink an entire bottle of wine; she's always been useless with alcohol.

She forces down coffee then squeezes a full two-pints from Freda's oranges, the whirring of the machine almost intolerable, her fingers sticky with their juice. And she really does feel quite peaky now, one lick of her fingers and something sour starts to swell in her mouth. She hasn't had enough sleep – she couldn't sleep, tormented by the calls she'd made, and the fear that she had slurred her words on Julian's machine.

But now her mouth really is filling. Thank goodness there's no one up to see her as she flees from the room with a tea towel to her face. She makes it to the bathroom, manages to sweep aside Claudine's flannel and toothbrush before letting go. Last night's wine comes up as pure acid, burns her throat. She dares herself to raise her throbbing head to the mirror; her pallid skin is filmed with sweat, consumptive. The shadows around her eyes draw her back and she groans with her hands to her face.

That night.

It was the shock of waking to find him there and his sour sick smell that sent her fleeing for the bathroom. Julian's breathing was amplified behind her, so loud it sounded more like a creature than a man. He slid shut the door while she gripped the basin – this basin, as she gripped it now – and retched so violently she thought the baby might come up her throat. Julian stood, radiating fever, pulling at his hair. The nightdress she was wearing was one of Ellie's, fine linen worn quite thin. She put her hands to her belly and his eyes followed them, widening in disbelief. 'You're pregnant.' She nodded, and after that the words came easily, like water through a dam.

'Sshhhh, shut up . . .' he said. The burning heat of his sickness was repelling her as well as his hands, which he held as though to halt falling masonry, saying: 'Please. Don't come closer. Flu. Mira. Don't wake Mira.' He was grappling with the door in his haste to get away from what she was telling him, half-falling, half-flying down the stairs.

Now she ransacks Heino's cupboard for Alka-Seltzer, sets up the percolator for more coffee. Flat Coca-Cola, isn't that supposed to be the best thing for a hangover? She wonders what sort of person keeps an open can at the ready. By the time Heino joins her she's downed a couple of Nurofen and gulped down a pint of tepid water. Her headache is starting to recede though her eyelids remain heavy. It was four in the morning by the time she got hold of Karl in Connecticut. They'd spoken and sighed and conducted long silences for over an hour. The things they said hadn't made for sweet dreams and she wonders who will apologise first. She fetches orange juice for Heino, puts bread in the toaster. Heino is smartly dressed as always, but this morning he is wearing his polished leather shoes rather than slip-ons and his cufflinks are the gold ovals with the hospital crest. He arrives carrying sheafs of papers in blue files.

Brandishing last night's empty Sauvignon bottle she confesses, 'I don't know what came over me but it appears I've drunk the whole lot. It was in the fridge, I hope it wasn't something precious.'

Heino takes the bottle from her, adjusts his glasses and reads the label. 'One of Claudine's, I think,' he says and returns it to her, his eyebrow raised. 'That's not like you, my dear.'

She slumps beside him at the table, they hold hands and she rests her forehead to his knuckles. 'Come, come,' he says. 'Tell me what's wrong. Oh, excuse me, silly old fool, of course. I'm sorry. It's one of the hardest things to lose a parent . . .'

'Oh no, Heino. I don't think it's him. I'm not upset. I mean, I'd rather he wasn't dead . . . I keep feeling a bit guilty to be honest.' She rests her head again, likes the smell of his skin and soap.

He pats her shoulder with his free hand. 'I'm sure I've bored you many times and so you know that after I came to England I never saw my father or grandparents again, all very sad. I got on with my life here, grew up, went to medical school. It wasn't until after the war that we got official confirmation about what had happened to them, but I didn't throw myself on the floor weeping,' he says. 'All my memories of Hamburg were happy ones and yet I was more upset by the death of our neighbour's dog a week or so before. I felt wicked, but that dog was my main companion. He and I went for long walks over the Heath every evening and I told him all my troubles. I used to sit high on a ridge with him beside me, looking across to Cherry Tree Woods, and when he was run over I wept many tears. He was a dear old thing, with big paws and an intelligent look on his face. I've thought about that since, especially since Ellie died. Now I think that grief is more connected to the loss of tangible things, the day-to-day doings, not simply memories.'

She forces herself to chew some dry toast. Swallows painfully.

Heino gives her a sad smile. 'You ran away from home very young, am I right? Sixteen?'

She nods. 'Well, it wasn't exactly running away. More like being pushed,' she says. 'But you're right. Perhaps grief is only as big as the hole it needs to fill and my dad didn't really figure in my life once I'd got away.' The toast goes down like gravel, her throat still raw from earlier. Heino shakes his head while she fiddles with her necklace, running the gold sun back and forth along its fine chain.

'What a shame for him. Missing out on a daughter like you,' he says. 'And, as I always tell you, how sad that my Ellie never got to meet you,' and Julia has to stop fiddling to blot her eyes with her napkin.

He's delighted by the idea that the juice they are drinking comes from the fruit of trees that she grafted and grew. He dabs his mouth with his napkin and proclaims it sweet and delicious, points to her glass. 'And you need the vitamin C this morning yourself, so drink up.'

Julia starts to feel more optimistic, a day working with Freda is just the medicine she needs. 'What time are you due at Great Ormond Street?' she asks. 'If Claudine's up I could leave the girls and walk over there with you.'

'I'd love you to accompany me there, my dear,' he says and muses for a moment, looking into his cup, before continuing. 'And I was wondering if we should leave half an hour early and take Mira. Do you think she'd be interested? I know some of those nurses would love to see her looking so fit and healthy.'

Julia takes another bite of toast, stalls while she chews. 'Oh, I don't know, Heino . . .'

'Some children find it a very reassuring thing to do, I mean, not that I'm a psychiatrist . . .' He searches her face then changes the subject. 'There are some terribly difficult questions in here,' he says and taps with a finger at his files. 'Today I find I am dreading the Ethics Committee. Sometimes it's too much like playing God. It is worse every year: these very sick babies that can be kept alive younger and younger, while the funding doesn't rise to keep pace with medical advancements and technology. That's what it comes down to. All these questions of life, and what can and should be done to prolong it, need to be asked with only thoughts of the child, not pounds and pence. The child first, always.'

Heino, like Karl, has soft brown eyes with bronze flecks around the pupils that flash when they get fired up, the same thick expressive brows, even in old age. 'So, shall we show off Mira to the nurses or not?'

Before she gets a chance to reply there's a thundering of feet on the stairs. 'Here they come.' Ruth screams as she flies into the room: 'Don't push me, Meeee-rah!'

The girls cheer when she tells them they'll be spending the day with Claudine and run to wake her. Heino is happy for her to keep using his car and, though it's mawkish, she finds herself once again at Burnt Oak on her way out to Freda's. When she gets to her old street she cranes her head to the top windows. She sees the curtains twitch, the pale moon of a face, then nothing.

Perhaps they were stuck there for ever in those sad December days. Julian, gaunt with loss, his library books piled up beside him, folded into their only comfortable chair. She, curled around a hot-water bottle in the bed, drifting and dreaming, barely able to admit to herself, let alone him, that what she felt for the poor lost baby was closer to guilt than grief. She bled quietly. 'Let's try again as soon as possible,' he said, though he was still only twenty-one. He wrapped her in the embroidered quilt and the weight of his dreams seemed to press down on her.

Despite the detour she arrives at Freda's early. 'My God, you look gloomy.' Freda tups her under the chin, draws up a stool and sits beside her. 'What's up?'

'Oh, you know, Mira . . .'

'Still grumpy?'

'And Karl not being here so that we can work out what to do,' Julia says. 'He's got this paper to prepare for the Administration by Friday, so it's no use trying to talk to him about anything else. And I've got a hangover. Have you got any painkillers?'

Freda motions for her to stay where she is, fetches some paracetamol and pops a couple from the foil for her.

'And one or two things she's been saying. The other night, I think Ruthie got wind of the fact I was married before . . .'

'Oh yes, I always forget him,' Freda says. 'The guy who taught you everything you know about, ahem, hydroponic gardening; it's why I offered you the job in the first place.' Freda winks and mimes rolling a joint, asks: 'What was his name? You so rarely mention him. Chris, was it?'

Julia visibly shudders: 'Yes, Chris. Best forgotten.'

'I'm sorry, I interrupted you,' Freda says.

'To be honest, Freda, just thinking about him makes me feel sick. But Mira was asking me where I lived when I left home and I just said 'With Chris'. And Ruthie is such a nosy little thing she pushed me for details. She wanted to know if he was a nice man and I had to admit that he wasn't. Mira was crawling around behind the sofa looking for her shoes, pretending not to listen, but muttered something I couldn't quite catch. She wouldn't repeat whatever it was, but I thought I heard the word

230

"Dadoo".' She gives Freda a rueful smile as she continues: 'Which was her name for Julian. Maybe I imagined it.'

'Come on,' Julia gives herself a shake, jumps down from the stool. 'Let's get on. I've had a good look through the architect's drawings and I've had some ideas. Can we make a list of the big trees, the fruiting varieties that you think would do well there?'

Freda rubs her hands together. 'That's more like it,' she says and, grabbing her notebook, scribbles across a page with a pen to get it working.

Julia blurts it on their way out to the greenhouses, the thing she's been longing to confess. 'I rang him last night.'

'Who?'

'Julian.'

'You did?'

'It was his voice on the machine at Firdaws, so I guess he's still there. You know we've not spoken since, not since . . .'

Freda lays a hand on her shoulder, gives it a rub. 'These are some knots you've got here,' she says. 'I often think about how awful it must have been for poor Julian that night . . . I mean, for all of you, him just walking in like that.' They arrive at the glasshouse and she props the notebook on a ledge and gives Julia's crunchy muscles the full benefit of her plantswoman's thumbs.

'As I'm sure you remember, it wasn't supposed to happen like that. Karl had come back on the red eye and I was dead on my feet. Mira was only just out of hospital. Karl came down from his shower in a bathrobe, we drank hot chocolate and took turns reading stories to her. We were tucked up on the bed. Somehow we all ended up falling asleep.' Even now she feels the need to explain herself. 'The stress of the hospital, and, you know, tired all the time from being pregnant with Ruth. We were going to tell him that day. Karl had flown in to talk to him: I mean, it was going to be gory. Just not like that. I can't bear to think how long he was standing there at the foot of the bed looking at us.'

Freda takes her hands from Julia's shoulders, sticks out her lower lip. 'No, finding out like that, poor man. And he was such a good soul.'

Julia's eyes well. 'Oh Freda, don't. Remember he was shagging that Katie.'

Freda resumes kneading her shoulders. 'Was he really?' she says. 'I mean, are you really sure about that?'

Julia sighs, says: 'Oh Freda, it's what I thought at the time.'

Freda rolls her own shoulders, checking for stiff muscles. Her face remains doubtful.

Julia places a hand over her heart. 'Sometimes I think about Firdaws and wonder if we could've been happy there. If things had been different. It was such a beautiful place. You never came, did you?'

Freda shakes her head: 'We had to keep putting my visit off.'

'Oh, yes, I remember now,' Julia says. 'Mira was ill both times. Shame, I wish you'd seen it. I'm not sure I ever truly appreciated it, how peaceful it was, no people or cars, nothing but birdsong and trees. I remember being led around by Julian, his love was infectious, every nook, every tree had a story from his childhood. The garden sort of drifted into the fields, seedy grass and wild-flowers, apple trees, and around the house every sort of climber covered the bricks like damask. At night the clearest skies: I've never seen so many shooting stars nor made so many wishes.'

Freda smiles at her to go on.

'When he took me there, I was quite overwhelmed. For the first time I understood why he wanted to sink everything we had to buy it back. You know, he never knew his father, and Firdaws connected him with all that. It was all beams and nooks and window seats, the walls were so thick and ancient that the doorways sort of bulged and you felt hugged each time you entered a room.'

'It was a gamble,' Freda says. 'With all your futures.'

'But it might have worked. There was a primary school in the village for Mira, so no fees, and she loved having a dog and running about. Maybe I would've become less stubborn about continuing with you and Arbour.' Julia gives Freda a rueful shrug. 'There was an old granary in the grounds and he showed me the place up against its wall that he'd thought of for my glasshouse. It couldn't have been a more perfect spot, with full sun and this lovely old granary for potting up. He'd done his research.

'We hadn't been there long before his mother – remember fearsome Jenna? – arrived with an entire team and a removal van full of furniture. It was everything from before, rugs, curtains, furniture, pictures, everything. Julian was crazy-happy to see it all again. "You sure this is OK?" he kept asking me and I told myself it would be piggish to object as they started unloading stuff, unfurling carpets, humping huge chintz-covered sofas through the door. His mother was re-creating their home, complete with dog-bitten carpets and rags. Our few bits and pieces from Cromwell Gardens were swamped. The men were uncomplaining, young, Australian. Jenna directed everything into its rightful place.'

'I bet she did,' says Freda.

'I started to feel a bit wobbly and lost when Julian took me to the attic room he'd earmarked as my workroom. He showed me where my drawing board would go, my pinboards, he had it all worked out. And while he was over by the bed clearing up a cluster of dead flies, Jenna popped her head around the door. "Julian's right," she whispered to me. "This is the perfect place to work. I can vouch for it." She pointed to the louvre window. "The light is good. I did all my drawing here . . ." And as she left she let slip that the granary he wanted for my potting shed had been her ceramics workshop, her kiln was still there . . .' Julia tails off as Freda opens her notebook and starts to catalogue the trees.

'Yes. You were always pretty wrung out after Jenna had been to stay,' Freda says. 'It's strange to think of the lives we could've led. I often wonder what would've happened if I hadn't left my husbands.'

'Oh, Freda. Do you really?'

'Yes. All my mother-in-laws despised me. I imagine myself in all sorts of depressing situations, going mouldy in that great big house in Dublin, or drinking myself into the grave with Monty, or, worst of all, having to bring up the boys with Eddie. Ugh. No. I much prefer things the way they are. Just me and the cat and whoever rocks up.'

Julia laughs. 'I think I'm prone to imagining my alternative futures every time Karl pisses me off.'

'Not surprising if you're feeling let down. He should be here, it would be the normal thing to do.'

'Yeah, well he's not normal, is he.' Julia chews her lip for a moment, repents. 'Arghh, Freda. If I'm honest, I think I'm having a jealousy attack.'

Freda turns to her, startled. 'You? What do you mean?'

'He's working with this woman, she's very sexy, Dutch, single . . . Yesterday Karl wasn't at the lab and I rang back and found out that she wasn't there either.' Julia lets out a wail of self-disgust before continuing. 'Karl thinks I've gone mad questioning his movements; he's terribly angry. I never used to be like this. Not before Julian. You know, before all that business with Katie, I was so trusting. I mean, I wasn't thrilled that she was living in the village but, you know, I didn't really think he would. And then, with Mira in hospital, that just made it all so much worse . . .'

She's been thinking so fondly of Julian, but she's talked herself right out of all that now. She forces herself to remember the moment she clicked about Katie, the twist of her heart when she did. It was well past three in the morning when he finally arrived at PICU stinking of her, that bluebell perfume she always wore. As she buried her face in his jacket Julia had told herself she was imagining it, was too swamped by need to consider it, a need which had grown more overwhelming with each frantic call she'd made to him, Mira looking as lifeless as a wax doll wired up to the machines, her liver failing and no one quite saying, 'Yes, yes, of course she'll live.' He was the only person who could hold her. There was no one else.

There were signs along the railings outside the hospital asking people not to smoke. They were both in shock, standing close. He'd been drinking whisky, never a good idea. He slid his tongue along the cigarette paper, his hand shaking, his rolly clumsy with tobacco falling out the end. He had taken a matchbook from his pocket, bent the cardboard match back in that way he did so it was still attached to the book. His top lip curled where it gripped the cigarette. The book of matches was upside down and she was trying to make out the name embossed in tacky gold letters. Julian's eyes followed her gaze. They both knew where Katie was staying. She'd swanked about it in the hospital playroom, saying she was going to 'hurt Adrian in the wallet'. Julian looked surprised by the matchbook in his own hand. She had been about to ask him where he'd been all night, but then he struck the match and there was no need.

Twenty-four

Julia sketches out the first draft for the atrium on tracing paper taped over the architect's drawing. She draws circles where conical holes can be sunk along meandering paths. It answers the brief perfectly – *a surprising green space within a geometrically perfect building* – and as she and Freda work side by side their excitement mounts. 'I think we're going to win this,' Freda says as she leans across to mark the junction spots of the underground watering system. 'So you think Julian was with Katie when you were at the hospital?' she asks.

Julia frowns to herself: 'If I was being kind I'd say he didn't stand a chance. Did I ever tell you about the letter she sent me, when Julian and I were first together? She was incredibly manipulative, you know.'

'What sort of letter?'

'As it happens, an incredibly effective one,' Julia says.

'So, go on . . .'

'I didn't get a whole lot of post at Mrs Briggs's – officially I didn't live there – so any envelope was a surprise and at first I thought it was something pleasant. There it was, the sole occupant of Julian's pigeonhole in the hall, a blue envelope addressed to me, attractive writing quite large, all hooks and flourishes.

'I started opening it but other tenants were moving about in one of the rooms off the hall, someone shouting for a loo roll from the bathroom upstairs. I wasn't dressed apart from Julian's dressing gown with one of his ties as a belt. I didn't have to go in to work that day, but I had to be careful not to be caught there too often by Julian's landlady. Mrs Briggs was a terrifying old toad. God, it was grim.

'The kettle was boiling as I bolted back up the stairs to Julian's room, the letter concealed in the folds of his dressing gown. He had his back to me fiddling around with the coffee pot, blending three different beans: for a cash-strapped student he was particular about things like that. I sat on the bed, unfolded three sheets of thick blue paper: her signature was at the bottom of the final page, no wishes or regards.

'She began by stating that she probably wasn't the first spurned girlfriend who wanted to set the record straight with her usurper.'

'Usurper?' says Freda.

'Oh, I don't know, perhaps it was "new lover", I can't remember now,' Julia says. 'She claimed she was writing not out of spite but out of genuine concern for Julian, who she called 'Jude' throughout. She said it was unlikely her letter would ever reach the postbox. I wish it hadn't.

'She went on about my great age: honestly, anyone would've thought I was an old crone who'd bewitched the poor boy. And to think I wasn't even thirty. By the second page she even invoked his mother, claiming that Jenna "who I happen to love very much" was heartbroken. "I want you to be aware of what you're destroying," she wrote. She described how they met on the first day of comp, how they'd grown from children who raced each other home on their bikes to adults and in great vivid detail of the balmy night that adulthood "came softly" upon them. At sunset in a bluebell wood, apparently. According to Katie, they marked the date every year by visiting the same grassy mound, where she lay in her garlands and he lit a fire. She was clever, her words chosen so carefully. Like Julian, she was studying English, harboured dreams of becoming a writer. She covered each sheet on both sides with that deceptively pretty script of hers, not a single crossing-out or clumsy phrase. She must've worked hard getting it right, writing it out many times before this final version.

'Clever Katie. I only read the letter once before setting fire to it but that image of them lying entwined and naked in the blue-bell woods never really left me. One read and it was spliced in, ready to thrive and blossom alongside Julian's relationship with me. Which is what I'm sure she intended.'

'Bitch,' says Freda.

'Yes,' says Julia. 'Bitch.'

'When Julian joined me on the bed her letter was already cinders in the ashtray. He pulled me close, asked me what she'd written. I couldn't tell him. His concern was sweet. I was feeling so squalid: old and pregnant and unemployed. No bluebell woods for me and him as we headed on a sea of disapproval to that grimy little room in Burnt Oak. I was on the run. Chris was handy with his fists.'

Freda's hands rise to her face.

'Oh, I never told you?' Julia says. 'Oh well, let's not talk about it now. Hadn't we better get on?'

She is a little out of breath. Freda rests a hand on her shoulder. 'Julia, you were married to this Chris for what, twelve, thirteen years and from all the time we've been friends I have only ever known two things about him. One: he had a hawk and two: he grew dope in his attic.'

Julia chews her lip, picks up a pencil. 'The hawk was the best thing about him but even that I grew to hate.'

Freda proposes a break before Julia gets stuck into her favourite part of any job: the artist's impressions. She finds it totally absorbing to commit what she sees in her mind's eye to the page, meditative. It was always a surprise to Julia when people couldn't draw: it was one of those things she'd grown up believing anyone could do. In the earlier part of her marriage to Chris she'd completed a foundation year in art. But then the nights were drawing in, and suddenly Chris had to work away; there was the new hawk to train and that ate eight hours a day. It was easier for her not to return to college after summer.

She sees him again, that husband of hers, shouting instructions, his streaky hair lifting in the wind, not one colour or another, a bit like the hawk's feathers. The spittle that always caught in the cracked corner of his mouth. The weight of the hawk on her arm making it impossible to run after him, the back of his van bouncing away, a temper tantrum because she hadn't managed to get it to fly to her glove, so they'd had to pull it back from the trees by the creance attached to its leg. He abandoned her there with the hawk in a windy field miles from home. She can never be too far from him, even now.

Freda rootles through a cupboard to find the Caran d'Ache pencils while Julia puts the kettle on. She thinks briefly, reluctantly, of the bony cavity at the junction of Chris's ribcage, how they used it as somewhere to flick the ash from their spliffs, sunk into piles of pillows in the bedroom at Wychwood, so sated and weak it was impossible to get up and find the ashtray. She cringes now to think of her compliance. He'd got her young; he knew what he could get away with. He bought her motorbike leathers and a silver helmet that matched his and took the corners so fast that their knees skimmed the ground. He made jesses of fine calf which he used to tie her to his bed, he taught her to cook rabbit stew, to skin and to gut. She made cakes and for a while was quite plump. He manned her as he would a hawk, building up trust while he touched her, withholding then rewarding only when she bent to his will. She got pregnant and had an abortion. The dope helped the years to pass while she tried to convince herself of the good in him: his amber eyes, his muscular arms, most of the records he bought. His talent for flipping beer mats had struck her as a mighty thing.

Freda passes her the tin of biscuits, says: 'How do you stay so thin?'

Julia shrugs, takes a couple of Hobnobs, waves one at Freda before dunking it: 'These were Julian's favourites, I once watched him eat a whole packet in one sitting.'

Freda is looking for snacks; she turns around with a pot of jam in her hand and grins at her. 'Mentionitis!'

'Actually, I was still thinking about horrible Chris, but . . .' She pauses. 'Yes, Julian *is* on my mind. I really must find a way to speak to him. I thought Karl would be here to help steer us through this Mira problem, but no.' She stops for another moment and fiddles with her necklace. 'I mean, we didn't kid ourselves that coming back here might not stir things up for Mira. I can't tell you how much I resent him staying behind.'

Freda gives up on her idea of a Ryvita thinly spread with diabetic jam and reaches for the Hobnobs. 'Have you and Karl ever thought you should just explain it to her?' she asks. 'Let her sort out what she thinks?'

Julia spins the gold sun on its chain. 'Just after we arrived in Connecticut we consulted a child psychiatrist. It did seem odd that she never ever mentioned Julian. The way she took so readily to Karl. I mean I'd be lying if I didn't admit that it was also a relief, especially with Ruthie on the way.'

'What was the advice?'

'Oh, you know, to answer any questions she had as honestly as we could.'

'But did you tell the shrink that Julian was refusing all contact?'

'I didn't imagine that would go on for ever. I don't think any of us expected him to disappear,' Julia says. 'Anyway, the gist of the psychospiel was that any information should be fragmentary, not a big sit-down-and-listen-to-us thing, and that it should all be Mira-led, that she might easily start to ask questions later. He felt that what she'd been through at the hospital and the new baby was quite enough for her to cope with, and his advice was that we should wait until she asked.'

She picks up a pencil and starts shading in shadows at the bases of trees, around the feet of a small cluster of people she's drawn drinking coffee beneath the canopy of leaves. 'She did ask for him for a while, and then she stopped,' she says.

But what if she had gone on asking? It seemed unthinkable that Julian would be so cruel. In Lamb's Conduit Street, Karl had been trying his phone constantly but only got the machine every time. When the tape was finally full he borrowed Heino's car and drove to Firdaws. He got no answer when he knocked on the door and all the curtains were drawn, though he swore he could hear the dog.

Julia moved out of Ellie's room. She and Karl were both sleeping on the top floor. Chastely. She slept, or rather tried to sleep, with Mira beneath the primrose quilt of the guest room and Karl next door in his boyhood bed, his Airfix planes circling. For several days she couldn't bear for Karl to touch her; the only place she found any peace was the bath. She thought the pain might never recede the night Mira sobbed and asked for her Dadoo. She lay in the dark while tears large as pearls rolled into her ears.

It was two days before she got hold of Jenna, who at last called her back but coldly refused to say what was happening with Julian, only that he wanted her gone from Firdaws: 'Every last trace, do you hear me? You and the child.' From her tone you'd have thought she was talking about an infestation of rats. Julia could imagine her having the place exorcised afterwards, burning sage in the corners.

It winded her most of all to hear Mira reduced to 'the child'. It was a struggle to know what to say. 'But Jenna, wouldn't you like to see Mira? You will always be her . . .' But Jenna cut her off before she could say the word 'grandmother'. 'My heart can't take this, Julia. So, no, thank you,' she said. 'Now, how soon can you get to Firdaws?'

They hired a van and her brother, Howie, agreed to drive her and do the hulking. While she and Howie set off for Firdaws, Karl stayed at Lamb's Conduit Street with Heino and Mira, trying every number he could think of for Julian, eventually reaching Michael at his office, who informed him that Julian was in hospital receiving treatment for suspected meningitis, but, with great civility, refused to tell him where.

Julia was too exhausted to think about any of it, slept the sleep of an invalid in the van. Howie drove in silence, only shaking her hours later when he needed to check the directions from the crossroads at Horton Station.

To her awakening eyes it was no less miraculous than the moment *The Wizard of Oz* turns Technicolor. The trees had been quite bare when she was last in the village and the fields still muddy. But now, beneath a cloudless sky, high grassy banks were bursting with leaf and flower. The tarmac flared with bright sunlight between spreading branches that made a green tunnel of the road. Down the hill and first left. Flowers flashed by in the hedgerows: pink campion, buttercups, frothing Queen Anne's Lace and dog roses. As they cleared the humpback bridge, the long bend of the river came into view, spreading itself like mercury through the valley.

Firdaws stood alone in a sea of wildflowers. The roses were in full bloom; 'New Dawn' rambled across the bricks, around the windows and the front door, dropping petals of tender palest pink, one or two splashed darker pink by the rain. The brickwork was a mellow ground for the brocade of leaves, the roses

– some blown almost to white – and twining clematis that hung purple stars from the lintels. Everything was still slightly steaming and glistening from that morning's drenching. Beyond the house the fields rolled away, rippling green and rich, gleaming with buttercups. It was quite breathtaking to see it in the sunshine, to smell the petrichor of recent rain and warm dust. She wound down her window as soon as they pulled up, had forgotten how sweet air could taste. The birdsong was almost deafening as she stepped from the van, her brother already unloading the empty packing cases. The smell of the wet warm earth made her heart ache, camomile and cornflowers brushed the backs of her legs. Swallows and house martins darted across the sky, she could hear the squeak of nestlings from the eaves. She looked at the windows, at the old frames in their chipping layers of forget-me-not-blue paint. A shower of petals fell on to Mira's toy pram. Julia stopped at the door and folded back the knitted blankets to check they weren't damp. Wee-Ro-Ro was tucked up inside. She imagined Julian wheeling the little pram back out here, washing the pearly knitted blankets at the sink, the care he'd have taken to make it seem to Mira that she had never been away. It was unbearable, all of it.

She looked up from the pram when she heard the door open. Katie emerged from the house, shrieking her name as though they were old friends. She was wearing a white sundress and her ponytail appeared extra blonde and swingy as Julia attempted to sweep past her to get inside. Katie tried to follow her. 'I've only come to change the sheets, is that OK?'

'Just leave me alone,' Julia said, attempting to hold back her tears.

Packing away the photographs was the worst of it. Julia wouldn't have had the heart to take them at all, but Jenna had been quite specific. Howie was outside working up a sweat strapping Julia's few bits of furniture to the roof, the van already full of boxes. Mira's high chair toppled above the pea-shoot-green chairs and a small chest of drawers from Cromwell Gardens that she'd painted with gold leaf. As it turned out, there wasn't much that was hers.

She grew numb with unhappiness as she stood in Julian's den going through all the photos. Only the pictures from the few months after Mira's birth were arranged in an album, everything else remained in polythene packets that had been laughed over, sighed over, and put away until the day when one of them would find a spare moment. They never had. They never would. The photos were stacked in two bulging shoe-boxes, in rough date order. The empty albums waited patiently beside them, a set of half a dozen, handsome and leather-bound, Michael's present to them at Mira's birth. Julia took just the one, quickly turning the pages. Mira's arrival, too heartbreaking to see her in Julian's arms like that; various family groupings around the bed; Mira's first smile; Mira playing peek-a-boo with her big nappy in the air and legs as bandy as sausages; sitting propped and importantly chinned between cushions at Cromwell Gardens or twirling in her baby bouncer, her brow creased with concentration. Julia gathered them all, checked drawers and cupboards for strays and found a few from when they owned a Polaroid. She felt the greatest twinge as she removed the framed pictures of Mira from his desk and from his side of the bed.

She didn't have long to dwell. As she took a last look around she was interrupted by voices. Through a gap in the curtains she saw Howie following Katie across the grass. Katie's white dress swung as she walked. She saw her come to an awkward stop at the open front door, the folds of white muslin settling around her legs.

Again Katie tried to waylay her: 'I can't believe you're doing this.' Julia swept past her to the van with Howie rushing to take the boxes from her. As they drove away, Katie stood at the front of the house, hands on her hips, and Julia dwelt on the five albums she'd left behind, their creamy blank pages.

You'd think it would be hard to remove every trace of yourself from a life, but really, it isn't.

Twenty-five

Claudine has waited up for her though it's past midnight when she gets back from Freda's. Claudine is wearing a yellow dress, a vintage one, with a daisy-chain belt. Her spiky hair is dip-dyed white at the tips, she looks like a little porcupine as she stretches and yawns. Her face, bare of its usual dark eye make-up, is as sweet as a principal boy's. There's nothing to dislike about Claudine, except maybe the large silver tongue stud that makes her lisp.

'We've had a fantastic day,' Claudine says. 'But if they tell you about it, make sure you know it was my fault we almost got chucked out of the V&A.'

Julia is pouring milk into a pan. 'What? Why? And do you want hot chocolate? I'm making some for myself.'

'Yes, please,' says Claudine. 'Oh, the security man was overreacting. There was an extremely tempting vacant plinth on the main staircase. It was sort of spotlit, you know? Light falling in a beam from the window. And I had my new camera.'

'Oh, Claud, you didn't?'

Claudine giggles. 'The girls take direction well. We did *The Kiss* and *Romulus and Remus* before he came flying up the steps. I thought they would be upset at being told off, but not a bit of it. We spent the rest of our time pretending to be fugitives from justice.'

'I hate to say it, but you're a very bad influence,' Julia pretends to admonish as Claudine continues: 'I've got the photographs downstairs and they're cracking. We must find a way to email them to Karl. Oh, by the way, he's been calling. I told him to try you at Freda's.'

Julia joins Claudine at the table, blowing on her cup. 'My stupid phone won't work in the UK and I haven't found a minute to do anything about it,' she says. She's sure the phone hadn't rung once at Freda's. Well, let him stew for a while longer. She decides not to call back.

'Any other calls for me here?' she asks, allowing herself to feel hopeful. Claudine shakes her head and Julia tries not to look crestfallen. She turns to the clock and checks the time. Too late now. She'll have to wait until breakfast to try Firdaws again. She gulps down the remains of her hot chocolate.

Upstairs the girls are sleeping peacefully, Karl's Airfix fleet watching over them. Julia bends to kiss Ruth's cheek, she smells of sweets and warm milk. She leans across to sweep the hair from Mira's face. Mira makes a snuffling noise and turns away. Ruthie smiles in her sleep. Julia suffers a rush of tenderness gazing at her younger daughter. She is overcome with yearning as she bends once more to Ruth, rests her hand on her brow, whispers: 'I love you.'

Julia had been crazy with anxiety and tiredness, truly out of her mind, the night Ruth was conceived – conceived in this very bed, as it happened. Julia had hardly slept at all for the first two nights of Mira's descent into sedation and Intensive Care. Julian was beside her, both of them sleeping fitfully, slumped into chairs beside Mira's bed. She needed him too much, was too full of fear for Mira to contemplate what was happening between him and Katie. On the third night the nurses insisted she go back to

Lamb's Conduit Street for a good night's sleep and she found herself glad to leave him behind. She wasn't expecting to see Karl's coat hanging in the hall when she got there, had no idea that Heino had called him in Connecticut to alert him to Mira's decline. Julia sniffed Karl's collar to confirm, though she already knew it was his. She stood there for a while with the tock of the grandfather clock and pressed the fabric to her face, the smell of him almost painful.

She thinks of Karl that night, his look of surprise when she came naked across the room, the draught from the door making his model planes spin. Afterwards they stared up at the bobbing planes, shaking their heads in disbelief, the frenzy absolute.

She feels the familiar deep ache just thinking about him now. Sometimes her mood seems to have little to do with her desire for Karl and on the nights he's made her furious she wonders if it is, as he once claimed, just an anatomical quirk: 'Simply a perfectly angled meeting of nerve endings, of Gräfenberg spot and penile raphe,' he said. Whatever it was, they were always left sweat-soaked and reeling.

Twenty-six

Batteries! Julia sprints to the corner shop leaving the girls in the kitchen in their vests and pants eating croissants. Mira is furious, indignant that anyone would expect her to travel the five hours to Vernow in a car without her Walkman and the stories she can recite by heart.

They're already running late, Julia can hear the build-up of traffic as she crosses back to the flat, the air thickening with fumes. She must remember to pack their new dresses still hanging in the wardrobe. The girls' outfits are perfectly plain black linen, high to the neck and full at the skirt with a penitent placket of buttons up the back. In the chi-chi shop where she chose them, shortly after hearing her father had died, she snorted with delight to think of her girls looking so Amish. The dresses were expensive and they'd never be worn again. She wonders if Claudine might lend her the camera but thinks it's probably bad taste to take photographs at a funeral. She can hear her mother going on about it already.

A pity. She pictures her daughters at the graveside, their lovely heart-shaped faces pale and serious above the black linen, Ruth's hair escaping from her thick braids, Mira's fine skin reflecting a single white Madonna lily she has clutched to her chest . . .

It's still too early for the flower shop, but she's shaken from this reverie by the rattling ching of its door. For a moment she thinks the blonde florist must have read her mind and be offering her lilies. 'I've something for you,' she says.

'Oh?'

'Hang on there a minute,' she says. 'You're Julia, right? Staying with Heino, right?' Julia nods and waits at the door while she turns and shouts into the back of the shop.

'There's a box been dropped off round the back for you. Someone's shoved it in the yard with one of our deliveries from Holland. It's quite heavy; if you wait there I'll get Ken to bring it up to you.'

Ken has the box. It is old cardboard, bulging between criss-crosses of packing tape, the tape wound round so many times it's impossible to tell what it might once have contained. A microwave oven or possibly a television, it's that sort of size. She turns and stops Ken halfway up the stairs, impatient to see the writing on the label. She braces herself and holds out her arms to take it from him. 'Honestly, Ken, I can manage.' He keeps hold of the box and though it's dark on the stairs she sees the familiar spaced block capitals and her heart starts to kick like a rabbit.

'You open up, love, just tell me where to dump it.'

Somehow she gets the door unlocked and directs Ken to leave the box in the hall. The grandfather clock makes her jump as it dings the hour. Her nails make little impression on the densely woven packing tape. Damn, they're seriously late setting off – and now *this*.

In the kitchen she kisses Heino good morning and flings the flimsy bag with the batteries at Mira, begs the girls to hurry up and finish.

Claudine holds out her hands for the Walkman: 'Here, Mira,' she says. 'Let me sort that out for you.' Heino proffers a cup of

250

coffee and she takes it from him before his hand starts to shake too badly.

She's still got things to pack and the hell of Ruth's knotted hair. Mira's kicking up the usual fuss about her vitamins, Heino wants to make sure she has his AA membership details. She bats them off and rummages through the drawer for the kitchen scissors, knows she has no option but to leave them all to it until she's seen what's inside the box.

It takes a few moments, alone with it in the dim light of the hall. The cardboard is deteriorating, spattered in places with pigeon guano – he'd clearly had it knocking around for a while. Her old jumper comes out first, half-eaten with mould, more mottled grey than lavender. It releases a cloud of dust when she shakes it. There are books: lots of musty paperbacks and the Andy Goldsworthy art books he'd bought her, with his inscriptions roughly ripped out, leaving only ragged margins. A broken radio spills leaking batteries, some old sketchbooks she'd somehow forgotten are stained on every page. She picks through it all, heart sinking, the dust making her cough, searching for a note among the tangles of filthy-looking clothing, but comes out with nothing more than the sorts of odds and ends you might find under a bed: single socks, dried-up old face cream in a lidless pot, an ancient gardening glove grown hard and calloused as a hand, bits of broken pottery, a tampon that has swelled and burst its wrapper, some crushed silk irises that he'd once bought for her hair, the brass padlock she'd given him in Paris. There was nothing more; no note, no further explanation. That was that.

She gathers the girls and their things and drives in hot silence, gulping back tears and furious with herself for allowing a box of rubbish to upset her so. The road is choked with cars beneath a smothering grey sky, there is nothing on the radio to distract her, only noise.

She blows a kiss at Mira in the rear-view mirror and Mira

instantly lowers her lashes in return. She starts overtaking, has to check herself for speeding, feels a surge of self-righteousness recalling the message she'd left on Julian's answerphone. She hadn't had time to work out what to say before she began speaking. How had she put it? That even after five years she still thought of him tenderly, with happy memories, and it was becoming clear that Mira did too. It really had been lovely to hear his voice on the machine and easy to summon warmth as she found the words. And his response? To send her that box of rubbish.

She brushes away a tear, checks in the mirror that the girls haven't noticed. However hard she tries she cannot summon up a picture of Julian being so hateful. Why didn't he simply bin those things? Did he collect it all up in one industrial-cleaning-style purge? It catches in her throat to think of him dangling her old jumper, transporting it to the box at arm's length with the sort of euwww on his face he reserved for clearing up one of the dog's accidents.

The girls are mercifully quiet in the back and, surprisingly, not squabbling. Mira is stupefied by her stories and Ruth has dozed off with the family-selection pack of sweets that Claudine gave them for the journey clutched to her chest.

There's altogether too much time to dwell as she takes the motorway, with only her mind's eye to fill the void between Karl's empty seat and the road. She's focused on the summer's night Karl came to Cromwell Gardens. Julian was in Paris and she hadn't been expecting him. Since the zoo, she and Karl had taken great care never to be alone together.

The first Julia had known of Paris was the morning Julian left. She came in from the glasshouse to find him running in little circles, his words erupting in great bursts, so it took a while to grasp what he was on about. His smile was infectious as he bounced from their strawberry-coloured walls, holding out his hands to her.

'Come on, Julia, come with me. A whole week in Paris at the film company's expense,' he said.

And she'd wanted to go with him, really she had, but she and Freda were in the middle of an installation and it couldn't have come at a worse moment.

She'd never seen him so excited. 'Wow, and I've always wanted to work with Claude De'Ath. Apparently he's fired the last guy and come up with my name and had them track me down.'

He wanted her to dump everything, had bodily lifted her, laughing and protesting, sat her on the kitchen counter to talk sense into her, but though the thought of being parted from him was almost unbearable, she promised instead that she'd fly out on the morning of his birthday. He punched her on the arm, called her a swot and a yuppie. She punched him back: 'Feckless loon.' There was barely time for a quickie before he ran for his flight.

The bath at Cromwell Gardens stood on four gilded feet cruel with talons and claws. It was double ended and so vast it took a whole boilerful of hot water to fill. The chipping and greening of the enamel made her think it was almost certainly original to the building. It was rare for Julia to find herself sloshing about in it without Julian, and she had to wedge her knees against its sloping sides to stop herself slipping under. She had the water as hot as she liked. When she climbed out for a flannel, an enjoyable scald was reddening her skin. She added some mandarin oil to the water, sniffed the delicious steam and added a second, bigger slug. With her hair wound and clipped to the top of her head, she pressed the nape of her neck into the roll-top and tried to relax. She thought of putting on some music, but that would mean getting out again, and decided instead to try and enjoy the absolute quiet of finding herself alone. She wondered what Julian was doing about dinner in Paris. She stretched a leg along the edge of the bath and, though she didn't normally bother, found a great luxury in soaping it and running Julian's razor along it and then its twin until they were slippery smooth.

She was having some success relaxing in the swirls and steam, when the doorbell burst in. The fourth ring came accompanied with knocking. The only thing to hand was Julian's old dressing gown so she wrapped it around herself and cursed him for its lack of a belt.

She opened the door to find Karl standing there. 'Sorry,' he said, looking quickly away, 'I thought your bell wasn't working.' His hair curled around his collar, a little longer and scruffier than the last time she'd seen him, yet he was so clean-shaven his skin shone. He was rumpled and hot from his journey, two bottles of wine gripped by their necks, one in either hand.

'I couldn't remember if you and Julian liked claret or Burgundy,' he said, showing her the labels. 'So I got both.' He leant and kissed her cheek. His lips were the only part of him that touched her because of the bottles in his hands. She gripped the dressing gown in a bunch at her chest. It had taken on a slightly doggy smell. She could feel her face sweating from the steam. Karl was looking expectantly into the hall behind her. 'He's in Paris,' she said, taking a step backwards.

Karl's eyebrows shot clear of the wire rims of his glasses. 'He isn't here?' he said. 'What, seriously? Paris?'

She nodded; if only she could get away from him, at least to get dry and put on some clothes. She twisted one foot around the other ankle, pulling Julian's dressing gown tighter.

'Why didn't he call to let me know?' Karl sighed deeply. 'Honestly, Julia, he's impossible. It's taken me ages to get here, the tubes are really fucked tonight. Oh, sorry . . .' He noticed her wet footprints, her bare feet.

'Hang on a minute,' she said, inviting him to follow her. The hallway was steamy from her bath. 'You know where everything is,' she waved in the direction of the kitchen.

She scarpered, down the hall, calling to him: 'I'll be right with you.'

In the bedroom she pulled on a jumper and jeans, sat briefly before the mirror and put cream on her face, released her hair from its band and brushed it free of knots. *That was all.*

Twenty-seven

Julia pulls into the services so that the girls can pee. Mira starts a fight with Ruth as soon as they leave the car. Her headphones have somehow become tangled around Ruth's foot – the Walkman clatters on to the tarmac and Ruth's heel briefly tramples the case. Mira runs at her, knocking her down, and Julia kneels to comfort Ruth and rub her knee, trying to simultaneously comfort the one and scold the other. She stands and places Mira's hand firmly around Ruth's. They both note the expression on her face and neither lets go.

She thinks of them the summer before, such good friends, bare-backed and tanned, holding hands without being forced to, rickrack skirts with ribbon waistbands, bright sunlight caught in their hair, Mira pointing to something in the far distance, and . . . Julia realises it's a photograph she's thinking of, one of a set on a sideboard at home, and despairs at how often and easily her memories seem to be replaced by snaps.

The girls brighten up when she buys them chips and allows them a Coke. Julian's brass padlock is weighty on top of her purse, green verdigris fills the swooping double Js of its engraving and around the lock, the key is greeny black. Mira and Ruth trawl the motorway store begging for sweets and come to a halt at the comics. Each one is gaudy, with its own free gift taped to the front, pink plastic, starbursts of glitter. The girls eye them up, grading the toys. Julia stems the urge to point out that they should choose based on what's between the covers. Instead she tells them to stay right there, and, sternly, that they are not to let go of each other's hands.

She selects the booth where she can still see through into the shop and dials home. It's eleven o'clock, six in the morning in Connecticut. She thinks of the Captain O'Shea House, the broad sweep of polished stairs to their bedroom. The light from the estuary bouncing on the ceiling, the walls chalk-white, the terrifying spectre of the unslept-in bed at its centre.

The phone rings on and on. She looks in disbelief into the receiver, its grime the colour of ear wax. She dials again, holding it an inch from her ear, but still Karl doesn't answer. She tries his mobile but that appears to be switched off. She replaces the receiver, stares at the girls sprawling before the comics on the floor of the shop, tries to push her misgivings away, but they gallop in anyway and give her a muscular kicking.

The girls are happy for a while as they leaf through their comics in the back of the car, which is just as well because the traffic slows through the valleys, the drizzle turning to dense fog. Julia fixes her concentration to the tail lights of the car in front. There really is too much time to think on this journey.

When she came back from her bedroom Karl was waiting on the plum sofa, his phone clamped to his ear. 'Bloody Julian. I can't even get hold of him now,' he said.

'I don't think there's any reception at all where he's working. Claude De'Ath's studio is underground. He's probably still at it,' she said and slipped past to draw the curtains.

The light was falling in the street. Some branches of orange blossom she had brought in from the greenhouse unfurled a deep scent into the room. She carried the vase and set it down in front of the fireplace, switched on some lamps, turned to the mantel

257

and fiddled with a little ivory monkey that belonged to Julian. She held the monkey to her lips and closed her eyes. If she wished hard enough Karl might just disappear. As she returned it to the shelf the light made its jet eyes sparkle with mischief. Karl was clearing his throat.

'Is it OK if I open this wine?' He lifted the bottle to show her. She turned and nodded, caught the twitching smile that those who didn't know him took for shyness. He'd already found the corkscrew and a couple of glasses. She was trying to remember the last time they'd met, caught herself glaring as she thought it must've been when he swaggered into town with those Dutch twins for Julian to drool over.

He noticed, said: 'Can't we try to be friends?' His thick eyebrows were set in the imploring triangles of a sad clown. She was instantly ashamed. He handed her a glass and she took a gulp, trying to shrug and smile as though not being friends was a shockingly false accusation.

He buried himself deeper into the sofa and raised his glass in her direction. When their eyes met they both had to look away.

'God, I need this.' He ran a hand inside the collar of his shirt as though loosening a noose and a sudden flare of desire made her feel guilty to be alone with him.

'What's up?' she asked. 'Why all the deep sighing?'

She was still standing and he waved an exasperated hand to the chair. 'Do you know, it'd be really nice if you sat down,' he said. 'I won't take up too much of your time because I can see you're busy, but I've had a hell of a day, and now to get here and find Julian hasn't even remembered I'm coming, well . . .'

She sat with her legs folded away from him in her peapod-green chair. Karl leant towards her, his hands planted on his knees. She was intensely aware that she must not look at him and instead fixed her eyes on the vase of orange blossom. As he spoke she started to understand the depth of his disappointment at finding

Julian not there. 'My mum is dying and there's nothing I can do,' he told her. 'Julian met her once, you know. Made a big impression. She told me tonight to send her love to my friend "that Adonis".' Karl's wire-rimmed specs were steaming up. 'I got quite a shock when I flew in yesterday. Dad didn't really prepare me for how it's progressed. All he wants is that she can remain at home. She's very weak now, and there's a nurse who stays.'

'Is there no hope?'

'No, none at all.' He was hunched against the arm of the sofa. Julia thought the normal thing to do now would be to hug him. He reached out a hand as though he was going to clasp her and pulled it back almost immediately.

'Denial is only a good option for a non-medical family; ditto crystals, healers, special herbs,' he said. 'But *we* know only too well what stage she's at. It's in the dying that you most clearly see the split between the cerebral and primitive brain. The intellect knows it must eat, but it gets harder to override the rest of the body. Soon my darling Ma will be down to crème caramel and formulations through a straw.'

He refilled Julia's glass and her fingers brushed his arm as she reached for it. She recoiled as though from static and almost spilled the wine. He took a gulp from his, and straight away another, shuffled closer so their knees almost touched.

'It's very hard for me to keep working through this, but I have to go to Brighton tomorrow, I can't see any way out of it. I've got three papers to deliver.'

'How long is the conference? Couldn't you come back to London afterwards?'

'I must be back in Rotterdam by the weekend. Oh, really, Julia, don't look so stricken. She's got a little way to go yet. It's just lovely to have time with her. My mother is very elegant, even in dying. Her skin has always been beautiful, but now she's almost luminous. She's tiny, as light as a moth. A pale and glamorous moth engulfed by her white nightdress. Just before I left tonight my dad and Jeanette, the nurse, managed to walk her from her bed to the piano in the sitting room. My dad sat on the stool to support her and she played the piano as though she was well again, preludes and nocturnes with the back of her head on his shoulder and her eyes closed, away with the morphine fairies.' Karl sat back, took off his glasses and wiped them with the hem of his shirt, blew his nose on a tissue from the box on the table. She was less tense when he wasn't so close.

He gestured around the room, taking in the bright fruit of the cornicing, the ripe-mulberry walls, the oriental vase with the fragrant blossom that made him sniff appreciately at its loveliness: 'Goodness, Julia, it feels great here. You've made this place gorgeous.'

'Oh, really?' she said, miming indignation. 'Last time you visited you said you needed sunglasses or you'd get a migraine.' She couldn't stop herself.

He laughed and set his face to bashful. 'Did I? Are you sure that was me? If it was, I was probably just jealous of you and Julian having such a lovely home when I can't seem to settle anywhere.'

Ribbing him lightened the atmosphere. 'Yeah, and you brought not one but two sexy girls with you. Now that wasn't very nice, was it?' she said, and put a chastising hand to her hip.

His smile twitched again. 'Aw, Julia. I was just showing them the sights of London.' And she had to restrain herself from leaping up to poke him in the ribs, tickle him, pinch him. She half rose from her chair but willed herself to back down and turn off the banter because who knew where it might lead.

He took a deep sniff. 'That smell of heaven . . . is it those branches?'

She nodded: 'Yes, they're from a Madagascan orange I was pruning earlier.'

'If you've got any spare I'd love to take some for my Ma.'

'Of course,' she said. 'You can take these, I'll wrap them for you.' She rose to see to it immediately, but Karl put out a hand to stop her. His fingers gripped her arm only briefly, but she felt them long after he let go. 'Are you throwing me out so soon? Can't we get a takeaway or something? Or have you already eaten?'

She assembled a tray in the kitchen while he pulled the cork from the second bottle of wine. Her hands shook as she sliced bright rings from the salami. He worked out the music, put on Neil Young and shouted through to see if that was OK with her. She revived a French stick by brushing it with milk and putting it in a warm oven. She tipped cornichons into a bowl, the Camembert oozed when she released its waxy wrappings.

Karl tore the baguette and handed her a piece. She concentrated on the food but it became difficult to swallow anything other than the wine he kept pouring. He was asking about Julian, about what he called 'his gig' in Paris. Her mouth was chewy with bread. She gulped at the wine. She knew she had to eat in order not to get too drunk but something was overruling her usual common sense. Her primitive instincts were winning. She wasn't putting up a very good fight as Karl refilled her glass. Her head started spinning and she retreated to the fireside chair to get away from him, turned the conversation to Julian.

'He's besotted with Claude De'Ath's films,' she said. 'Have you seen any? No? Me neither,' and she started giggling. 'But he's so excited, he's only called once since he got there. He's even forgotten that we're supposed to be making a baby.' She placed her hand on her belly, thought, why am I telling him this? But continued anyway.

Karl's face paled. He put down his glass, stood up and sat down again.

She felt herself grow hot, said: 'I mean it's the right time of the month . . .'

Karl buried his head in his hands.

'My God, Karl, what's the matter?'

His shoulders were shaking.

'I can't do this any more,' he said. 'Oh God, Julia. This is the conversation I came here tonight to have with Julian.' He was barely whispering. She stood and took a step towards him to hear what he was saying. He held out a hand, motioning for her to stay put. She sank back into the chair.

'Karl, what is it?' She tasted the first salt of tears but had no idea what she was crying about or why her heart was hammering.

His shoulders were heaving. At first she couldn't make out what he was saying. He had to repeat it, looking straight at her. 'Julian can't have children,' he said. There, he'd said it again. 'His sperm has zero motility. I've seen it. I've actually tested it several times.' He managed to hold her gaze. 'Zero,' he said, making a perfect o with his finger and thumb.

She burst out laughing. 'That's not true, Karl. That's a terrible thing to say.' She snapped her fingers in front of her face: 'That's how fast we got pregnant before. It's only my age that's making it take so long now.'

Karl stood up. 'Yes, almost four years. Is that how long you've been trying?'

She thought she should slap him, or at least ask him to leave.

'That's a long time, Julia. It's what I was trying to tell you at the zoo.' He pointed to her stomach. 'That baby wasn't Julian's.'

Twenty-eight

Peace has broken out in the back of the car: Mira is indulging Ruth by allowing her a turn with the Walkman. Mira's face is turned to the window, though there's not much to see through the mist. Julia twiddles through the radio stations. There's nothing to distract her from her thoughts.

By the time she arrived at Charles de Gaulle Julia was swollen with secrets. She had never known herself cry as she cried on that flight. She had checked herself in the mirror of the airplane loo, spidery red legs shot across the pink whites of her eyes and still the tears wouldn't stop. She pulled away the blue scarf she'd wrapped around her head. It was still damp. She'd washed her hair before leaving, there hadn't been a choice: the strand she pulled to her mouth had tasted of the sea. There wasn't time to dry it, she'd been an idiot not to allow longer at home. It was only at the last moment she'd wrapped and added the padlock to her hastily assembled bag. Shamefully, she had completely forgotten whatever it was she'd been intending to buy for his birthday. She'd wound the scarf around her wet hair like a turban and if she hadn't run for the tube would've missed her flight. Her brown T-shirt was saggy at the neck, around her face an unruly mass of snakes. She redid the blue scarf, despaired that she hadn't thought to dress in something lovely for his birthday.

There hadn't been a moment to think: they almost hadn't let her through to the gate. She splashed her face with water in the pongy cubicle, didn't have a clue what to do about the racing of her heart.

Julian was in impossibly high spirits; he came bounding towards her across the concourse with his huge grin. It was a wonder he didn't notice her swollen eyes. Grabbing her, not her bag, which had been cutting into her shoulder, he was covering her in kisses and bouncing in his trainers. 'Thank God you're here,' he said. If he'd had a tail he'd have been wagging it. 'Mmmm. You smell delicious.'

She shifted the bag to her less-troubling shoulder, could feel herself flushing with guilt as he snuffled her neck, thinking of the bath she'd taken that morning, of how carefully she'd washed the salt from her skin and hair. He sensed no change in her as he zigzagged to the taxi queue, looping back a couple of times to embrace her. He had no reason to be anything but happy.

She eased her bulging overnight bag from her poor ancient shoulder. 'So, twenty-five, how does that feel?' Her voice sounded brittle and false, but he was oblivious. He put his lips to her ear: 'Randy is how it feels right now. Let's go straight to the hotel.' She felt herself freeze, closed her fingers around the gift-wrapped padlock in her pocket, griping it to give herself courage. Although Paris was warm, almost muggy, she had a chill realisation that at that moment sex with Julian was something she would only be able to do if she were very, very drunk.

They came to a standstill at the taxi queue. She suggested they get the taxi to drop them close to the Pont des Arts. There was still sunshine to walk in but rain forecast later. He slid his hands to her bum and pulled her in close.

At the Pont des Arts she urged him to lock the padlock to the railings. On the plane she'd made a pact with only the devil knows who. Their love would be safe locked to the bridge, something like that. Silly.

She had to make herself stop biting her lip because she'd made it so sore willing him to do it, to throw the key to the jaded waters of the Seine. He was apologetic. He wanted to own the padlock a little longer, he said. They wandered on, getting drunker in the warm Parisian sun. She gulped from various glasses until her legs were wobbly and she had to clasp his arm and let him carry her heavy bag. She was trying to lose herself to pastis and wine. His gaze never left her.

Sometimes it was irritating, that sense of being watched, to look up from something absorbing, like a book, to find him staring at her from across a room. When she had a bath he was always there. She had been glad of the bathroom with the egg-shaped bath at Firdaws because it was the only one with a lock. At mealtimes his eyes followed the food from her plate to her lips. He blamed it on writing in dog voices, told her to thank her lucky stars he didn't shag her leg when she walked through the door. She never once conquered the shyness she felt while he watched her undress.

The hotel in Paris was the swankiest place she'd ever stayed, him too. Dark panelling from the lifts to the bar displayed paintings of slightly debauched little boys in lace collars, pansy-eyed comtes and aristocratic papas with cruel moustaches and military honours. The faces and their gilded frames shone only by the light of candles. At various points bucket-sized vases of roses with blown petals in lingerie colours of blush, peach and cream flickered and glowed. Ornate mirrors were dappled with mercury, turning passers-by to ghosts. The hotel was so dimly lit it was an effort not to stumble around like a blind person, even the lift was muted so she couldn't make out the numbers without her glasses, and Julian laughed and said maybe that was how the place stayed hip, by making it impossible for oldies like her, and she kicked him.

In the hotel bar the music was trancey and loud enough for a gym. The pictures of petal-eyed ducs in the vestibule gave way to erotic nudes. Arching her back on one side of the rear wall, in tasteful sepia and crackled glaze, a nymphet displayed the pale patisserie of her buttocks and, on the other, her caramel-tipped breasts. The light flickered with cinnamon candles and dim gold, the chandelier drops were the colour of burning sugar. There was a man in a brown corduroy suit whose breath stank of old meat. She was grateful to him.

Julian's face rises above her. 'You wanted to fuck him, didn't you?' Lights come straight at her out of the fog. The lorry is on the wrong side of the road. She's swerving, hears Ruthie's scream as the windscreen explodes and the world turns red. 'I did. I did. I did.'

Twenty-nine

Brighton was overcast, hazy white, the seagulls swooping and flapping about as though they'd been cut from the same cloth as the sky. The sea was pearl grey. There was barely a ripple and it merged with the sky in a rolling bulge so it was impossible to tell where water finished and air began.

She left her van at Hove Lawns, anxious that she might not find another space closer, and stopped at a café to ask for directions to Karl's hotel. 'The Ida Heights.' The man pointed east. 'A couple of miles that-a-way.' The traffic had been on her side all the way from North London and she was fretful as well as early. A walk along the seafront might help to settle her nerves.

The tide was almost halfway in or halfway out, she couldn't decide. Karl would be at the conference all day; there was no point coming sooner, he said. She passed the Conference Centre: an incongruous lump that hogged the sea view. He'd be back at his hotel with 'a window' at six. A dinner he couldn't miss with some French biochemists at eight. *A window*.

She wore a dress to meet Karl in Brighton. She wouldn't want Julian to know that, nor the care she'd taken with her appearance before setting off. None of it would make her look good in the eyes of the prosecution.

The dress was vintage rose brocade, sleeveless. It swirled

around her legs as she walked and its many tiny mother-of-pearl buttons glinted. Her hair was loose and shining clean. Her sandals were supple leather with a braiding of pale gold, comfortable. Before dressing, she kneaded her skin to a glow with a breathtakingly redolent olive rub that she'd found in the back of a drawer.

The air was warm beneath its white blanket of sky, the gentlest of breezes brushed her face. She cast layers of clothing as she walked, swinging her coat from her shoulder, tying her cardigan around her waist. She stuck close to the railings and looked down at the pebble beach and a group of young gulls hunched in drab feathers receiving instruction from a debonair elder in splendid morning dress. A canoeist was coming to shore with slow, deliberate strokes, his head bowed like a mournful boatman, and she stopped to watch him, her elbows to the iron rail. Stones washed to and fro at the edge of a sea that was strangely monotone, with bulging clouds in shades of grey where the horizon should have been.

She was thinking only of Julian as she drew closer to the Ida Heights. Not that he would ever know.

Again and again she imagined him transfixed over the microscope in Karl's student room. She suffered a stab of jealousy each time she thought of the girl who was with him that night getting the sample.

'Azoospermia.' Karl had been quite explicit in his explanation. 'This means there are no sperm cells at all in the semen.' He'd hung his head between his hands and shook it. 'I was stupid. I switched the slide,' he said, hiding his face. 'I wish I hadn't.'

'I tested him again, several times. It wasn't hard to persuade him, he needed the money. He donated at the lab. It was for research, not reproduction, so he didn't worry. And it was quite natural that I should ask him for blood tests.'

Julia held out her hands to make him to stop. She kept saying,

'No,' as he lobbed facts at her, because now he'd started it seemed nothing would make him stop.

'I'm sorry, but Julian's condition is not a blockage, which was what I'd been hoping – against all the evidence. I consulted a professor: in every sample his FSH was elevated, inhibin was absent. There was fructose in the semen, which indicates that the channel from the epididymis is open. I'm afraid the defect is in production and the professor confirmed my diagnosis. Zero means zero and that is unlikely to change.'

He looked straight at her into the silence that followed, reached out to where she'd fallen back in her chair. His brows were steepled with misery.

'Oh God, Julia. I am so sorry and now I've made it worse by telling you instead of him.'

'Well yes,' she said. 'But I suppose you've at least told me.' She felt a rush of fury. 'You've managed to tell a woman who would very much like to have Julian's baby, in fact.'

Karl hung his head so she could see only the thinning curls at his crown. 'I've been on the verge of confessing for years, but something always makes me chicken out. Once it was confirmed, I wrestled with my conscience night after night. In fact, it was my despicable moral cowardice in this matter that made me decide I could never become a doctor.' Karl raised his eyes. They blazed straight into hers as he told her of the evening he'd finally won over his conscience and set off to Julian's digs. His mouth twitched in the tiniest of sneers. 'When I got there he told me you were pregnant.'

Karl leant in to where she sat slumped in the peapod chair. Through the shock of it all, a sudden vision: Wychwood, her red shirt in tatters, Chris kneeling over her and spitting into his hand.

'Listen, Julia,' Karl was saying. 'It's not the end of the world. I can give you some telephone numbers. It is not difficult to obtain what you need.'

She shook herself. 'Oh yes, easy for you to say.'

'Listen. Throughout my first and second year of studies, I was able to buy myself good dinners with wine every Saturday night with what I made at the wank bank – sorry, crude, I know. We med students were targeted as soon as we arrived on campus. It was twenty quid a pop and I didn't think about it too much then. Now, of course, I can't help wondering about how casually I scattered my DNA.'

Julia used the back of her hand to wipe a tear from her cheek and her voice surged forth, interrupting him, forming the words unbidden: 'I'd rather you than a stranger.'

Now she stood at the rails and closed her eyes. The wash of sea on shingle took the edge off, like a dream that she might wake from. Hush little baby, don't say a word.

It was quiet all along the prom: only the occasional serial-killer breath of a runner coming up behind shook her from her thoughts, or a dog skittering for a stone. A man and a woman stood hip by hip painting the door of their beach hut, companionably touching as they worked, Blur from the radio at their feet. She was almost soothed by the shush of sea against shingle. She swung her arms a little as she walked, licked the back of her hand and found it was salty. She passed students hunched over tables outside a bar, a few skateboarders, the two piers, the wrecked one glittering with broken glass, its walkway rusting and forbidden with notices. Beyond it the iced white peaks of the Palace Pier called to punters with lights and union flags, a red, white and blue helter-skelter pointing a finger to the sky.

Julia turned off the seafront, crossed to a faintly sinister rise where latticework iron arches enclosed the pavement. She climbed a steep flight of concrete steps. Clumps of yellow wall-flowers grew in the cracks and she stopped for a moment and, seeking calm, took a breath or two of their sweetness. There was an elevated walkway, which at first seemed deserted. She heard scufflings in the bushes, and grunting, and bolted up the second flight, found herself on a street of bus fumes and furious cyclists. She weaved through the traffic to a crescent where the houses were gracious, even the crumbling ones, windows curving to the sea, and passed through a square where a gang of happy children played in a communal garden, hanging from a tree and whooping like gibbons.

She arrived at Karl's hotel on the dot of the hour. He'd left a message with the concierge and she was shown straight up to his room on the first floor. As she was ushered from the foyer into the lift she just about had time to pull her dress straight and run her fingers through her hair. She waited a moment outside his door before knocking, flushed with shame when he opened it and caught her glossing her lips with balm.

Karl wasn't long out of the shower; there was warm steam and bath essence, something woody, cedar maybe. He was half-dressed for dinner in a smart silk shirt, untucked and the deep blue of permanent Quink. The cuffs were yet to be fastened, his forearms dark with hair. His charcoal wool trousers made his bum look neat. They were part of a suit, the jacket was slung over the back of a chair with his tie.

They didn't touch one another. He looked as nervous as she felt as he gestured for her to come inside. He had shaved closely. His forehead was shiny with sweat. She went across the room, gripping her basket, and stood at the window looking out at the sea.

'Did you find the list I left you?' he asked when their silence became intolerable. 'Shall I order up some drinks? Some medicinal cocktails?'

She nodded to both questions but didn't turn around. She had found his list as soon as he'd gone from Cromwell Gardens, tactfully sealed in an envelope that he'd stolen from the kitchen drawer. He must've tucked it into the frame of the bathroom mirror while she was calling him a minicab. The second bottle of wine was empty, the table a mess of crumbled bread, smears of cheese, greasy bracelets of salami skin.

She continued staring at the sea. Now here they were, like strangers, tongue-tied, their words few and stilted, peppered with nervous laughter. And across the water came a thick mist that not even the sharpest eye of the sun would pierce. She took the cardigan from her waist to hang it over her shoulders. Her stomach knotted to think of the way she had blurted it out. 'I'd rather you than a stranger.'

She remained at the window while he perched on the edge of the bed with the phone to his ear. He didn't ask her what she'd like: vodka martinis, crisps, olives. She took a carrier bag from her basket, walked to the bed and offered it to him. 'It's all in here,' she said. 'You were right about Wigmore Street.' He took the bag and patted the bed for her to sit beside him, started to open it. 'OK, let's have a look at what's to be done.'

There was a knock at the door. 'Oh, please put it down,' she was already reddening at the thought of its contents. 'Here's our drinks.'

The martinis were strong and came with a twist. She sat at the window to drink hers. Karl remained on the bed.

Eventually he checked his watch, went back to the plastic bag. 'Julia, if you're still really sure about this, we'd better get on.'

She sat beside him, her hands in her lap, while he emptied the contents on to the pristine bedspread. She was glad that he hadn't turned on the light as he picked through the surgically sealed packages, through the shiny, crackling cellophane, all too clearly the coiled loop of a catheter, a syringe, a cup with a screw-on lid, a speculum like the bill of the nastiest duck moulded in transparent plastic that made her shudder just to look at it.

'These are all sterile, good.' He reloaded the bag, and it was a relief not to have it all there, laid out like that. 'I'll need to go and wash my hands in a minute, but let's get you comfortable first.' She was instantly flustered. He gestured for her to lie on the bed. There were cushions and pillows; he arranged them, one for her head, the others set aside for her legs.

'And you're definitely ovulating?'

'The line on the stick was pretty unequivocal this morning. I took it as a sign . . . that this was, you know . . .' She trailed off, unsure what it was she took it as a sign of. She always felt ovulation as a swelling dull ache, the tester merely confirmed it once a month. A blessing perhaps?

A canopy fell from the ceiling and parted like a bride's veil at the head of the bed. She stared from the folds of celadon silk up to the looped ring from which it flowed. The cornicing of the room was ripe with plaster pomegranates and lilies. It was silent but for their breathing, a chalky twilight through the window.

She lay on the bed, a pillow beneath her head, a sense of unreality as though she was floating in and out of a dream. He perched beside her, inspecting the backs of his hands, barely making a dent he'd positioned himself so gingerly on the edge.

'It'll be best if you remain lying here with your legs elevated for half an hour or so afterwards.' He was pushing back each cuticle in turn. He showed her how to arrange the cushions, one beneath her bottom. She felt a fluttering hysteria, the quiver of a childhood memory of doctors and nurses, the cool slide of a stethoscope. He looked up from his fingernails with his twitching smile and her hysteria became a pulsing rush.

'So, I'll wash my hands now,' he said, standing to go. Another smile, slightly apologetic. 'And you will have to remove your pants, of course.'

He came back with his cuffs rolled to his elbows, rubbing and shaking his hands dry as he approached. The room was thrumming with her heartbeat. Fine drops of water fell from his hands.

She lay ready on the cushion with her dress hitched up her

thighs. He sat with his back to her and emptied the bag of its contents, turning to show her each item like a visitor bringing fruit. He wouldn't look at her while he spoke. So, not a kindly visitor at all, rather a doctor somewhat hassled on his ward rounds.

'I'm going to talk you through this, OK? We should repeat this procedure tomorrow as well, if you can get here, but in the meantime we need to optimise your chances. I will have everything in place for when I come back. You know about the speculum?' He held it up in its package.

'Yes, awful. I dread every smear.' Julia tried to repeat a joke, some old comedian or other who described it as like having a Ford Cortina driven up your fanny, which frankly had never been a helpful image.

He ignored her, turning her attention to the remaining items. 'Once I've got this speculum in place it will be easy to guide this catheter to the cervix and then I'll go to the bathroom with this cup . . .'

There was a sharp rap at the door. Karl put down the packet containing the plastic cup and scooted from the bed to answer it. She heard a woman with a throaty voice cry his name, saw the pointy tip of a shoe, an ankle. He was blocking the door, in the end he walked right around to the other side. Still, Julia could hear them.

'No, Sofie, I said I'd meet you at the restaurant. I can't see you now, I have something to do.'

The woman objected with a blast of scorned laughter: 'I can see her on the bed through the door behind you, you must think I'm really stupid.' Karl shushed her further: 'Really, Sofie. You have to go. I have an old friend in here who has had a bit of a shock.'

Karl looked as cheerful as a man heading for his own execution as he returned to the bed. Before he picked up the cup she caught him glancing once again at his watch, and fury hit her quick as the snap of a hypnotist's fingers. She sat bolt upright, kicking away his cushions. She was reaching beneath the pillow for her pants. He stopped tearing open the package. 'Julia, wait. What's up?'

She didn't care what he saw as she pulled her pants on, turned around, tossing her hair from her face.

'I don't want to make you late for . . .' she couldn't help but sound childish as she said the name, 'Sofie.' She was wrestling with her cardigan, her fingers shaking, uncooperative, as she buttoned it stiffly over her dress. He sank with his head in his hands. She waited for him to speak and when he didn't, swept past him. She turned to look at him from the door, the detritus of their venture scattered across the bed.

'I can't do this, Karl. Not like this.'

Her eyes stung as she headed out into the hazy street, the sea obscured by clouds.

She descended deeper into the mist, sliding her hand down the iron railings of the steep steps, her feet strangely noiseless on the concrete, the fret rolling in to greet her. She couldn't see any distance at all, but there were streetlights. They appeared one by one, beacons in a sulphurous haze. The sea was muffled, she could barely hear it meet the shore and it gave no clues as to whether it was near or far. A foghorn sounded somewhere out there, the most baleful noise she'd ever heard. Her face and hair quickly became wet on the side turned to the sea. It had grown chilly and she realised, cursing, that she'd left her mac in Karl's hotel room.

She tried to make herself think ahead, to bring on a cheering lurch of excitement. She'd be in Paris with Julian in time for his birthday. Just two more days. She made a mental note to ring around a few antiquarian booksellers to see how interesting an edition of *Paradise Lost* she might be able to afford. She thought about lingerie, of his voice on the phone telling her the bed in the hotel had black sheets.

She thought too of the first time they met: Julian a windswept boy lolloping towards her across the Downs with his trouser leg tucked into his sock. Up close his breath was last night's party: not a boy after all. He was tall and lanky with the widest grin she'd ever seen – it didn't seem possible that one face could contain it. His skin, hair and eyes had a unifying metallic gleam, a fine dusting of gold, his irises more golden than brown, his pupils pinholed by the sun. Even his hangover didn't spoil his looks. His eyelashes were a gift from the desert, as long as a girl's and so thick it appeared he was wearing kohl.

She couldn't imagine that such a beautiful boy would fall for someone like her, nor that in the arms of this 'boy' she would feel safe and comforted for the only time in her life.

She put a hand to her crown, remembered the touch of his fingers as he parted her hair to swab the patch of scalp that Chris had left bare and bleeding. She'd buried herself in his pillow, even the smell of him gentle, and he'd eased her out of her ripped shirt, peeled away her filthy jeans, her torn pants. He had a bowl of warm water, a sponge. He dried her with a clean towel, covered the dirty fingerprints of her bruises with calendula cream. He pressed coins into the meter to keep the gas fire burning, gave her hot milk with brandy, wrapped his softest jumper around her to stop her teeth from chattering.

On the radio Billie Holiday cracking her heart into pieces while he danced her slowly. *What do I care how much it may storm. I've got my love to keep me warm.* Her head to his shoulder and his breath at the patch of her crown where the hair would grow back.

People loomed out of the mist along the promenade, voices muted and sudden, some pushing bicycles, others with bottles of beer in their hands, everyone a little startled to find someone

276

coming towards them, emerging first as silhouettes, faces only visible for a moment. An Alsatian dog appeared and disappeared, looping back wraithlike, and emerged with its owner, a man with a proud belly, the fur around the hood of his parka glittering with moisture.

After a while the foghorn becomes the only noise, she can't even hear the fall of her own feet. There are no more people, she's lost track of how far it is to her car. She misses Julian so acutely that tears run down her cheeks. That's something she'd like him to know.

She hears footsteps, running, her name being shouted. Karl is coming to get her. Karl is beside her, bent over, grasping his thighs to catch his breath. He stands up and wraps her mackintosh around her shoulders, using its lapels to pull her towards him, she can feel the rapid rise and fall of his chest, his arms holding her as if he might never let her go. He bends to kiss her.

'I love Julian,' she says, kissing him back.

'Me too,' he says, breaking the kiss and spinning her around. A lone rollerblader curves out of the mist, graceful as a needle trailing black silk, and is gone. They follow him, catching sight of him once more on the glide of a turn, and then disappear into the mist as into the pages of a book, their arms entwined.

FIRDAWS
August 2012

S he arrived at Firdaws on an August day beneath a sky of airmail blue. It was Jenna's birthday, as it happened, that one day of the year when the sun wouldn't dare not shine.

She was dressed in many layers, her long hair was wispy, neither up nor down. A loopy grey vest hung over a T-shirt on top of a thin jumper worn with the sleeves rolled up. Her arms were skinny as saplings, her eyes the same surprising blue as her mother's and ringed by the black smudges of her make-up, her nose a freckled snub. She had bitten nails and many silver rings, beaded cords around her neck, amber, turquoise, Eliana's gold sun on its fine chain. Beneath her short denim skirt her legs were comical in black and white hooped leggings; she carried her stuff in a brown school satchel, fiddling constantly with its buckles as she stood at the end of the lane where the minicab had left her.

The sun was high in the sky, blinding, as she squinted across the unknown meadow to a house of warm terracotta bricks. The dog-daisies, buttercups and various weeds of the meadow had been trodden into a path where people cut straight through to its wonky front door. It was as strange to her as a dream: no fences, just this wide-open view. The trees and shrubs and tough little flowers surrounding the house simply dissolved into the landscape, and, though she could commit to no memory of having been there before, she could sense there was water nearby.

She closed her eyes: the idea of a river shimmered tantalisingly, a hazy sky buzzing with insects. As hard as willing a dream. She thought of his book, almost stamped her foot with fury. The dark flowing water with floating lillies of Japanese porcelain had been put in her memory by him.

Dr Wiseman, the first shrink they took her to, stared out of his window, tapping his teeth with his specs while she answered his questions. He told her it was unusual to have no memory at all of a long stay in hospital, or something as traumatic as a head-on collision. Unlike Ruth, she told him, she did not recall the stiff black linen dresses that their mother had made them wear on the day of the crash.

Ruth was able to re-create the whole thing in sensuous detail, she whispered its horrors to her pillow: the screech and boom, exploding glass, the smell of burning rubber and the final sickening swerve that went on for ever. Their mother being pulled from the wreckage with blood all over her face, the snipping of scissors through black linen, even the names of the ambulance men. Their mother calling, 'Ruthie, Ruthie . . .'

It was Ruth who told her that the airline had lost the trunk containing all of their toys when they left Connecticut. When it seemed their tears might never stop, Grandfather Heino had taken them to Hamley's. 'Remember Heino? With his hump and his cane with the snake carved on it?' Ruth embroiders her memories with other things: a cat called Marcel who only liked Ruth and hissed whenever Mira came too close, a bad-tempered Mira who peed in her knickers at school and took things from Ruth that weren't hers to take. Sometimes, Mira told Dr Wiseman, she felt she existed only in second-hand memories. As if to compensate, Mira's dream life was unusually vivid. She drifted back and forth in the rich tide, was always slow to rise and late for school. Ruth had given up waiting for her even when she was still young enough to find the long bus ride frightening on her own.

Nothing had been kept from Mira. In fact, with all this talk of childhood amnesia, people around her seemed all too happy to fill in the blanks: the hospital, her kidney, the brightly painted flat in North London. All elaborately described but not remembered. The stuff about Julian had been mildly intriguing the first time they explained, but it was really not such a big deal that they had to keep going on about him. Julian's photograph was in a review of one of his books in the *Guardian*. He looked tanned and friendly, with dark hair and sombre eyes. He didn't look like anyone she knew.

Her amnesia was the root of her problem, Dr Wiseman said, whatever her problem was supposed to be. Some sessions with a child psychotherapist might help to unblock things. Sofie arranged things, efficient as bleach, though was careful to stand back and allow Karl to do the talking.

Mira didn't mind seeing Mr Gabriel Rubin, Gabriel, Gabe. He was actually quite cool. His room was peaceful, the couch she lay on every Friday at four was perfectly comfortable, with a velvet cushion for her head. He made no demands, she didn't even have to look at him. It was a nuisance that he wouldn't let her smoke, but you can't have everything. Mostly they just talked about whatever she'd been reading on the bus over.

Apart from sticking around in Lamb's Conduit Street to let in Sofie's decorators, Mira was at a loose end. Even Gabe had cancelled their appointment. Her dad and Sofie might just as well have let her join the rest of them in Marrakesh for all she had to do here.

She was supposed to be going through the listings on UCAS. 'See if something will raise even a flicker of interest,' her dad had said. 'Failing that, you can bloody well find a job.' So that was it. Right up until the day they left, she couldn't believe he would go through with it and she cried like a baby in her room while they packed. She was saved by her little brothers fighting in their bedroom; she could feel their thuds against the wall, the screaming of insults and was at that moment struck by a sudden joy: oh, let Ruth be the unpaid babysitter this time. She was even thinking of helpfully gathering a few books together for the boys' backpacks, when she heard Sofie, sotto voce on the stairs. 'It's good that you stuck to your guns and made her stay here. Much better she keep her appointments with Gabriel Rubin,' she said. As usual Karl didn't do a thing to stand up for her, barely a sigh. 'I'm not taking someone with an eating disorder on our holidays again and that's final,' Sofie hissed and Mira's stomach clenched with rage.

Mira had been standing across the meadow for a while when Dolly arrived. The little girl was pretty, the sun threw bright dots on to her face through the holes in the brim of her hat, she had the same double dimple when she smiled as her mother. A dog with a white ruff and springy haunches ran around her in circles. She grasped a corkscrew in one hand and in the other a stick that she threw for the dog. The throw wasn't good and the stick didn't go far. The dog picked it up and bounded across the grass to Mira, dropping it at her feet. It sat thumping its tail, looking longingly from the stick to her face and back again. The little girl trotted across the meadow, grumpy with the dog, who didn't come when she called.

'Is that her name? Muriel?' Mira handed over the stick. 'No, not *Muriel*, he's a boy,' the girl giggled. 'His name's Uriel, but I call him Uri and Uri-bear, but not when he's naughty.'

Mira held out her hand. 'I'm Mira. What's your name?'

The girl stalled for a moment. 'Dolly.' From her voice Mira knew she was weighing up the dangers of talking to a stranger. She felt a stab of unearned guilt.

'Dolly. Hello,' Mira smiled to reassure her and Dolly dropped her stick into the jaws of the dog. 'I like your dress,' Mira said and Dolly decided to trust her enough for a twirl. 'It's new,' she said. 'Daddy bought it for me and I have growed into it now.'

Dolly skipped along with the dog trotting beside her and Mira followed them on a magical mystery tour beyond Horseman's gate, through long seedy grasses of pale gold and rutted stubble and on into the dip by the barns where the figs grew – places Mira knew only from his book. Then down through a field of cows. At least Mira hoped they were cows, especially as they drew closer and she saw they didn't have udders.

'Don't run away from them,' Dolly told her authoritatively. 'Just flap your arms at them and say "No". That's what my daddy does. Look, like this.'

Within moments the two girls were doing what you should never do in a field of young bullocks. Down at the river they could hear the stampede. Mira flew into view grasping Dolly by the hand; Dolly's straw hat flew away, creating a diversion before being eaten.

For Julian it happened in broken flashes, like a flickbook or strobe lighting. His knees were already tensing to follow as Jenna left the bank in a perfect arc. Dolly's scream cut through the air and he turned. Dolly bawling, 'Daddy!' Katie with firewood, dropping it, running, blonde hair flying, William shouting, Michael staring, the dog barking, and at the crest of the field, partly obscured by a patch of white angelica, a girl. He tried to stop himself mid-leap but was already falling as he shouted her name.

Except it wasn't her name, it was Julia's. He exploded into the cold water, cursing and coughing from the mouthfuls of river he'd swallowed. He knew it was Mira he'd seen, not Julia. The current was strong, sweeping him along, and he had no option but to swim the mile to Swan Bank; there was no way out

285

through the blackthorns and nettles. He powered through the water, leaving Jenna far behind to battle her imaginary snakes alone.

With each stroke he feared she might be gone. He became breathless and scraped both of his shins scrambling out, but still he managed to bellow her name. The right name: 'Mira!' He ran through the hay fields, his legs bleeding, the stubble painful on his bare feet. 'Mira!'

She was waiting beneath the shade of an oak, sitting with her back to its trunk, chewing skin from her thumb, her satchel beside her. Her eyes were prominent in her face and though she looked up at him boldly, he was afraid that she might take flight. He stopped before he reached her. 'Mira?'

She nodded. In one movement she straightened and lifted the layers of clothing from her left side, revealing the triangular jut of bone above her denim skirt and above that the scar at her waist like a thread of pink silk. She let the clothing drop but kept her face turned away from him and he wondered if she was crying. His arms and chest ached to hold her and he took a step closer. She turned, stopped him in his tracks. 'I don't remember you,' she said, and her eyes were defiant, not tearful. He reached for her hands, suddenly aware that he must look ridiculous in the middle of a field wearing nothing but his bathing trunks. He looked down at her fingers. He was too scared to squeeze them. Her arms had no more weight or shape to them than bone.

Back at the house Mira folded herself into the window seat, while he drew up a chair and tried not to stare at her. Katie came in and clasped her to her bosom and Mira mouthed sideways to him that she *didn't* smell of hyacinths as he'd said in his book. He winked and cocked his head to William: 'Scent gives her husband a headache.' Jenna kept looking from Mira to Michael as though for reassurance, holding out her arms and withdrawing them several times, before finally sweeping

286

her up. 'But darling girl, you are too thin,' she said, and started weeping. Dolly stared wide-eyed and miscomprehending, as William took her on to his knee and told her that Mira was his goddaughter. 'So Daddy, does that make us godsisters?' she wanted to know, and William laughed. Eventually they all drifted off, following Jenna to the kitchen. Mira's knees were drawn to her chin.

He leant towards her. 'Why now, Mira?'

She tugged at a cord around her neck and he saw that she wore the little brass key to the heart-shaped lock Julia had given him in Paris.

'It was my eighteenth in February . . .'

'Oh, I know,' he said, and again her eyes were challenging.

'And obviously you know what this is the key to?' she said, and he nodded for her to go on.

She tucked the key away; her voice had a crack to it, just as it had as a child. 'I already had a key to the house, so I suppose it wasn't that weird. We never had any secrets. The pretty brass lock was on the box in my mum's wardrobe for as long as I can remember.'

She laughed ruefully, adding: 'And actually that isn't very long at all.' And this puzzled him.

She described for him the contents of the box: the photographs, the keepsakes and cards that she had no memory of creating but which made him chuckle with recognition, wavy pencil lines of writing following the dots. *I love my Dadoo.* She looked up at him and stuck out her lip before carrying on. There were photographs that the nurses had taken of her at Great Ormond Street. A hollow-eyed, sickly child she couldn't recognise as herself, festooned with plasters and wires. And beside her bed a man she had no memory of meeting until this moment.

'I'm sorry,' she said, picking at the baggy sleeves of her sweater. 'But I don't remember you at all. Is it bad of me to say so?'

He was overcome with sadness as she turned her head away. 'Oh Mira. I'm sorry. I thought I was doing the best thing . . .'

He was making excuses: 'I assumed you were all living in Connecticut . . . I had meningitis . . . I wasn't even conscious . . . I thought I was doing the right thing for you. A clean break.' He bowed his head: 'Forgive me,' he said as Katie came crashing through from the kitchen chasing Dolly with a squirty bottle of water. Katie's sprigged dress had a broad wet strip where Dolly had surprised her at the sink. Katie skidded to a halt, noticed Julian rapt on the edge of the chair, Mira's eyes huge and anxious. 'Goodness,' she said. 'I think you two need a cup of tea.' She returned to the kitchen to put the kettle on, ushering Dolly through with her.

'All your books were in Mum's box too. I read the dog ones first. They're funny.' Mira shifted her position, her legs tucked up beneath her, barely denting the cushions. Her fingers toyed at the stained centre of the seat. The nap was rough there, the mark from her long-ago ice-cream showed up more since Julia's papal velvet had faded to the palest of mauves.

'And I read your other book, that was in there too. The one you dedicated to me.' Again her eyes flashed and he bowed his head.

'I'm glad she got it. Freda's was the best address I could think of.'

'It was freaky, reading it,' she said. 'And when I went to talk about it Mum told me she'd never read it.'

He felt the blood rush to his head. Julia hadn't read his book? He'd done her the kindness of being generous in his portrayal of her treachery, so sure had he been that she would read it.

'At first I didn't believe her. But she swore she was telling the truth. She said she was too frightened to face even a page of it,' Mira said.

'Is that so?' He was leaning right out of his chair.

Mira started to giggle. 'She's probably reading it right now though,' she said. 'Ruth's gone with Dad and Sofie and our brothers to Marrakesh, so she'll be able to give it her full attention.' Mira was giving him a cheeky look, sideways through her lashes; he remembered that look and it made his heart swell.

He was attempting to stay calm, to piece these bits of information together.

'What brothers? How many?' he said.

'Dad and Sofie have three boys. Little devils: ten, eight and six, Max, Sam and Lucien. Not bad going for a couple who met researching male contraception, huh?' she said, and his head started to spin a little. He had a sudden urge to waltz her around the room.

He gulped to find himself asking: 'And is she OK? Your mum?'

'Well, she was fine last time I saw her, but that was before I persuaded her to read your book. God knows what state she's in now.' That look was unmistakable mischief. 'Maybe you should go and see her and find out for yourself.'

He motioned at Mira to move over, and mirrored her position in the window seat, close enough that their shoulders touched.

'So she never read my book. You're sure of that?'

Mira shook her head. 'Not until now,' she said. Again the puckish grin. From the kitchen door came delicious wafts of the lamb that Jenna was taking from the Rayburn. It had been cooking slowly in the bottom oven all night. Their stomachs rumbled in noisy unison. 'Man, I'm hungry,' Mira said, and laughed to hear herself say it. He reached out an arm and pulled her head to his chest, where she laid her cheek flat and closed her eyes. 'You smell the same,' she mumbled. 'Cigarettes, chewing gum, something like dry bread.' She raised her head to look up at him – 'And vanilla ice-cream' – and pointed to the stain on the seat. 'You were here in the window and I was trying to climb to you with it in my hand. The cushions were dark purple then.'

Jenna poked her head through from the kitchen to say they'd eat the lamb outside at sunset. The evening light was already turning them golden.

'Come,' he said, leading Mira by the hand. 'There's something I want to show you.'

The room became amber. At the window, jasmine wreathed across the leaded glass, vines reaching and twisting in double helixes, throwing patterns across the surface of his desk. The little shoe was red leather, scuffed to pink across the toes. She sat on his chair and pulled the strap back and forth through the silver buckle, fixed it at its usual hole, looked up at him and smiled.

ACKNOWLEDGEMENTS

I have been lucky to have Cressida Connolly as my first reader and Damian Barr as my first editor. I am hugely grateful to them both, as I am to David Gilmour for unwavering support and insight.

Thank you Claire Singers, Louise Allen-Jones, Justine Picardie and Charlie Gilmour for reading and commenting on early versions, and thank you Clare Conville for making invaluable textual suggestions. Thank you Gabriel Gilmour for saving me from an Air anachronism.

I am grateful to Tony Wolff for sharing medical knowledge and ideas. Thank you Ghislaine Stephenson, Emma Sturgess, Renate Tulloh, Charlotte Jenkins and all the amazing staff at Great Ormond Street Hospital. Professor Kathy Pritchard-Jones made me feel that Mira was in the best possible hands and she, together with the generous recollections of Brian and Susan Hickey, helped me to build and shape the hospital chapters.

Grateful thanks to all the Blooms – it is such a joy to be published by Bloomsbury. Alexandra Pringle is as great an editor as she is a friend. Thanks to Robin Jack for the Milton tutorials and to Hugh Lillingston for the beautiful ratios. Thank you Esther Samson, Romany Gilmour, Joe Gilmour, Cassandra Jardine, Mike Moran, Gala Wright, Adam Phillips, Victoria

Angell and Jaz Rowland. Thanks to Amanda and Chris Dennis of the Citrus Centre, Pulborough for the lessons in grafting.

I am grateful to Lisa Allardice at the *Guardian* for commissioning the story *The Man Who Fell* which laid the bones for this book. Thanks to Joe Winnington who sent me the little shoe from East Berlin that set the pulse and to my father, Lance Samson, who gave me the two stories that lie at its heart.

A NOTE ON THE AUTHOR

Polly Samson is the author of two highly acclaimed story collections and a novel, *Out of the Picture*, which was shortlisted for the Authors' Club Best First Novel Award. Her most recent linked story collection, *Perfect Lives*, was a *Sunday Times* Fiction Choice of the Year and was read on BBC Radio 4. She has been shortlisted for the V.S. Pritchett Award and the Edge Hill Short Story Prize. She recently wrote the introduction to Daphne du Maurier's *The Doll: Short Stories*. She has written lyrics for three bestselling albums and was a Costa Book Awards judge in 2007. Polly Samson lives in Brighton.

A NOTE ON THE TYPE

The text of this book is set in Linotype Sabon, named after the type founder, Jacques Sabon. It was designed by Jan Tschichold and jointly developed by Linotype, Monotype and Stempel, in response to a need for a typeface to be available in identical form for mechanical hot metal composition and hand composition using foundry type.

Tschichold based his design for Sabon roman on a font engraved by Garamond, and Sabon italic on a font by Granjon. It was first used in 1966 and has proved an enduring modern classic.